Advance Praise for
The Secret Life of Kitty Granger

"You'll root for Kitty Granger, a heroine for our times, from the first to the last page."

—Sarah Ahiers, author of *Assassin's Heart* and *Thief's Cunning*

"Falksen's portrayal of a multifaceted girl who comes into her own while being thrust into an intriguing world of espionage is at turns delightful, poignant, and suspenseful. I couldn't stop turning the pages to find out how Kitty Granger would triumph!"

—Jennieke Cohen, author of *Dangerous Alliance*

THE SECRET LIFE OF
KITTY
GRANGER

G. D. FALKSEN

Carolrhoda LAB
MINNEAPOLIS

Carolrhoda Lab®
An imprint of Lerner Publishing Group, Inc.
241 First Avenue North
Minneapolis, MN 55401 USA

For reading levels and more information, look up this title at
www.lernerbooks.com.

Image credits: AMR Image/Getty Images (female); crossbrain66/Getty Images (Westminster); Yamko/Getty Images (flag); ilbusca/Getty Images (triangles); Milanares/Getty Images (border).

Main body text set in Janson Text LT Std.
Typeface provided by Linotype AG.

Library of Congress Cataloging-in-Publication Data

Names: Falksen, G. D. (Geoffrey D.), 1982– author.
Title: The secret life of Kitty Granger / G. D. Falksen.
Description: Minneapolis : Carolrhoda Lab, [2020] | Audience: Ages 11–18. | Audience: Grades 7–9. | Summary: "In 1960s London, sixteen-year-old Kitty Granger, a working-class girl on the autism spectrum, is recruited as a spy for the British government and must help bring down a group of covert fascists hiding in plain sight" —Provided by publisher.
Identifiers: LCCN 2019034442 (print) | LCCN 2019034443 (ebook) | ISBN 9781541599314 | ISBN 9781541599314 (ebook)
Subjects: CYAC: Spies—Fiction. | Autism—Fiction. | Nazis—Fiction. | London (England)—History—20th century—Fiction. | Great Britain—History—Elizabeth II, 1952—Fiction.
Classification: LCC PZ7.1.F352 Sec 2020 (print) | LCC PZ7.1.F352 (ebook) | DDC [Fic]—dc23

LC record available at https://lccn.loc.gov/2019034442
LC ebook record available at https://lccn.loc.gov/2019034443

Manufactured in the United States of America
1-47984-48583-8/17/2020

For anyone who has ever been told
that being different is wrong.

Differences are good.
They make us human.

CHAPTER I

It was midmorning, and Kitty Granger sat huddled in her seat on the crowded London bus, sandwiched between a very stylish Indian lady and a big pasty-skinned man who smelled of tobacco. She eyed the man beside her and shuddered. His tie was decorated with little horseshoes, and it looked ghastly. Also, it was lime green, but the horseshoes were the worst part.

It had rained earlier, and the smell of damp fabric mingled in the air with the unpleasant odors of cigarette smoke and cheap perfume. Half the time Kitty felt like she was choking. The other half, she was too overcome by the crowd to notice anything else. The people all blurred together until they were just a jumble of motion and noise that seemed poised to crash down upon her like a giant wave. But despite all else, the damned lime green tie with its little horseshoes kept staring at her out of the corner of her eye.

Taking the bus might have been a mistake, but it was the easiest way to get downtown. This was her first day off work in two weeks, and she was determined to visit the British Museum—and have a good time doing it! Kitty clenched her jaw and gave a firm little nod to remind herself of that. It probably appeared odd, but no one was looking at her. She was just an ordinary teenage girl on an ordinary London bus. No one knew that she really just wanted to scream and hide, to huddle in a safe dark corner away from all these people.

Kitty rubbed her fingertips against the rough wool of her skirt. To any observer, it would just look like she was brushing away wrinkles, but in fact she found the texture of the fabric very calming, and the repetitive motion soothed her nerves.

She should have bought a newspaper before leaving. There was a book in her handbag—a delightfully lurid detective novel—but she'd never be able to concentrate on reading. Kitty needed a puzzle to distract her from the loudness of the world.

She glanced awkwardly at the woman seated next to her, who had gotten on ten minutes ago and spent the entire journey reading a copy of *The Times*. Well, no, the woman wasn't actually doing much reading. Kitty had noticed that. She was watching a man in a Mackintosh raincoat a few seats in front of them, rather like how Kitty kept watching the hideous green tie. No one else noticed, but Kitty did. It often felt like she noticed everything all at once, and it was exhausting. Maybe the lady next to her was the same way.

No, Kitty took another look and knew that couldn't be the case. Her accidental traveling companion was far too glamorous to be peculiar. The lady looked very chic and modern, with a short bob haircut tucked under a newsboy cap, blue flared trousers, and a matching jacket worn over a white sweater. All that stylishness made Kitty feel hideously plain by comparison. But somehow the lady didn't look out of place, even here in the East End. She was just a person who belonged wherever she decided to be. Kitty imagined the lady could wear a fur coat in the middle of the Sahara and still look natural.

Then Kitty realized that she was staring, a moment after the lady did. The lady slowly turned her head toward Kitty and arched an eyebrow. Kitty shrank back, afraid that she had done something wrong. She was never sure how long was too long to look at another person. All those social cues everyone else seemed to know instinctively, Kitty could never quite get right. She had to pretend to understand the game without actually knowing the rules.

"May I help you?" the lady asked in a very crisp Mayfair accent. She spoke softly and kept the newspaper up, still hiding from the man a few seats ahead.

Kitty quickly looked down at her hands, and folded them to keep from fidgeting. The lady had a very direct stare and it made Kitty uncomfortable.

"Pardon, miss," Kitty stammered. "But, um, could I trouble you for . . . ?"

"Yes?"

"Could I trouble you for the *Times* crossword?" Kitty asked, internally wincing with each word. God, it sounded so stupid when she said it. Imagine her, mousy little Kitty Granger from East London, asking this very refined woman for a crossword puzzle! The lady was probably a model or an heiress or something. She had better things to do than talk to a peculiar girl who couldn't even make eye contact when having a conversation!

The lady's eyebrow arched a little more. Then she shrugged and smiled, like she was amused.

"Certainly," she said to Kitty, shuffling through the pages of her newspaper.

When the bus came to a halt at the next stop, the lady's eyes darted toward the man in the raincoat, and Kitty looked too, sizing him up at a glance. The man was on his feet, heading for the front door in haste. He was carrying a leather briefcase, and his hand gripped the handle as if for life itself. That was odd. Kitty sometimes did that when she was nervous, but she had learned a long time ago that most people didn't unless they were outright terrified.

Why would a man in a raincoat carrying a briefcase on a London bus be terrified? People got on buses in raincoats all the time and nothing bad happened to them.

The lady frowned and shoved the newspaper into Kitty's hands. "You can have the whole paper if you like," she said.

Kitty watched the lady set off in pursuit of the strange man. She had no idea what to make of it, so she just shuffled through the newspaper until she came to the crossword. It was still untouched, and a glance at the questions suggested it would be a good one. Kitty grinned and pulled a pencil out of her handbag. She felt a glimmer of safety again. The puzzle was like a wall she could use to shut out the world around her.

Three words in, the bus started moving again. Suddenly, Kitty heard a commotion from the back door, and she looked to see what was the matter. She saw the man in the raincoat clamber aboard, breathing hard like he had just made a dash for it. That was *very* odd. Why would he get back on the bus he had just left?

The conductor apparently had the same question. "'Ere, didn't you just get off?" he asked.

"Um, wrong stop," explained the man in the raincoat. He fished money for another fare out of his pocket and offered it to the conductor. "Sorry, I'll pay again."

The conductor just sighed and jerked his head toward the seats. "Get on."

As the man in the raincoat pushed his way the middle of the bus, Kitty hid behind the newspaper and fixed her eyes on the crossword puzzle. There was something strange going on here and she wanted nothing to do with it.

Except that it made her curious, and that curiosity began twisting around in the back of her mind, worming its way through her self-imposed disinterest.

She was so preoccupied with not looking up from the paper that she didn't notice the man in the raincoat approaching until he dropped into the seat next to her. A shiver of alarm shot through Kitty, but she fought back the urge to squeak in fright.

The man set his briefcase on his knees and looked out the window. An unpleasant smile curled the corner of his mouth. Kitty stole a glance too and saw the Indian lady standing on the street corner at the bus stop, watching the bus depart with a furious expression. She'd been following the man and he had given her the slip. Kitty wasn't imagining things.

What was going on?

Kitty sank back in her seat and kept her eyes fixed on the crossword puzzle, trying to block out the world. It was fine. It was none of her business. She was going to the British Museum to have a nice afternoon. She wasn't going to let her curiosity get the better of her.

And for a little while, she almost believed that.

CHAPTER 2

Kitty spent the next few minutes in total silence, keeping her gaze focused on the crossword puzzle. It was suddenly very hard to concentrate on the words. The man in the raincoat was distracting, worse than the man with the green tie. He was trying to keep his cool, but Kitty felt nervousness rolling off him in waves. Every forty seconds or so, the man would drum his fingers against the side of his briefcase. It was practically clockwork, a constant annoyance.

Within minutes, the annoyance had become a fascination. Who was this strange man? Why was he so nervous? And why was that lady following him?

Maybe the man was having an affair. Maybe the lady in blue was his wife. Or maybe she was a private detective! That was it. She was following him with a camera to take photographs of his scandalous doings, which she would then sell to his wife, destroying their marriage. Perhaps he was a banker or even a minister of the Crown, only in disguise for meeting his fancy woman in secret. When news of the affair came out, it would be in all the papers and it would bring down the government and scandalize the Queen and . . .

Stop it! Kitty hissed inside her head.

But it was too late. The absurd notion had dug its hooks

into her and suddenly Kitty couldn't think about anything except finding out what was going on. She was still staring at the newspaper in front of her, but all her attention was focused on the man in the raincoat.

A moment later, the bus stopped and the man in the raincoat jumped to his feet. Kitty gripped the corners of her newspaper and tried not to shake. She didn't like sudden movement, and the man's agitation just made it all worse.

Don't get up. Don't get up. Just let him walk away.

It wasn't going to work. The stress of the crowd and the strange man's manner had already worn away at Kitty's resolve. As the man pushed his way to the door, Kitty got up, tucked the newspaper under her arm, and slipped out the back of the bus. She told herself she was just going to see which way the man went and leave it at that, but she knew it wasn't true.

Kitty watched the man from around the corner of the bus. He seemed even more on edge than before, and he looked around a few times before walking away from the bus stop at a quick pace. A few other people on the street were going in the same direction, so Kitty fell in among them. She kept her head down and tried to look inconspicuous. That part was easy: even being peculiar, she rarely stood out.

Following the man wasn't all that difficult, even after the crowd thinned out. A block from the bus stop, he turned down a side road and Kitty followed, pausing at the edge of a building before hurrying after. He looked over his shoulder every few minutes, and Kitty only narrowly avoided detection the first two times by ducking around corners and waiting until the coast was clear. After that, she had worked out how to tell when the man was going to look again. He always shifted his shoulders before turning, and it gave Kitty enough warning to hide.

Kitty knew she was being reckless. If the man realized she was following him, there was no telling what he would do.

A few blocks from the bus stop, he turned onto a one-way street that ran between two large brick warehouses. A few cars were parked near the intersection. One of them had someone behind the wheel. Kitty noticed that but didn't think much about it. She should have.

Kitty hurried to the intersection and pressed herself against the wall of the nearest building. Something told her that the man in the raincoat had begun to suspect her. If she rushed around the corner, he would be there, waiting to confront her. And then she would have to run very fast to get away.

But to her surprise, when she peeked out, she saw him standing midway along the street, looking back and forth nervously. Kitty ducked back behind cover and took some deep breaths. This was very stupid. She shouldn't be doing this. And yet, for some reason she couldn't shake the feeling that something important was going on. All the little pieces making up the past half hour were starting to fit together into something very suspicious.

She looked out again and saw the man farther down the street, walking very quickly. A couple of times, he glanced over his shoulder, and Kitty was forced to stay where she was to avoid being seen. By the time she was able to get moving again, the man in the raincoat was too far ahead to follow. He promptly disappeared down the next street.

Kitty inhaled the chilly, damp air. The fixation was starting to fade. With the man gone, there was nothing left to keep her focused on her absurd adventure.

"Well, Kitty," she muttered, "you must be awful proud. You've made an ass of yourself, and now you'll be late."

Kitty went down the street, following the route the man had taken. In her mind, she pictured a map of the London bus routes, which she knew almost by heart. She had wandered far enough that she could reach another stop closer to the museum if she kept going this way.

As she walked, something about one of the buildings troubled her, and she stopped near where she had seen the man standing. She looked at the wall and it made her uncomfortable. After a few seconds, she realized why.

There was a small line of chalk marked across two of the bricks, the dull white standing out against the red clay and gray mortar. No one else would give it a second thought, but Kitty noticed it. It was out of place. It didn't belong. Things that were out of place always made her uneasy.

Unable to control the impulse any more than her curiosity, Kitty knelt and brushed the chalk away with her thumb. It was stubborn and didn't want to go. In the end, Kitty just managed to smudge it and get bits of chalk on her fingertip. She sighed and looked at her hand. Now the chalk stain was going to bother her until she could wash it off.

I'm a bloody mess today, she thought dejectedly. Maybe she was tired. She'd been up late helping her father rearrange the stockroom, since he would have to mind the store by himself today.

As she looked at the smudge of chalk, Kitty noticed a new feature of the wall that troubled her. A few inches below the mark, one of the bricks jutted out from its place slightly more than the rest. The lack of symmetry made Kitty twitch. She pushed at the brick a couple of times, even though she knew it was probably the work of bad placement on the part of the mason who had laid it.

Except that the brick was loose. And there was something behind it. Kitty tilted her head and pulled the brick away. It came free very easily. Behind it was small hole hollowed out from the wall. Kitty peered inside and saw a little metal canister.

Leave it, Kitty told herself, as she reached in and pulled the canister out.

Don't open it.

But open it she did. Inside was a roll of undeveloped film. Kitty felt herself grow cold with fear. This wasn't right at all. The man *had* been up to something, probably something criminal. Had he left the film canister behind the brick in the wall? What was on it? What secrets did it conceal?

Put it back! Kitty shouted inside her head, but as usual her impulses didn't listen. She got up and shoved the film into her bag. The movements were almost mechanical, like someone else was doing it.

Kitty started walking quickly. Despite the cold, she felt sweat on her forehead and the palms of her hands. She had made a terrible mistake coming here, but it would be all right. No one knew what she had done. She'd find a rubbish bin somewhere and throw the canister away, and no one would be the wiser.

Only she knew that wasn't true. She was fixating again. Her curiosity was running wild. If she didn't shake this soon, she might actually find a chemist's shop and get the film developed.

Kitty clenched her hands shut. *Get yourself together. Put the film back!*

She was too caught up in her thoughts to pay attention when one of the cars behind her pulled out from its parking space. Kitty only heard the roar of the engine when it sped up to reach her, and then the squeal of tires as it lurched to a stop in front of her. She stared, dumbfounded, as the side door opened and a grizzled man in a leather jacket got out.

Run! Kitty screamed to herself.

This time she did listen. Her instinct was to freeze in shock, and that was what her conscious mind did, but the impulsive part of her subconscious wasn't having any of it. The same part of her brain that had driven her to follow the man, to wipe away the chalk, to remove the brick, and to take the film assumed control again. Kitty dashed for the intersection.

As she rounded the back of the car, a second man with an unpleasant-looking mustache grabbed her from the side and slammed her against the wall. Kitty started to scream, but the man with the mustache covered her mouth with his hand. His companion reached them and pulled out a knife.

"Don't you dare make a sound, girl," he growled, waving the knife in front of her eye. "One peep and I'll slit your throat."

Kitty froze in terror, unable even to whimper. She was going to die.

"Christ!" the mustached man said. "She's just a kid."

"I don't care if she's your bloody gran," snarled his companion. He grabbed Kitty's handbag and pulled out the film canister. "The boss was right: they're onto Higgins. Girl must've followed him when he left to make the drop."

"We can't stay here," Mustache said, glancing down the street. "They wouldn't send a girl to follow him on her own. There's probably someone else a few minutes behind."

The other man nodded and grabbed Kitty by the scruff of the neck. He dragged her away from the wall and toward the back of the car.

"We take her to the boss," he replied. "Open the trunk."

"No! No, please!" Kitty cried.

She tried to explain that she didn't know anything about Higgins or the film or anything at all really, but each time she tried it just came out as a confused jumble of words that didn't make sense even to her. She kept trying to explain as the men dragged her to the car and shoved her into the trunk. Kitty was sobbing and shaking, overwhelmed as much by the looping thoughts inside her head as by abject terror. Never in her life had she imagined something like this might happen to her, and she still didn't fully understand what was going on.

Have to get out. You're going to die. It's all a mistake.

Have to get out. You're going to die. It's all a mistake.

Have to get out. You're going to die. It's all a mistake.

The trunk slammed shut, sealing her in darkness, leaving her alone in the embrace of fear.

CHAPTER 3

Kitty huddled in a ball on the floor of the trunk, arms wrapped around her knees to make herself as compact as possible. She felt herself shuddering, but it was a strange, disassociated experience. Her mind turned in circles as it tried to make sense of what had happened, and she found it impossible to do anything but stare ahead into the darkness.

The kidnappers drove slowly, probably to avoid attention from the police. That was good: it meant Kitty wasn't sent sliding around the trunk, banging into everything. Not that it helped her situation at all. She tried to count the number of turns, how many minutes had passed, anything to give some sense of where they were going. It didn't work, but at least the counting became a half-hearted distraction.

Eventually the car turned another corner and slowed to a stop. Kitty had fallen into a kind of motionless trance, which sometimes happened when she started to panic. She shook herself and shivered. The air smelled like petrol, and it was disgusting.

She heard the kidnappers get out of the car and start speaking to someone. A few moments later the trunk door opened, showering Kitty with bright light. She had been in the dark long enough that it hurt her eyes, and she squinted to keep from being blinded. Hands reached for her and she started thrashing around, feebly trying to fight back.

Her resistance was met with the back of someone's hand across her face. She didn't give up struggling, but the sudden pain startled her long enough for the men to drag her out. The man with the mustache held her arms with a painful grip and forced her to stand up.

Breathe. Breathe. Breathe, Kitty told herself. *Stay calm. Stay in charge.*

She wanted to scream and panic. She wanted to lash out at the men and run for her life. Right now that wasn't going to work.

Kitty looked around to get her bearings. She was in a large garage, which was filled with so much assorted junk that it somehow managed to feel claustrophobic despite its size. Three cars stood in a row near the doors, waiting to be serviced, underneath the watchful eye of an upstairs manager's office with wide glass windows. Barrels and crates lined the walls, and Kitty's gaze was drawn toward a towering pile of boxes that looked like it might topple over in a strong breeze. It was so precarious, it made Kitty uncomfortable just to see it. The whole garage screamed *danger!*

Near the office stairs was a table occupied by four men in work coveralls who were playing cards. Well, had been playing cards. As Kitty was hauled out of the trunk, they got up and approached the two kidnappers. A seventh man in an everyday suit came down from the office to join them. This man was older than the rest, probably about fifty. He looked angry, and Kitty wasn't sure if it was because of her or someone else.

"What the hell is going on?" the older man demanded, pointing at Kitty. "Who is that and why is she here?"

"Sorry, boss," said the man in the leather coat. "Higgins is compromised."

"What?" The boss practically spat with anger. "Are you sure?"

Mustache answered. "This girl was following him. After he made the drop, she snatched up the film. Good thing you had us watching the site, or we'd never have known."

"Dammit," the boss said. The men in coveralls exchanged looks, and one of them muttered something that Kitty didn't understand. The boss snapped his head around and shouted at his underling, "You know the rules! No Russian!"

"Yessir," the underling replied.

The boss turned his attention to Kitty. He approached her, studying her with an intense stare that made Kitty shiver. She didn't like being looked at directly, and she turned her face away. The boss grabbed her chin and forced her to look at him.

"Well now, young miss," the boss said, "who are you?"

"I'm—I'm nobody," Kitty whispered, still trying to turn away. Her eyes darted around, trying to look anywhere but at the man and his angry expression.

The boss answered her in a cruel, half-singsong voice. "That's not true, missy. Everybody's somebody. Now, you should answer my questions when I ask them. This will go better for you."

A lump formed in Kitty's throat and she swallowed.

"I'm, um," she stammered, "I'm Kitty."

"Kitty, eh?" the boss asked. He chuckled. "Well, Kitty, you're in a lot of trouble." He snapped his fingers and addressed his men. "Chair. Now."

Before Kitty could ask what was going on, the man with the mustache dragged her over to a chair and shoved her into it. Kitty gripped the armrests, shaking with fear. She looked around for an exit. There were two big garage doors for the cars, but they were both closed. A side door stood on the other end of the room, just past the boxes, but she couldn't tell if it was locked.

The boss pulled up another chair and sat across from Kitty. "Now then, Kitty," he said to her, "I want you to tell me who you work for."

Kitty shook her head. "I don't work for nobody. Honest, sir."

"Then why were you following Mr. Higgins?"

The boss spoke in a soft, patronizing tone, like he was trying to be kind and considerate when both of them knew he wasn't.

"I—I just were curious, sir," Kitty answered.

"Curious?"

"I were seated beside 'im on the bus," Kitty explained. "An' 'e were just so fidgety, I wanted to follow an' see why. I didn't mean no harm, honest." She gave a nervous smile and hoped it was disarming. "Just curious, like I said."

The boss chuckled and patted her knee, which made Kitty shudder and pull away.

"Well, Kitty, you know what they say about curiosity and the cat, don't you?"

"Please, I dunno nothin'!" Kitty cried.

The boss glanced at the two kidnappers and asked, "Did Higgins deliver the film?"

"Yes, boss," said the man in the leather coat, as he handed over the film canister. "Girl had picked it up when we found her. Put the thing in her bag, was gonna run off with it."

"Now why would an innocent girl do a thing like that?" the boss asked Kitty. He waved the film canister in front of her nose. "Were you 'curious' about that too?"

"I just—I noticed the brick were in the wrong place an' I thought I'd take a look." Kitty tried to sound calm and sensible, but everything was coming out frantic and muddled. "I would've put it back where I found it, honest!"

The boss gave her a dramatic sigh. "Listen here, girl: we both know you're lying. Now, if you tell me the truth, you won't get hurt. But if you keep lying . . . well, it won't go very nicely for you. Understand?"

Kitty nodded quickly.

"Good." The boss handed the film canister to one of his men and murmured, "Put this in the safe until we can get it to Dmitri."

"What about Higgins?"

"Find him and dispose of him. Our friend at the Ministry of Defense has outlived his usefulness."

The underling nodded and went into the upstairs office with the film. The boss turned back to Kitty, still pretending that there was a way for her to save herself if she cooperated.

"Now then, girl," he said, "tell me who sent you to follow Higgins."

Kitty shook her head. "No one, sir, I swear—"

"Ah!" the boss held up his hand. "One more lie and I will lose my patience. Who sent you? Was it Gascoigne? Jones?" His expression twisted into a hideous snarl of impatience. "Give me a name!"

Kitty pressed herself deeper into the chair and held up her hands as a shield. She had to delay long enough to think of some way out. But what could she say that would convince them to keep her alive?

"There . . . there were a lady on the bus!" she exclaimed.

"A lady?"

Kitty nodded. "An Indian lady. Very posh. She—um— she paid me to follow that man Higgins an'—an' she said if 'e dropped anythin' along the way, I were to take it an' bring it back to 'er."

She tensed, afraid that the lie wouldn't be believed. To her surprise, the boss smiled.

"That wasn't so hard, was it?" he asked, patting her cheek. Kitty pulled away. The touch made Kitty want to scrub her face until it was raw. Chuckling, the boss got up and approached his men. "A posh Indian lady?" he asked.

"Sounds like one of Pryce's lot," said the man with the mustache.

The man in the leather jacket frowned. "Odd. I saw a posh Indian lady while I was watching the docks last night. She had on this fancy fur coat. I assumed she'd been at a club. Came up to me drunk, asking for directions." The man laughed at the memory. "Before I can say 'clear off,' she trips over herself, falls flat on the pavement, then gets up and wobbles away."

His laughter died away as the other men stared at him.

"You don't think it was the same person, do you?"

"You're an idiot, Mark," the boss snapped. "Ten to one Pryce knows who you are now."

"She didn't take photographs or anything, I'm certain of it," Mark insisted. "And she just came straight to the side of the car. Never saw the license plates."

"Someone change them anyway," the boss said. "I'll deal with you later," he added to Mark. Then he called to Kitty, "How were you supposed to meet this woman, to give her the film?"

Kitty searched around for an answer. "Um . . . we were to meet at the British Museum at three, an' I'd give 'er whatever I took from Mr. Higgins."

"Good." The boss rubbed his hands together, looking pleased. "Boys, I think we're due a trip to the British Museum. I daresay our mystery woman can tell us how much Pryce knows about our little operation here."

Mark looked at Kitty and asked, "What about the girl?"

"Put her upstairs. You'll have to stay behind anyway. Work the girl over a bit, see if she knows anything else." The boss cast a glance at Kitty. "I think she's hiding something."

Kitty shrank back more, until it seemed she couldn't get any smaller in the chair.

The boss rubbed his chin with his thumb and asked, "Mark, which car were you driving last night?"

"Same one as today," Mark began. His voice faded away and he turned pale. "You don't think—?"

The boss turned bright red with anger and shouted, "Tripped over herself, did she? Fell onto the pavement? You mean this mystery woman was lying down next to your car and you never thought to check what she was doing?" He snapped his fingers and pointed at the car. "Search it! Search it now!"

Three of the men rushed to obey him. They began crawling around the car, looking at every nook and cranny.

Kitty's eyes sifted back and forth as she watched the men. They weren't paying any attention to her now. Kitty glanced at the side door. No one was near it. It might be unlocked. That was better than nothing.

Moving cautiously, she got up and tiptoed toward the door, casting glances back at her kidnappers as she went. Once they saw her, she would have to run. But if she ran now, she'd make too much noise and they'd immediately notice she was trying to escape.

One of the men pulled a small metal box out from under

the car. He held it up for the boss's inspection, and the boss started shouting.

"A radio beacon. You bloody idiot, Mark! They know where we are now! They could've been following you all day!"

Mark backed away and raised his hands. "Easy, boss. I messed up, I know, but we can fix this. Those radio devices, they can't work miracles, can they? If someone's followed us here, they'll have to search the buildings one at a time to find us." Mark looked around at the other men to back him up. "Let's wait in ambush, and if someone shows, we'll kill 'em."

The boss slowly nodded. He reached inside his coat and pulled out a short revolver. "That's good. That might work. Someone get upstairs and watch the road. I want to know when they arrive." He turned and pointed toward the empty chair. "And tie up the g—bloody hell!"

His eyes locked on Kitty, who was only a few paces from the door now. Kitty ran.

The door was unlocked. She shoved it open and bolted outside. She was in an alleyway that ran alongside the garage, leading toward a long courtyard shared by several different buildings. She couldn't tell if any of them were occupied.

Kitty screamed for help. She kept running, of course, but a person could scream and run at the same time. Kitty had always been rather good at it.

She made it around to the front of the building before the man called Mark caught up with her. He grabbed her from behind and clapped a hand over her mouth, stifling Kitty's cries. Kitty struggled with all her might, but there was no contest.

Kitty had made her grand escape and it had failed. She was done for, and she knew it.

CHAPTER 4

Kitty didn't stop fighting even as Mark dragged her back inside the garage. She kicked and squirmed and thrashed violently, almost knocking her attacker off his feet twice. He practically threw her back into the wooden chair. Kitty flinched from the impact but she was on her feet again in an instant. That impulsive part of her brain that refused to sit still had taken over. All she could think about was the one-track idea of escape. There was the door: she had to get to the door.

Two of the other men grabbed her shoulders and slammed her back into the chair, hard. That was almost painful enough to break Kitty out of her fixation. She shook her head a few times, trying to make sense of the fact that she was sitting rather than running. Finally, conscious thought took over again and her eyes focused on the face of the boss gazing down at her.

The impulse to flee finally died away, and Kitty shrank back in fear.

"That was a very foolish thing to do, girl," the boss snarled. "You are going to regret that."

He was lying and Kitty knew it. That made her angry.

"What can you do that you weren't plannin' on a'ready?" she retorted, though the words came out in a half-stutter. "Gonna kill me twice? That it?"

"I . . ." The boss wagged his finger at her, but having reality presented to him, he had no rebuttal. "Well, you're going to regret it anyway. Simon, get the blowtorch!"

Kitty shuddered, inwardly casting about for some way to avert her fate. She couldn't run. She couldn't fight. They were all too big and too fast.

Beg, Kitty told herself. *Beg for mercy.*

Except that Kitty couldn't form the words. Panic overwhelmed her. She tried to pull away from the men holding her down, but they tightened their grip and forced her against the chair. She was trapped.

Kitty started thrashing violently. It was practically automatic, something she did when her mind just couldn't cope anymore. It had been the worst when she was a small child. Since then, she had taught herself how to keep most of it suppressed, but now the fear and the noise and the boss's shouting were too much for her to handle.

She swung her head back and forth, trying to sense something—anything!—through the haze of fear and noise. She felt her head connect with someone's face and one of the kidnappers started screaming in pain. That only made things worse.

Someone was shouting "No! No! No!" It took Kitty a few moments to realize it was her.

"Christ!" the boss swore. "Someone shut her up!"

Mark grabbed Kitty by the chin, forcing her mouth shut and pinning her head in place. He glared into Kitty's eyes. "I say we just kill her," he said. "Less trouble."

Before anyone else could speak, there was a loud knock on the side door. The kidnappers turned around, and Kitty looked past Mark to see what was happening.

A man stood just inside the doorway, holding an umbrella, which he tapped against the door to get everyone's attention. The man was in his late forties and a little jowly, giving him the look of an English bulldog. He was very smartly dressed in a tweed suit and a matching bowler hat, and he smiled politely when everyone turned toward him.

"I say! Roughing up a young lady? Quite unacceptable. A gentleman can't stand for that."

The boss made a face. "Pryce."

"Ivan."

The man named Pryce advanced into the garage, walking with the air of a man out for an afternoon stroll. "I heard shouting and I thought I'd take a look," he said. "Lucky I did. Why don't you let the young lady go, Ivan? This is between us."

"She's not one of yours?" The boss sounded surprised.

"She most certainly is not." Mr. Pryce nodded to Kitty and tipped his hat politely. "Don't worry, miss, we'll have you safe and sound in just a moment."

The boss pressed the barrel of his revolver against Kitty's temple. Kitty clenched her eyes shut and waited for the gunshot.

"Wishful thinking, Pryce," the boss said. "But if you try anything, the girl dies. Now drop your weapons."

Kitty opened one eye. The boss was making threats. He didn't plan to kill her. Yet.

Mr. Pryce tossed his umbrella away and held up his empty hands. "I'm unarmed, Ivan," he said. "Why don't you return the favor? Let's settle this like gentlemen."

The boss scoffed and nodded at his men. "Take him." But as two of the kidnappers approached Mr. Pryce, the boss hesitated. "Just a minute. You said '*We'll* have you safe and sound.' What did you mean, *we?*"

The answer came from behind him, spoken by a woman with a cool tone and a crisp Mayfair accent: "He meant you shouldn't leave your windows unlocked, Ivan."

Kitty looked up, and the boss turned to see the lady in blue standing behind him. One of her hands was already balled into a fist. As the boss turned, the lady punched him across the face and laid him out on the floor of the garage. His revolver went skittering across the floor and disappeared under the car.

"Perfect timing, Mrs. Singh!" Mr. Pryce exclaimed.

"One tries to be punctual, Pryce," Mrs. Singh called back.

The two men holding Kitty released her and backed away, reaching for the nearest weapons to hand. One pulled out a knife, while the other grabbed a crowbar from a nearby table.

Mrs. Singh stepped in front of Kitty. "Find someplace to hide," she said quietly as she faced the two men. She put her hands on her hips and called to them, "Come along then. Who's first?"

It was a silly question because both of the men attacked her at once, but they seemed unnerved by Mrs. Singh's bravado. Their apprehension was well-founded. As they came at her, she ducked under the crowbar and met the knife-wielding man with two fists to the gut. Across the garage, three of the kidnappers had rushed at Mr. Pryce, while the last one ran to help the two fighting Mrs. Singh.

Kitty was surrounded by noise and violence. She ducked and covered her head with her arms, flinching each time she heard someone get hit. It wasn't like in the films. The sound was softer, but more visceral. Kitty could practically feel each blow. She tried to work up the courage to peek out at the fighting, but she couldn't. Her mind was caught in circles, divided between the impulses to hide and to flee, and the confusion left her rooted in place.

The fear paralysis was suddenly broken when one of the kidnappers fell to the floor in front of her. Kitty cried out and bolted, knocking over the chair.

The fighting had devolved quickly. Mr. Pryce and Mrs. Singh were now back to back, surrounded by the remaining five men, who seemed dead set on killing both of them, through weight of numbers if necessary.

Kitty's gaze turned toward the side door. It was open. She could make a run for it. But then, what about her mysterious rescuers? They hadn't come there to save her, but they had saved her all the same. Kitty knew that if she ran, she'd never forgive herself.

But what to do?

Her eyes snapped toward the stack of boxes across the room. It was quite near the brawl. A good push would bring the whole thing down and hit at least two of the kidnappers. That would even things up a little.

One, two, three, go, Kitty thought.

She didn't move.

One, two, three, go! she repeated silently.

She remained rooted to the spot. The haze of panic was too strong. Her body felt like it was made of lead. It was all she could do to keep from cowering, let alone run toward danger.

No, you have to do this! Kitty insisted to herself. *You can't hide and you can't do nothing!*

Kitty shook herself and dashed to the boxes. The kidnappers weren't paying any attention to her. They were now down to four, but Mr. Pryce and Mrs. Singh had been hit a few times too. There was blood on Mrs. Singh's nice white sweater, and Mr. Pryce's fancy suit had been slashed here and there by knives.

You can do this, Kitty. So do it.

Kitty braced her hands against the box at eye level and pushed as hard as she could. There was something heavy inside that resisted her, but she planted her feet and kept pushing. The box started to slide forward.

There was movement by the chair. Kitty looked and saw the boss get up, rubbing his face where Mrs. Singh had punched him. He and Kitty stared at each other, and for a moment Kitty was certain he was going to come for her. Instead, the boss took advantage of the opening and ran across the room. A moment later, Kitty heard the rattle of the garage door opening. The boss was fleeing like a coward.

Stay focused. The boxes.

Kitty gave a last hard push and the stack of boxes tumbled over onto the fight. The top two boxes landed with a crash, hitting three of the kidnappers and knocking down two. Mr. Pryce jumped backward to avoid being hit as well, but he looked relieved when he turned toward Kitty.

"Much obliged, miss," he said, tipping his hat to her.

Mrs. Singh knocked the final kidnapper down with a quick one-two punch and looked in Kitty's direction. "I thought I told you to hide."

"Yes, miss," Kitty answered meekly. She paused and added, "I didn't."

"I see that," Mrs. Singh said.

They were interrupted by the roar of an engine. Kitty and her rescuers turned in time to see one of the cars drive out into the yard, its tires squealing and leaving rubber marks on the floor. The boss was behind the wheel. He looked afraid but determined.

Mr. Pryce and Mrs. Singh ran to the garage door and watched it go.

"Dammit!" Mrs. Singh exclaimed. "If we've lost Ivan, the whole operation's gone up." She swept her hand in the direction of the kidnappers sprawled out on the floor. "These fellows are all replaceable."

Mr. Pryce frowned and pulled a notepad and pencil out of his jacket pocket. "Did you get any of the license number? I think there was an A in there."

Mrs. Singh shook her head. "There was a five or a two, I think. He was going too fast for me to see more."

"Well, at least it's something to go on." Mr. Pryce tried to look positive, but Kitty felt the defeat on him.

"Um . . ." Kitty began hesitantly. She wasn't sure if she should interrupt.

"Yes?" Mr. Pryce asked.

"I—um—I saw the license plate," Kitty explained. "All of it, I think."

"Really?" Mrs. Singh asked, giving Kitty a look caught between skepticism and suspicion. "You only saw it for a moment. Can you be sure?"

"Absolutely sure, miss. I sometimes 'ave trouble with names, but I always remember faces and numbers."

"Faces and numbers?" Mrs. Singh repeated, still staring at Kitty.

Kitty glanced away. Mrs. Singh had a very intense stare, which was hard for Kitty to meet. But she did remember the plate number exactly. She closed her eyes to picture it, like a photograph imprinted in her head, and recited it aloud. When she opened her eyes again, she saw Mr. Pryce scribbling in his notebook, looking very pleased.

"It's worth a try anyway," he said. "I'll call from the telephone in the street in case this one's been tapped. Don't want to alert Ivan's compatriots, do we?"

"Not if we can avoid it," Mrs. Singh agreed. "Go. I'll keep an eye on our new friend here." She turned to Kitty. "Who are you, by the way?"

"Um," Kitty stammered, "Katherine Granger, but everyone calls me Kitty."

Mr. Pryce smiled at this and raised his hat. "Kitty Granger, very nice to meet you. I am Mr. Pryce, this is Mrs. Singh. We work for Her Majesty's government."

CHAPTER 5

"**Y**ou're spies!" Kitty exclaimed, too excited to hold her tongue. Ivan and his men were probably spies too, but these were British spies! Queen and country and all that! That meant they were on her side and this whole wretched ordeal was finally over.

Mr. Pryce drew himself up like a bird with ruffled feathers. "Certainly not! Spying is what the other side does. Now, if you ladies will excuse me, I have a telephone call to make."

Mr. Pryce hurried outside with a spritely gait. Kitty watched until he was out of sight, and then flicked her eyes toward Mrs. Singh. The woman was studying her with folded arms and an arched eyebrow.

"Am I in trouble, miss?" Kitty asked nervously.

"Missis," came the correction. "And that remains to be seen. You were on the bus with me, weren't you? The girl who wanted my newspaper."

"Just the crossword," Kitty said.

"How did you come to be here?"

Kitty fidgeted, playing with her fingers nervously. Everything had been so completely overwhelming a few moments ago, but direct conversation really was the *worst*.

"Well, um, you see, that man Higgins, 'e got back on the bus after you followed 'im off."

"I know. I was there," Mrs. Singh said.

"An' I got curious," Kitty explained.

Mrs. Singh arched both eyebrows this time. "*Curious?*"

Kitty nodded. "Curious. I do that sometimes. So when Mr. Higgins got off the bus a few minutes later, I followed to see what 'e were about." She twisted her face into an awkward expression of embarrassment. She knew exactly how absurd it sounded.

Whatever Mrs. Singh thought of the explanation, she didn't react. Instead, she asked, "And that's how they caught you? Higgins saw you?"

"Oh, no, miss—er, missis." Kitty shook her head. "Higgins never saw me, not for the five blocks I followed 'im. I'm good at not bein' seen, you see."

Mrs. Singh considered Kitty's words, looking skeptical. On the ground, one of the men started to groan and shift in place, so Mrs. Singh knelt, removed his belt, and used it to hog-tie his wrists before he could wake properly. Then she began tying up the other kidnappers while she continued her questioning.

"How *did* you get caught?"

"Well, that man Higgins got ahead of me a ways, on account of me needin' to stay outta sight, and I were goin' to give up followin', only I saw this chalk mark on the wall an'—"

"Chalk mark?" Mrs. Singh asked.

"Just a little line of chalk on a brick. I saw it an' I . . ."

"And you got curious?" Mrs. Singh finished for her.

"Yes, missis." Kitty shrugged. "Then I noticed there were a brick loose, so I took it out the wall and inside there were this little canister of film. So I took that, only a couple of that fellow Ivan's ruffians was waitin' in a car down the block an' saw me. I tried to get away but they nabbed me an' took me 'ere. I think they meant to kill me till you an' Mr. Pryce showed up. They thought I were workin' for you."

"I can see how they got that idea," Mrs. Singh said. She folded her arms and cocked her head at Kitty. "What were you doing on the bus anyway? Shouldn't you be in school?"

"I'm sixteen," Kitty explained.

Mrs. Singh frowned at her. "I understand that you're legally allowed to leave school if you want. I said *shouldn't* you be there?"

Kitty sighed. "It's me da, you see. Needs me to work in the family shop ever since me mum's passed." The moment she said it, she knew it was too much information, and she clammed up.

Mrs. Singh's expression softened. "My condolences for your loss." She paused as Mr. Pryce rejoined them. "Good news?"

"The police are on the lookout for Ivan's car," Mr. Pryce replied. "He'll abandon it before long, but hopefully we've put some pressure on him. You know, I didn't realize he was back in the country."

"Ivan's a bad penny," Mrs. Singh said. "He always turns up. You remember Cairo?"

Mr. Pryce smiled wistfully. "I remember a delightful sunset dinner along the Nile with a charming companion."

Mrs. Singh rolled her eyes. "I was thinking more about the ambush ten minutes into the second course."

"Oh yes, I'd forgotten about that part." Mr. Pryce shrugged and rubbed his hands together cheerfully. "Now, what have you learned about our young friend here?"

Mrs. Singh summarized what Kitty had told her.

Mr. Pryce gave Kitty a stern look. "Quite a story."

"I think she's telling the truth," Mrs. Singh said.

"I am!" Kitty exclaimed. "Honest! It were all a mistake!"

"Perhaps," Mr. Pryce said. He went to the staircase and climbed a few steps. "In the meantime, I think we should have a look around the place before the police arrive and make a mess of things."

"A capital idea, Pryce," Mrs. Singh said.

She took Kitty by the arm and led her up the stairs. Kitty's gaze shifted around nervously. Neither of the spies seemed threatening, but after what had just happened Kitty found it hard to be calm about strangers.

The upstairs office looked very commonplace, and Kitty couldn't imagine anyone using it for illicit purposes. She sat in a chair by the wall and folded her hands in her lap, trying to keep out of the way while Mr. Pryce and Mrs. Singh searched through the desk and the room's two filing cabinets. She watched them in silence, noticing the growing frustration on their faces. The two spies were not finding the information they wanted.

There was something about the room that made Kitty uncomfortable, and she shifted in her chair, trying to detect what it was. This was how she felt when the silverware was crooked, or when someone left a book sticking out on a shelf. Something was out of place, like the chalk mark and the broken brick that had started all this trouble.

Kitty's gaze ran along the far wall, following the grain of the wood. The fingers on one hand flexed unconsciously, like she was running her fingertips against the wall, feeling the texture. She couldn't actually feel it, of course: it was just something her hands did sometimes when she was focused on something.

After the third pass, she found what was bothering her. The wood paneling was different midway along the wall. Kitty got up and walked across the office with slow, almost mechanical steps. Her eyes remained focused on the wall, searching for the outline of the wrong wood. The seam was nearly invisible, but it was there.

"What are you doing?" Mrs. Singh asked.

Kitty glanced over her shoulder and saw the two spies watching her.

"Um . . ." Kitty shifted her feet nervously and pointed her finger at the paneling. "The wall's different over there. I think the wood's been replaced."

Mr. Pryce stepped away from the desk and joined Kitty. "Really? It looks the same to me, but . . ." He ran his fingertips across the wall where Kitty pointed. It took his a few times, but he finally found the seam that Kitty had detected. Mr. Pryce pressed his ear to the wall and tapped his knuckles against it, and what he heard made him smile with genuine delight. "Aha! I think there's a safe back there. Clever girl."

Kitty, caught off guard by the compliment, bobbed her head and mumbled, "Thank you."

"We should be thanking you," Mrs. Singh replied. She examined the wood paneling. "I don't think I would've noticed it until we started tearing the walls apart."

She reached into her sleeve and pulled out something long and metal, sort of like a screwdriver but obviously a weapon. Kitty's eyes bugged at the sight of it, and she shrank back.

"Don't worry, Kitty, this is for the wall, not you," Mrs. Singh said.

Together, Mrs. Singh and Mr. Pryce began prying the planks of wood away from the wall until a little panel sprang open, revealing a metal safe.

"Will you look at that, Mrs. Singh?" Mr. Pryce mused.

"I am looking, Pryce," Mrs. Singh replied. "I see a safe and no key."

"Ivan must have taken it with him."

Mrs. Singh nodded. She tapped her wristwatch and added, "I also see an impending deadline of when the police are going to arrive and start getting in our way."

Mr. Pryce laughed. "Don't be pessimistic," he said. "I've been hoping for a chance to crack a safe. It's been ages since I've had a go at one."

"That's what concerns me," Mrs. Singh told him.

Mr. Pryce made a disappointed face at her, but he removed a small set of lock picks from inside his coat pocket and knelt down to examine the lock.

"Um . . ." Kitty ventured softly, afraid to speak up and interrupt them.

"Yes?" Mrs. Singh asked.

"What's gonna 'appen to me when the police get 'ere?" Kitty asked.

"They're going to ask you some questions about what happened," Mrs. Singh replied. "They will be very curious about why you were following Higgins."

Kitty made a face. "Must I talk to 'em?" The thought of police questioning made her nervous. "Only, if me da knows I've gotten into trouble, 'e'll be furious with me."

"Not to worry, they'll be discreet," Mr. Pryce assured her. "I'm old friends with the head of Special Branch. We have an arrangement."

"Special Branch?" Kitty echoed incredulously. "Special Branch of the Metropolitan Police?"

"Yes, they handle all espionage-related arrests," Mrs. Singh said. "Pryce and I are like MI5. We investigate, but we can't actually apprehend anyone."

"What if there's a problem Special Branch can't manage?"

"Then . . ." Mrs. Singh chose her next words carefully. "Then there aren't any arrests to be made, understand?"

Kitty shivered. "Yes, missis."

CHAPTER 6

The policemen from Special Branch arrived about twenty minutes later, and they set about searching every last inch of the garage for evidence. Ivan's men were taken away in handcuffs like it was all very routine. No one seemed surprised at seeing Mr. Pryce or Mrs. Singh, or at least the police had been cautioned not to interfere with the two spies. Mr. Pryce had taken photographs of the safe's contents, but he left the documents inside for the police to confiscate. The roll of film, however, disappeared into Mr. Pryce's pocket and nothing was said about it.

One of the men from Special Branch sat Kitty down in the main part of the garage and took her statement, under the watchful eyes of Mr. Pryce and Mrs. Singh. Kitty explained that she had seen Higgins acting strangely on the bus and had followed with the intention of reporting him to the first policeman she saw. That seemed more believable than admitting she had been overpowered by curiosity, with no motive or plan beyond that.

The interview lasted about half an hour, and by the end of it Kitty was on the verge of shouting just to make it all stop. The whole day had been a nightmare, and being questioned over and over again frayed her nerves almost to the breaking point.

But she didn't break. She kept her cool, sitting with her hands folded tightly in her lap so they wouldn't shake. Under her chair, she kicked one foot back and forth slowly to relieve some of the stress, and it helped her get through the worst of it.

She also forced herself to look distressed and fearful, like how girls did in the films: on the verge of tears but not quite crying, gushing with relief at being rescued, that sort of thing. In reality, the more upset Kitty got, the quieter she became, trying to hide from the world until she could figure out how to get away. But the police would find that suspicious, so she did the opposite and it seemed to work.

At the end, the policeman took her address and stood up. "Right, miss, you're free to go. My sympathies for your ordeal."

"Thank you, sir," Kitty exclaimed. "I didn't mean no harm, I swear it. I were only tryin' to help."

That was true, even if the finer details were distorted.

"Take my advice, young lady," the policeman said. "Next time, leave the sleuthing to professionals. You see something suspicious, you find a policeman straight away instead of following a stranger. This could have gone very badly for you."

Kitty lowered her head and mumbled, "Yes, sir."

"She's all yours," the policeman said to Mr. Pryce.

"Much obliged, detective," Mr. Pryce replied, touching the brim of his hat. He smiled at Kitty and then looked to his partner. "I think it's about time for Miss Granger to go home, don't you agree, Mrs. Singh?"

"Quite," Mrs. Singh said. She motioned to Kitty. "Come along, I'll drive you. My car is on the street."

Kitty followed Mrs. Singh outside. More policemen from Special Branch were scouring the surrounding buildings for evidence. Kitty quickened her pace to get past them. Right now crowds of people were the last thing she needed to be dealing with.

Mrs. Singh's car was parked around the corner. It was a simple black sedan, and it looked far less dramatic than Mrs. Singh herself. That surprised Kitty. She had expected something flashy and fast.

Mrs. Singh noticed her expression and chuckled. "Disappointed?"

"No, missis," Kitty answered quickly. "I just assumed it'd be a bit more . . . excitin'?"

"To be fair, it's technically Pryce's car," Mrs. Singh said as they climbed in. "I do prefer something with a little more panache and acceleration, but you can't really tail people in the city with a Lotus Elan."

"Missis, 'ow did you find me?" Kitty asked as they drove.

"We found *you* because of your screaming," Mrs. Singh said. "Smart, that. I assume you tried to escape?"

Kitty nodded.

"Well, that's what saved your life. As for finding the garage . . ."

"That man Ivan said you used a radio device," Kitty interjected. Then she shut her mouth. It was rude to interrupt and she wasn't sure if it was a good idea to let on what she had overheard.

Mrs. Singh chuckled and opened the glove box in front of Kitty. Inside was something that looked like a small television set.

"We managed to get a bug on one of Ivan's cars last night," she explained. "Pryce was tracking it all morning, and after Higgins gave me the slip, he picked me up and we went looking for Ivan's hideout. Lucky for you we did."

"Yes, missis," Kitty agreed.

"That was a neat trick with the policeman, by the way," Mrs. Singh added.

Kitty froze in fear. "What trick?"

"The rescued damsel act." Mrs. Singh laughed softly. "Done it a few times myself, but you are a natural."

"I weren't lyin'!" Kitty insisted. "Honest! It's only, when I'm nervous I get all quiet, an' I thought it might look suspicious! I ain't done nothin', I swear!"

"I know," Mrs. Singh said with a grin. "If I still didn't trust you, Miss Granger, we would be having a very different conversation right now."

They drove in silence for a little while, heading toward the East End. Almost mechanically, Kitty gave Mrs. Singh the address of her father's shop when asked, and the rest of the time she rested her cheek on her hand and stared out of the window, watching the buildings pass. She had never actually ridden in a car before, not even a taxicab. It was very different from the bus: quieter, far less chaotic. Kitty found it strangely relaxing to just sit there and stare at nothing in particular, enjoying the experience of not being crushed by a mob of strangers.

After a little while, Mrs. Singh glanced over and asked, "You said you were good with numbers and faces, is that right?"

Kitty looked up, startled at being addressed. "Um, yes, missis. I just . . . remember things sometimes."

"You notice things too. That hidden panel with the safe, for example."

"I notice when things seem outta place," Kitty said. "It's nothin' special. You could do the same, couldn't you, missis?"

Mrs. Singh shrugged a little. "I'm trained to. You have a knack. There's a difference." She paused. "We passed a lorry at the last intersection. What color was it?"

"What?" Kitty asked, confused. Why ask something like that? Were they being followed?

"The lorry. What color was it? I'm just curious if you noticed."

Kitty closed her eyes and pictured all the cars they had passed recently. The memories rolled along inside her head, and several of them were indistinct or confused, but there had only been one truck.

"Red, I think."

"And the car we just passed?"

Kitty blinked. She had barely glimpsed it, since she'd been busy thinking about the truck.

"Blue? No, wait—yellow."

Mrs. Singh gave an approving nod. "Not bad."

Kitty was still confused at the questions. "Is this a game or somethin'?"

"You could call it that," Mrs. Singh replied. "Watch the road and try to remember everything. Let's see how much you notice."

<hr/>

It actually proved to be a rather fun memory game, and a very good way to pass the time on the drive. Kitty watched the road and every few minutes, Mrs. Singh would ask her to remember something they had just driven past. Kitty got most of the questions right, but even when she lost it didn't bother her. This was a distraction, and her mind desperately needed distracting.

Finally, they reached Kitty's block and Mrs. Singh dropped her off down the street from the shop.

"Thank you for the lift, missis," Kitty said as she got out.

Mrs. Singh raised her eyebrows. "The lift and not the rescue?"

Kitty grimaced with embarrassment. "That as well, 'a course."

The woman smiled. "Good day, Miss Granger. Try to stay out of trouble."

Kitty nodded. She watched Mrs. Singh drive away before she walked up the street to the family shop. It stood on the corner, once a prime location for customers but now overshadowed by almost everything around it. The building was a relic of the last century, and no amount of repairs and refurbishment would hide the fact anymore.

Kitty went inside and smelled the familiar scent of meat, shoe polish, and mothballs. There were half-filled shelves of small goods, and a counter where Kitty's father waited on customers and served cured meats and snack foods that no one ate.

Mr. Granger was behind the counter, arranging a tray of sugar candies for sale. There weren't any customers. They were lucky to get two or three any given day. It had been like that for years. Sales were just barely enough to keep them afloat, but Kitty's father wouldn't hear of selling the place. It had been in the family for five generations. A person didn't just walk away from five generations of history, even at the risk of starvation.

"Kitty! You're back!" her father exclaimed. It had been a few hours, but not long enough for Kitty to have finished her outing to the museum.

"Yes, Da," Kitty said.

Mr. Granger hurried around the counter and took Kitty by the shoulders. He peered at her, searching for signs of trouble. Kitty hid the last vestiges of her earlier distress and smiled. No reason to upset her father. That just led to trouble.

"You're very early. Did somethin' 'appen?"

"No, Da," Kitty replied, shaking her head. Well, she had to say something. She had been going on and on about visiting the British Museum all week. "I, um . . . It were very crowded so I didn't stay long."

That was a plausible excuse. It had happened before, for real. Once, a few years ago, Kitty had been so overcome by a crowd that she had hidden right then and there, unable to move for almost twenty minutes. She had made sure never to let that happen again, though. Now she looked for the signs of panic before they started, and escaped before the worst struck. It was safer that way.

"Oh, Kitty," her father said. His tone was sympathetic, but also pitying, which just made things worse. "You shoulda just stayed 'ome, like I said."

Kitty bit her lip to stop her retort. It always angered her when her father talked to her like that. *You should have . . . like I said.* As if he knew better than Kitty. As if he understood how she thought or felt. As if he had any idea what she went through when the panic or the fits hit her. She had almost died today, but if she said anything about it, her father would act like it had been all her fault for going out in the first place.

"I know, Da," Kitty said softly.

Mr. Granger smiled. "'Tis fine, though. You're safe with your ol' dad now. Why don't you put on your apron an' take a look at the stockroom for me? I can't make 'eads nor tails of your invent'ry."

Kitty had to stop herself again. The inventory list was perfectly fine. She had worked hard to make sure everything was accounted for and clearly noted. Why did her father have to be so thick sometimes?

Instead she said, "A'right, Da. But first I think I'll go upstairs for a bit. I just need some quiet."

"As you like," her father said. Sternly, he added, "But don't be long. If you're not usin' your day off, there's work to be done."

"Always is," Kitty muttered as she walked away.

"Wha's tha'?"

"Nothin'!"

Kitty went into the back hallway and up the stairs to their home above the shop. She went into her room and sat at the window overlooking the street. Outside, people went about their ordinary lives, uninterested in her or what had just happened to her. They all got to be ordinary. She was just boring. Boring and peculiar. Peculiar little Kitty Granger who got frightened at crowds and followed suspicious people into alleyways and got herself kidnapped. Today had been so utterly horrible, and yet it was probably the only exciting thing that would ever happen to her.

Sighing, Kitty flopped back onto her bed and reached for the book in her handbag. At least that was comforting. Here, alone in her room, she felt safe. Here she could be herself. She could be peculiar and mousy and uninteresting, and no one would hurt her for it.

CHAPTER 7

A few weeks later, Kitty was serving behind the counter when the shop door opened and in walked Mrs. Singh. She was dressed fashionably but less dramatically in a green dress, white gloves, and a matching pillbox hat. She looked like she should have been shopping in the West End, not here in the East.

Kitty quickly finished with her customer, only briefly taking her eyes from Mrs. Singh as the lady wove her way along the shelves, inspecting the contents. Once the customer had left, Mrs. Singh approached the counter. By then, Kitty's father had arrived from the back room, carrying two salamis under his arm. He stopped at the sight of Mrs. Singh, unsure of what to make of her.

"Oh," he said gruffly. "Afternoon, miss . . ."

"It's missis, actually. Mrs. Nisha Singh. I was just passing in the street and I thought I'd see the inside of your shop."

Mrs. Singh was very friendly and polite, but this just made Mr. Granger act gruffer. He hung the sausages from a hook behind the counter and frowned.

"Don't get many posh ladies in 'ere," he said. "You sure you're in the right place?"

Kitty turned bright red with embarrassment and exclaimed,

"Don't be rude, Da!" She turned back to Mrs. Singh and asked, "What can I get you, missis?"

"Actually, I'm here to see you," Mrs. Singh said to her. "Do you have a moment to talk?"

The question took Kitty by surprise. She glanced at her father and saw him narrow his eyes at Mrs. Singh.

"What business 'ave you got with my daughter?" Mr. Granger demanded. He looked at Kitty. "You know this woman?"

"Um . . ." Kitty stammered. She had no idea what to say. She couldn't tell him the truth.

Mrs. Singh smiled demurely and said, "My apologies, Mr. Granger, please allow me to explain. Your daughter and I happened to cross paths last month, and she just about saved my life."

"That so?"

"I was in the middle of several very important meetings, and my secretary at the time had simply bungled my schedule," Mrs. Sing explained, with absolute sincerity. If Kitty hadn't known better, she would have easily believed the story. "Inside of fifteen minutes waiting for a bus, your daughter rearranged everything marvelously and quite saved my bacon. A very capable young woman, your daughter. I'm certain she gets it from her father."

"Oh." Mr. Granger puffed himself up a little and seemed pleased. Still, the skepticism didn't go away. "So why're you 'ere? You givin' her a reward or somethin'?"

Kitty groaned. "Da!"

"In a manner of speaking," Mrs. Singh replied. "Mr. Granger, I would like to offer your daughter a job."

"A job?"

The astonishment in her father's voice matched Kitty's own amazement. This didn't seem real.

"As my secretary," Mrs. Singh clarified. "You see, in the past two months I've gone through five different secretaries, and they've all been absolute rubbish. Can't keep a schedule, can't balance an account. Two of them couldn't even type!"

"Kitty can't type either," Mr. Granger said, which wasn't true.

"Yes I can, Da," Kitty interrupted. "Mum taught me, remember?"

Her father grumbled. "Oh, well, aye. Still—can't let 'er go." He gave Kitty a stern look. "Need you at the shop, don't I? Can't do everythin' on me own."

Mrs. Singh coughed softly. "Mr. Granger, I can assure you that the salary I am offering is very competitive. I daresay that, if she shares her earnings with you, you could afford to hire two assistants to replace her."

Kitty's father seemed to mull this over, and Kitty felt his mood shift. Money was very tight at the moment.

Kitty tapped her fingertip against the counter a few times until Mrs. Singh looked at her. "What would I 'ave to do, missis?"

"Generally speaking, you would type my correspondence, keep my schedule, make certain that things don't get ahead of me." Mrs. Singh smiled. "Unfortunately, I'm rather busy these days and I've never had a head for numbers."

This was all quite strange. Kitty was certain that Mrs. Singh didn't actually need a secretary—but Mrs. Singh couldn't possibly want to hire her for something else, could she? Kitty Granger, a spy? That was absurd. Surely, accidentally getting kidnapped by Russian spies didn't qualify her for a career in international espionage.

And yet . . . Mrs. Singh wouldn't be making an offer if

Kitty couldn't do the job. Besides, whether it was being a spy or a spy's secretary didn't really matter in the end. This would be a chance for Kitty to do something meaningful with her life, something that didn't involve wasting away behind the counter of the family shop.

"When would I start?" she asked.

"I ain't said you can do it yet," her father reminded her.

"Look, Mr. Granger," Mrs. Singh, "it's no trouble for me if you refuse. Your daughter mentioned you had a shop in the area, I happened to be passing and decided to stop in. I'm certain the agency can send me dozens more secretaries if necessary, I just don't know if they'll be any good."

Mrs. Singh removed a calling card from her purse. She set it down on the counter and Kitty snatched it up immediately.

"Here's my card," Mrs. Singh continued, still speaking to Kitty's father. "Talk it over with your daughter. If you decide to take me up on my offer, simply call the number and make an appointment. We could give it a two-week trial to make certain Miss Granger is suitable for the position."

Kitty's father grunted and gave a curt nod. "Aye, we'll think it over."

"Splendid." Smiling, Mrs. Singh took a small shopping list out of her bag and offered it to Kitty. "In the meantime, I'm on my way to a picnic and was wondering if you could put together a basket for me. It's all in there. Sandwiches, sausages, jellied eels . . ."

Kitty took the list and looked up at her father.

"Aye, get to it, Kitty," he said.

"Yes, Da."

Kitty hurried around the shop, filling a basket with the items from the list. Some of it was very odd—not just food and drink, but various utensils: a bottle opener, a pocket knife. For a few minutes, Kitty entertained the idea that Mrs. Singh was secretly on a mission, and that she was going to foil a Russian spy ring with the contents of a picnic basket. It was fun to imagine, but Kitty knew it couldn't possibly be true. Who ever heard of jellied eels being used in espionage?

All the while, Mrs. Singh leaned against the counter and chatted with Kitty's father. The lady's tone was light and friendly, and Mr. Granger's standoffishness slowly mellowed into something a little more neutral. By the time Kitty returned to them, her father was bragging about how they were carrying on the tradition of the family shop, started in the days of his great-grandfather.

Mrs. Singh gasped in astonishment. "It can't be that old!" she protested, in a tone that Kitty almost believed was sincere. "Why, Mr. Granger, it's so well maintained!"

Kitty's father seemed unsure whether this was a joke at his expense. "Well, a little rough 'round the edges, I'll grant you."

"Nonsense, nonsense. It's very orderly. I'll admit, Mr. Granger, I had terrible preconceptions of what an East End shop would be like, and I'm pleased to say they have all been dispelled."

"Oh, aye!"

As Kitty joined them, Mrs. Singh paid for the goods and rewarded Kitty's father with a sweet smile. "Thank you very much, Mr. Granger. You've been a great help. Do have a lovely day."

"You as well, missis," Kitty's father said with sincerity.

Mrs. Singh turned to Kitty. "If you would be so good as to carry that out to my car, I'd be much obliged."

Kitty bobbed her head and followed Mrs. Singh out into

the street. A blue Jaguar sports car was waiting at the corner, and to Kitty's surprise, she saw Mr. Pryce in the passenger seat, reading a newspaper. As Kitty and Mrs. Singh approached, Mr. Pryce looked up at them and raised his hat.

"Miss Granger," he said. "Very nice to see you again."

"Mr. Pryce? Why are you 'ere?"

Mr. Pryce seemed surprised at the question. "Didn't Mrs. Singh explain? She and I are going for a picnic."

"Don't be coy, Pryce," Mrs. Singh said, taking the basket from Kitty. "I already told her about the job."

"And I'm very excited about the opportunity, sir." Kitty lowered her voice and asked, "It's not really secretarial work, though, is it?"

"That remains to be seen," Mrs. Singh replied. She handed the picnic basket to Mr. Pryce and got into the driver's seat.

"Secretarial work cracked Enigma during the war, you know," Mr. Pryce added. "It's very important stuff."

"Call the number on my card, make an appointment, and we'll run some tests to see where your aptitude lies," Mrs. Singh said.

Mr. Pryce tapped his chin, evidently deep in thought. "Have you ever fired a gun before, Miss Granger?"

"No, never," Kitty replied, shaking her head.

"Well, there's a first time for everything, isn't there?" Mr. Pryce mused. He tipped his hat to Kitty again. "Have a nice day, Miss Granger. We hope to hear from you soon."

Kitty watched them drive off down the street, astonished at what had just happened.

Her mouth slowly opened in a grin. This morning, she had just been boring old Kitty Granger. Now, she was going to be a spy.

Despite the good impression made by Mrs. Singh, Kitty's father dithered for the rest of the day, unable to decide whether he should let Kitty take the offer. He would talk loudly to himself whenever she was in earshot, listing the reasons why she shouldn't be allowed to work away from home, and then in the next breath grumbling about needing the money. It was all so transparent, Kitty wanted to scream.

Instead she held her tongue and smiled sweetly like everything was fine.

"What d'you think, Da?" she finally asked as they closed the shop for the night. "About the job?"

Her father was counting out the money in the till. He stopped and took a deep breath, like he was thinking very hard about it even though his mind was mostly made up. "Well, I . . ."

Kitty forced herself to talk over him, despite how uncomfortable it made her. "Good money, innit?" she said as she began tidying up the goods on the nearest shelf.

"Aye, maybe . . ."

"*Competitive salary* she said," Kitty added. "I mean, posh lady like that, eh? Must be quite a lot for the likes of 'er to think it's competitive."

"Aye," her father grunted. He hesitated and looked down at the money in his hands. Kitty stole a look, but she already knew it wasn't much.

"Probably more 'n anyone in the whole neighborhood makes," Kitty said.

She saw her father turn a bit pink at the observation. A frown creased his mouth and Kitty felt his mood turn sour.

"Not that we need it, 'a course," she quickly added. "You always took such good care of me, provided for everythin' an' such, especially since Mum passed. I only wish I could do more to help, is all. I mean, I'm no good with the customers, am I? You're practically doin' all the work yourself."

It wasn't true, but she knew her father believed it.

"And then 'ere comes this Mrs. Singh offerin' work I really could do—typin' an' such. Pro'ly pays well enough you could bring on a couple local lads to take me place in the shop. Better for everyone, innit?"

Her father was still looking at the money. He shuffled the bills between his hands again and again, as if trying to conjure more. Kitty felt a twinge in her heart. He was upset, and she couldn't understand why. They needed the money. This was a solution. Why did he have to be so thick about it? Why did *he* have to be the one providing for them if Kitty could do it? All that mattered was that they were both fed and happy and safe.

Kitty crossed the shop and put her hand on her father's arm. He looked at her, his mouth twisting with words he clearly didn't want to say.

Kitty smiled at him. "Seems to me, it's a good opportunity for us, Da," she said softly.

Very slowly, her father nodded in agreement. "Aye, I s'pose it is. But are you sure you can do it? You'll be out there," he said, looking toward the door, and beyond it the outside world. "I can't protect you if you're on your own out there."

Kitty bit her tongue to stop her instinctive retort. That was her business, not his. Yes, she had trouble sometimes, but he didn't have to talk to her like she was still a child!

"I'll just be typin' letters in an office, Da. It won't be that bad."

Father went quiet all of a sudden and looked down at his hands. "I know," he said. "I just want to do what's best for you, Kitty." He looked at her, his eyes two big saucers of uncertainty and guilt. "It's only, since your mother died, I dunno what to do 'alf the time."

So that was it. He was certain he was raising her wrong, so he'd rather have her do nothing at all than risk a mistake.

"Oh, Da," Kitty said softly. "There's no call for that, honest. You've raised me right, I promise. Mum would be so proud of how good a father you've been."

It wasn't entirely untrue. Kitty knew that he meant well, and that the incidents of unkindness were mistakes rather than malice. There was no point in fighting about it now.

She put her arms around her father and hugged him, hoping to comfort him and reason with him at the same time. "You've worked so 'ard all these years, an' now I've got a chance to 'elp. So please say that I can."

Her father took a deep breath and looked down at her. It took him a few tries to form the words, but finally he managed it.

"I s'pose so, aye. We'll ring this Mrs. Singh tomorrow an' make an appointment." He chuckled to himself, probably to hide his apprehension about letting Kitty take the job. "Hehe. Ring Singh."

Kitty looked away so that he wouldn't see her roll her eyes at him.

"Oh, very funny, Da. You're always so clever."

CHAPTER 8

The next morning, they rang Mrs. Singh's number and made an appointment. The date was set for the middle of the next week, and Kitty spent the intervening days brimming with excitement. Her head was filled with a thousand different thoughts that ran into each other even though they had little in common. What would the appointment be like? How was Mrs. Singh to work for? Did she have a cat? It almost drove Kitty to distraction.

When the day finally arrived, Kitty took the bus downtown. Mrs. Singh's address was in Kensington, which was a stark change from home. Everything looked terribly expensive. Mrs. Singh's office was a few streets away from the bus stop, in a tall brick building with a view of Hyde Park. Kitty took a deep breath and went inside before she could second-guess herself. She headed to the elevators as quickly as she could and rode to the top floor.

The doors opened on a mod spectacle of bright colors—nothing like what Kitty had expected. She stumbled out of the elevator into a little reception area with red carpeting, turquoise walls, and sofas and chairs colored a crisp shade of off-white. The art on the walls was very modern, all geometric shapes and lines that made Kitty dizzy to look at them. A receptionist lounged behind a wooden table, reading a fashion magazine and ignoring everything else.

Kitty looked back at the elevator in time to see the doors close. She exhaled slowly and brushed her fingertips against her skirt to calm herself. After a few moments, the receptionist lowered the corner of the magazine and flashed Kitty a grin.

"Well, don't just stand there!" she called. "Come here. I don't bite."

Kitty approached, sizing up the receptionist. The girl was a few years older than she was, with an easy self-confidence that Kitty immediately envied. She was dressed smartly in a suit and skirt, and her jet-black hair was trimmed into a short pixie cut that made her look very daring.

The receptionist grinned at Kitty. She leaned over the table and stuck out her hand. "Hello, I'm Verity. Verity Chase."

Kitty looked at the hand, uncertain of what to do. She wasn't fond of touching strangers, so she just stood there, clutching her handbag and hoping that she wasn't being rude.

"Kitty Granger. I'm, um, I'm 'ere to see Mrs. Singh. About a job . . ."

"I know why you're here," Verity said, laughing. She bounded out of her chair and walked around to Kitty's side of the table. "Come along, let's go see the boss."

Kitty followed Verity through a nearby door and found herself in a large, brightly-colored suite of offices. The place was bustling with activity, and she heard typing and talking coming from most of the rooms.

"What is this place?" Kitty asked, turning her head in circles to take in everything.

"Didn't anyone tell you? It's the magazine."

"What magazine?"

"*The* magazine."

Verity handed Kitty the magazine she had been reading. It was a fancy fashion publication, and the cover featured three very chic-looking young women in bright pastel dresses.

Kitty read the title aloud: "*La Mode.*" She gave Verity a puzzled look. "That's French, innit?"

"The title is, not the magazine," Verity explained. "*Haute* fashion for the average lady. The everywoman's window into Paris and Milan. Personally, I like it because it means I get to go to all sorts of fancy parties 'for research.'"

Kitty blinked and looked at the magazine a second time. This was not at all what she had expected. "I'm confused," she admitted.

Verity winked and whispered, "It's a cover."

Kitty sighed with relief, and at the same time she felt a little embarrassed at her momentary confusion. Of course the magazine was a cover! Spies didn't go around advertising that they were spies, did they? No, they had disguises, and code names, and photos of the latest French fashions, apparently.

She followed Verity to an office at the very back of the suite. It was a big room painted red and blue, with wide windows along one wall that gave a splendid view of the park. Mrs. Singh was there, waiting for them behind a fancy metal desk that looked like it was straight out of a science fiction film. She glanced at her watch as Verity closed the door behind them.

"You are *late*, Miss Granger."

Kitty looked down at her hands and mumbled, "I know. I'm sorry, missis."

"Don't apologize, just be punctual next time," Mrs. Singh replied. Her tone was stern, but not harsh. "You will find that being on time is very useful in this job."

Kitty nodded timidly. Then, spurred on by the gnawing curiosity she had felt since arriving, she asked, "Um—missis, what exactly is this job anyway? I mean, am I to be workin' for your magazine? Only, I thought it would be . . ."

"The magazine is part of your cover," Mrs. Singh explained, "just as it is for me and for Verity. Officially you'll be my assistant, like Verity. Part of the time you'll have something to do in the office, to keep up appearances. But mostly you'll be off helping me in the field or running errands."

Verity grinned at Kitty and mouthed the word "spying."

"You will find that working in fashion is a rather useful cover," Mrs. Singh said. "Thanks to the magazine, we get to rub shoulders with some very rich and powerful people."

"Rich and powerful people are usually up to something," Verity added.

"So is everyone 'ere a spy?" Kitty asked.

"Just us three," Mrs. Singh replied. "The rest of my employees are actual journalists. Helps with the authenticity. We avoid discussing sensitive information here, but my office is soundproofed for times like this. The actual magazine is managed by a team of editors, so I practically don't have to do a thing unless it's glamorous and exciting."

Verity held out her hands and pantomimed shooting a gun at the far wall.

Mrs. Singh frowned and gently pushed Verity's hands down. "Stop that." She turned her attention back to Kitty. "Now Verity is going to show you around the office and introduce you to the staff as part of your cover. After that, she'll take you to our second place of business and introduce you to your real coworkers."

Kitty nodded to show that she understood.

Mrs. Singh suddenly became very serious. "Let me emphasize, Miss Granger, that once you leave here, the information you'll be privy to is highly sensitive. You cannot divulge it to anyone, or else there will be consequences."

"I understand, missis. I won't tell a soul." Then she shrugged. "Honestly, there's no one to tell, apart from me da. He wouldn't even believe me. Just say I were makin' stories."

"It doesn't matter if someone believes you or not. In our line of work, if you tell people secrets they aren't supposed to know, they *will* get hurt, and so will you. Do you understand?"

"Completely, missis."

Mrs. Singh's expression softened a bit and a glimmer of concern appeared in her eyes. "If you are having second thoughts, now is the time to decide about them. You can take some time to think it over if you want."

Kitty shook her head firmly. "I've thought about it for days," she said. "Me mind were made up when I came 'ere, an' it's still made up. If I really can make a difference like you an' Mr. Pryce, I'd like to."

Mrs. Singh nodded. "One last question, Kitty. It might seem odd, but it's really very important. Would you have any qualms about working alongside someone . . . unlike you?"

"Unlike me, missis?" Kitty furrowed her brow in confusion. Everyone was unlike her. She was reminded of it nearly every day.

"For example, would you find it difficult to work alongside a black person, or a Jewish person?" Mrs. Singh asked. "Does it trouble you at all that I'm Indian?"

"What?" Kitty said, unable to disguise her bewilderment. "Why would that bother me?"

Mrs. Singh gave her a stern look again. "That is either a

naïve question or a disingenuous one. Pretending that prejudice doesn't exist isn't the same as not being prejudiced."

"Oh!" Kitty exclaimed, louder than she had meant to. "Yes, missis, I understand. There won't be no trouble from me, I promise. I'm 'appy to work with whoever you need me to. It's me job, after all. If I've got the job, that is."

"Good," Mrs. Singh said. She handed Verity a set of car keys. "Once you're done here, take Kitty to meet the Orchestra."

"May I take the Jaguar?" Verity asked excitedly.

Mrs. Singh sighed at her. "No, you may not. You'll take the Vauxhall, and you'll drive it under the speed limit like a normal person. Try to set a good example for Miss Granger."

Verity sighed and slumped her shoulders. "Yes, Mrs. Singh."

"You're not comin' with?" Kitty asked.

"Alas, I have a prior engagement," Mrs. Singh replied. "I'm going to interview the president of the Hawksworth Armaments Company."

Verity frowned. "So you think the rumors are true? Hawksworth's running guns?"

"Possibly," Mrs. Singh said. "I'll have a much better idea of it after I tap his phone. But," she added, "it's neither of your assignments, so the two of you keep your noses out of it."

"Yes, missis," Kitty said, echoing Verity.

After Mrs. Singh departed, Verity gave Kitty a grand tour of *La Mode*. Even though the job was only a disguise, Verity made it all seem very official and convincing. Once that was done, she led Kitty outside to a nondescript sedan parked by the road.

Verity gave a dramatic sigh as she unlocked the car and got into the driver's seat.

Kitty climbed in on the opposite side and sat with her hands resting on her knees, trying not to fidget. "Somethin' wrong?" she asked.

"I never get to drive the Jaguar," Verity replied mournfully. "Mrs. Singh says it's too conspicuous. That, and I tend to go racing." She smirked and gave Kitty a wink.

Kitty laughed, but she gripped the edges of her seat to be safe. "We're not goin' racin' now, are we?" she asked nervously.

"In this thing? Perish the thought. No, I'm taking you to meet the rest of the Orchestra."

"What's the Orchestra?"

"Our little spy network."

"Oh, I see. Odd name, innit?"

Kitty had always imagined spy networks would use fancy names like The Brotherhood of Spies or complicated acronyms so that they could go around calling themselves GHOSTS.

"It comes from a saying of Pryce's," Verity explained. *"An orchestra cannot play without diverse instruments.* We recruit people with valuable skills who might otherwise go overlooked by the intelligence agencies."

"Like workin'-class girls from the East End," Kitty said.

"Exactly."

Verity pulled the car out into the street and drove toward central London. Despite her talk, she kept to the speed limit and obeyed the driving laws to the letter. Their nondescript car had soon blended into the flow of ordinary traffic. Kitty waited in silence for a little while, but she had questions and eventually she decided to ask them.

"Mrs. Singh said I'm to be tested?"

Verity nodded. "Nothing to worry about. It's what we do with everyone. Over the next few weeks, the team will show you how to do the sort of work we do, and they'll decide what you're best at."

"Will I 'ave to do somethin' to prove me loyalty?" Kitty asked.

"Prove your loyalty?" Verity exclaimed, astonished at the question. "No, of course not. We've already vetted you."

Kitty didn't recognize the word. "You've what?"

"Vetted you. Verified who you are, made sure there aren't any dangerous attachments in your family. Mr. Price and Mrs. Singh started looking into you right after you met the first time. You'd never have been offered the job if they didn't believe you were reliable and trustworthy. We take our security very seriously."

"Oh gosh, I didn't realize."

Kitty narrowed her eyes and stared out the window, working over how she felt about having been spied on for weeks. Eventually she accepted it with a measure of caution. Mr. Pryce and Mrs. Singh couldn't start revealing state secrets to her without being sure she was who she claimed to be. That man Higgins had been trusted with information from the Ministry of Defense, but he'd turned around and given it to the Russians. Who knew how many people had been hurt because of him?

Besides, that was what spies did, wasn't it? They spied on people. And Kitty was going to be spying soon too. She couldn't very well complain about something she herself was doing. There couldn't be one rule for her and another for everyone else, that wasn't fair. As long as the spies were trying to keep people safe, spying was all right. If the spies were trying to hurt people, it wasn't right. That felt like a very clear line to Kitty, and she didn't intend to cross it, no matter what.

Kitty was pulled out of her thoughts as the car slowed. Verity drove around the back of a nondescript gray building belonging to an import-export business. If Kitty had only passed it on the street, she never would have given it a second look.

"Where are we?" Kitty asked as they got out of the car. She suddenly felt apprehensive again. The walls loomed over her, blocking her in. She brushed at her sleeve and tugged the cuff to make it look like she was straightening it.

"I'll explain once we're inside," Verity replied, "but we're going to see Mr. Pryce."

She led Kitty into the building, which was just as nondescript inside as it was outside. The doorway led into an open office area, with some desks arranged in neat rows. There were only a few people around, either typing or looking over paperwork. A couple of them greeted Verity, and everyone noticed Kitty, but they didn't seem surprised that she was there.

"Do they recognize me?" Kitty whispered to Verity.

"Everyone here was shown your photograph and told that I might bring you over today," Verity explained, as she led Kitty through the office and down a flight of stairs into the basement. "The building's just a cover for our real work."

"Like at *La Mode*?" Kitty asked.

"Sort of, except that *everyone* here is in the know. Most of the 'secretaries' are actually security."

At the bottom of the stairs they entered a short hallway ending at a closed metal door. A man in overalls and a long brown coat was seated next to it, reading half of a newspaper. He looked like a janitor, but Kitty spotted a gun on the crate next to him, mostly hidden beneath the other half of the paper.

Kitty suddenly realized she was in a building full of armed people who were all pretending not to be armed. This was going to take some getting used to.

"Mornin', Miss Chase," the janitor said, tugging on the brim of his cap.

"Good morning, George!" Verity exclaimed. She motioned to Kitty. "This is Kitty Granger, the new girl. Kitty, this is George Harman. He helps look after the place. Keeps it nice and safe for the rest of us."

"How d'you do," Kitty greeted him. She bobbed her head politely and tried to keep her eyes focused on George rather than the weapon hidden under his newspaper.

George gave Kitty an appraising look, then grunted softly and answered her with another tug on his cap. "Miss."

"Is Mr. Pryce in?" Verity asked.

George pointed his thumb at the door. "With Saul in the armory, last I heard."

"Then off we go!" Verity said. She opened the door and led Kitty through. Once it had shut again, she chuckled. "Don't mind George. He's a dear, he really is. It's just part of his job to be cautious about strangers, even ones Pryce brings in."

"Oh good. I thought I'd done somethin' wrong."

"If that happens, I shall tell you," Verity promised.

CHAPTER 9

Beyond the door lay a long corridor with concrete walls. They were painted a shade of dull white to make them less unbearable to look at, but the place was a far cry from the glamor of *La Mode*. Glancing into the rooms on either side of the corridor, Kitty saw a few scattered people, all of them busy with an assortment of tasks that made no sense to Kitty.

"That's the analysis department," Verity said, pointing. "Armory's down the hall, signals room over there, and the workshop is this way. Come on, I'll introduce you to the rest of the Young Bloods."

"The who?"

"Us under-twenty-fives. The other agents are older, so we stick together. Sometimes the oldies have to be reminded that we're perfectly capable of getting things done ourselves."

They turned down the side passage, and Kitty heard voices from a nearby room.

"Christ, Faith! The bloody thing's on fire!" exclaimed a boy with an Irish brogue.

"It's not on fire, Liam!" protested a girl whose accent sounded Jamaican.

There was a popping noise and then the faint crackle of something burning.

"*Now* it's on fire," Kitty heard Faith and Liam say in unison.

Verity dashed into the room, with Kitty close at her heels. It was a large workshop filled with machinery and benches and scattered tools. The air smelled like oil and metal, and there was a distinct odor of char to go with it.

A girl and a boy in their late teens were seated at one of the workstations, looking strangely calm given the circumstances. The girl had large horn-rimmed spectacles perched on her nose, and tightly braided hair that was tied off into a bun. The boy was heavyset, and his mop of ginger hair looked like an animal that had taken purchase atop his head. Neither of them seemed troubled by the flaming tin can the girl was holding with a pair of metal tongs.

"Good God!" Verity cried. "What have you done?"

Faith, the West Indian girl, looked at Verity with an astonished expression. "We're miniaturizing a flamethrower," she said, like it was the only possible explanation.

She dropped the burning can into a metal bucket on the floor, and Liam, the Irish boy, dumped a pile of sand in after it.

"Well, that's a bust, and no mistake," Faith grumbled. "I thought we had it, that time."

"What's this *we* nonsense?" Liam asked. "It's your idea."

"That it is, and it's a good idea," Faith replied. She snatched up a pencil from the workbench and began spinning it around her fingers. "I shortened the fuel pipe and everything," she mused. "Must be a problem with the pressure."

Verity cleared her throat. "This is Kitty Granger, Mrs. Singh's new hire. Kitty, this is Faith, our technical wizard. Half the equipment we use is either invented or improved on by her. If she had twenty more years on her, she'd be our quartermaster, but she isn't, so she just sets things on fire when she's bored."

"Can't make discoveries without experiments," Faith said sagely.

"Aye, what's a little accidental fire between friends?" Liam agreed.

"And that's Liam," said Verity. "He works with the surveillance boys, but he has a good head for electronics, so he's always in here finding new ways to help Faith blow us all to Kingdom Come."

"Pleased to meet you both, I'm sure," Kitty said.

Faith reached out to give her a handshake, which caught Kitty off guard. Why was everyone always so interested in shaking hands? There was an awkward pause, but before Kitty could force herself to move, Faith retracted her hand and gave a little wave instead. "Welcome to the Orchestra."

Liam tapped his fingers to his temple and gave a little salute. "Glad to have ya here."

Just as Kitty was about to feel relieved that she hadn't botched these introductions, someone appeared in the doorway behind her. She turned around and saw a black boy of about her age, dressed in oil-stained overalls. He was middling-tall and lanky, and there was a smudge of grease across one cheek, like he had brushed his thumb against it in passing and not realized it was there.

As the lad leaned in through the doorway, he shouted across the workshop, "Oi! Faith! I need them injectors! What's takin' so long, eh?"

He spoke with a noticeable East End accent, one that could easily have come from Kitty's father or one of the neighbors. It was very pleasant to hear, and it made Kitty feel a little more at ease.

Faith turned in her chair and waved the young man away.

"They'll be ready when they're ready, Tommy. I can't be rushed like this."

"You gone mad?" Tommy demanded, stepping into the workshop. "I've gotta get the bloody instillation done by three . . ." He trailed off as noticed Kitty. "Oh, 'ello."

"'Ello," Kitty answered, giving a small wave.

Verity clapped her hands together. "Ah, Tommy, just the fellow I wanted to see. Saves me a trip to the garage." She put an arm around Kitty's shoulders and said, "This is Kitty Granger, who just joined the cause today. She's smart as a tack and an absolute delight, and I just know we're going to get on. Isn't that right, Kitty?"

Startled at being addressed in the middle of someone else's conversation, Kitty just stammered, "Oh, yes, I 'spect so."

At hearing Kitty's accent, a smile tugged at the corner of Tommy's mouth. "You from East London, eh?" he asked.

"That's right," Kitty said, returning the smile.

"Tommy here is one of the mechanics who keep our cars running," Verity explained.

"Right, an' it's an uphill struggle, with how you treat your vehicle, Verity," Tommy retorted. He turned back to Kitty. "It's good to meetcha, Miss Granger. Glad to 'ave an East Ender round 'ere."

"Likewise," Kitty agreed.

"So . . . injectors, you said?" Verity asked, looking first at Tommy, and then casting her gaze toward Faith. "Not miniature flamethrowers?"

"Aye," Tommy answered. "Nitrous oxide injectors for the engine. Wait, did you say *miniature flamethrowers?*"

Verity chuckled. "I think that is our cue to leave," she said, taking Kitty by the arm. "If you'll all excuse us, I'll let Faith explain why she and Liam are trying to burn the building down, while I introduce Miss Granger to Debby."

"Signals room, last I saw," Tommy said. "Nice meetin' you, Miss Granger. See you again soon, I 'ope."

"Well, I work 'ere now, so . . ."

Kitty hadn't meant it as a joke, but everyone laughed anyway.

She followed Verity back to the main hallway and into a wide room filled with all kinds of complicated-looking radio equipment. Two men and a woman were seated at a long desk, listening through headphones and sometimes speaking to one another. There was a dull hum in the air, and it made Kitty twitch.

Verity leaned against the doorframe and waited silently until the woman at the desk happened to glance in their direction. Verity waved, and the woman flashed a grin in reply. She scribbled something on a notepad, whispered a few words to one of the men, and joined Kitty and Verity in the hallway.

"Well, well, Verity Chase," the woman said sternly, trying not to crack a smile. "Got bored with the French Riviera and decided to join the rest of us back here in dreary old England, I see."

"Two days in Monaco!" Verity protested. "Two!"

"And not doing a spot of honest work there, I imagine."

Verity snorted to cover up a laugh and slapped the woman's shoulder. "Honest work? Not on your life." She motioned to Kitty. "Debby, this Kitty. Kitty, Debby. Kitty's the—"

Debby interrupted, "The new girl. I know. Pryce told us to expect her." She turned to Kitty and offered a friendly hand. "Hi, I'm Deborah. I'm one of the Orchestra's cryptographers."

Kitty forced herself to accept the handshake. She suspected

there were going to be a lot of them, so she'd better get used to it.

"Debby's also the oldest member of the Young Bloods, so she's unofficially mother," Verity interjected, a mischievous giggle hiding behind her words.

"I never agreed to that," Debby said severely.

"See?" Verity said to Kitty. "Isn't she just perfect?"

Debby tapped Verity on the nose. "You're bloody incorrigible, you know that?"

"And you love it!" Verity retorted. "Anyway, we should let you get back to work. I'm just showing Kitty around the place before I take her to meet Pryce. George said he was in the armory with Saul. Think he's still there?"

"Undoubtedly," Debby replied. "If I know Pryce and my uncle, they'll be trading old war stories until sundown, unless a crisis rears its head."

"All quiet on the intelligence front?" Verity asked.

Debby shrugged. "Quiet as it ever is. There's always something that needs decrypting."

"Apparently Kitty is very good with puzzles," Verity said. "She might end up working with you."

Debby gave Kitty a pleasant smile. "Well, that will be fun. We can always use an extra hand cracking the intercepts." From inside the signals room, one of the radio operators started waving at her. "Ah, that's my cue. Best get back to it."

"Cheerio!" Verity called after Debby as the woman rushed back to her workstation.

"She seems nice," Kitty said.

"As I said, we Young Bloods stick together," Verity explained. "There's a fair bit of teasing, but when it comes down to it we back each other up. We're plenty used to people not taking us seriously, so there's no point in doing that to each other."

Verity took Kitty to the very end of the main hallway and down another side corridor to the armory. This proved to be a grim concrete room with a heavy metal door and countless shelves of guns and ammunition, all securely locked behind bars. The sight of the weapons made Kitty very uneasy, but at least they weren't lying around out in the open.

Mr. Pryce was there, once again dressed in a fancy suit, and with a purple carnation on his lapel. He was talking to another man, who was short and broad-shouldered. The man was probably nearing sixty, but he looked very robust. Kitty assumed he was Debby's uncle Saul. Either he or Mr. Pryce had evidently just said something very amusing, as both men were laughing uproariously.

"I'll never forget the look on that colonel's face . . ." Mr. Pryce trailed off as he looked toward the door. "Verity! And Miss Granger!" he exclaimed. "Come in, come in. I'm so pleased you're joining us."

"'Ello, Mr. Pryce," Kitty said timidly. "I, um, I've decided to take the job."

"Well, of course you have," Mr. Pryce said. "Otherwise you wouldn't be here." He motioned to his companion. "This is Saul, our armaments master."

Saul nodded to her. "Welcome, young lady. When it's time for you to start shooting guns, I'm the one you see."

"Saul's an excellent teacher," Verity said. She added ruefully, "He won't even let you pick up a loaded gun until he's certain you know how to use it safely. A bit of a spoilsport, that way."

Saul just chuckled.

"Of course, weapons handling will come later in your curriculum, Miss Granger," Mr. Pryce said. "The rest of today will be nice and quiet. Just a few exams for us to start determining your aptitudes." He turned to Saul and gave a quick salute. "Be seeing you, Saul."

"And you," Saul said, returning the salute.

Kitty followed Mr. Pryce and Verity to a little office with a table and some chairs. Mr. Pryce motioned for Kitty to sit, and then unlocked a filing cabinet and took out a folder. He placed it on the table in front of Kitty and set a pencil down next to it.

Kitty picked up the pencil, very confused. She hadn't expected the "exams" to be quite so literal. She had sort of assumed spy training would involve a lot of running and jumping and understanding table settings.

"I understand you like crossword puzzles, Miss Granger," Mr. Pryce said.

"Yes, sir. Very much so."

Mr. Pryce opened the folder and turned over the top piece of paper inside. It was a crossword puzzle. A somewhat tricky one at that. Kitty suddenly felt more comfortable. She hadn't expected this, but it was a very welcome reprieve from all the new people.

"I want you to complete as much of this puzzle as you can, as quickly as you can," Mr. Pryce explained. He took out a small notebook and sat in a chair on the other side of the table, while Verity leaned against the wall. "You have ten minutes to complete that one, and ten minutes for the one under it, and ten for the one after that. And after *that*, we'll do some mathematics."

"What if I don't get it all finished?" Kitty asked.

"Then you move on to the next one. Sometimes we can't complete every objective we want to, and we need to be able to move on to the next task with a clear head. Do you think you can do that, Miss Granger?"

Kitty took a deep breath and nodded. "Yes, sir."

She picked up the pencil and turned her eyes toward the puzzle, already determining which questions she could answer most easily, and which ones would make it easier to decipher the others. Maybe Mr. Pryce didn't expect her to finish them all in time, but Kitty Granger had never met a crossword puzzle she couldn't complete, and she bloody well wasn't going to be stumped by one now.

She turned to the first question:

What goes up a chimney down, but can't go down a chimney up? Eight letters.

Kitty smirked to herself and scribbled *umbrella* in the boxes. With an easy first victory achieved, she narrowed her eyes and got to work.

CHAPTER 10

"**K**itty, can you hear me?"

Faith's voice echoed in Kitty's ear. The sound was fuzzy, broken up with little pops and crackles that drowned out the edges of the words. Kitty reached up and tapped the little metal earpiece a couple of times to settle it in place better. Then she lifted her wrist and whispered into the microphone concealed in her bracelet.

"Loud an' spotty," she replied.

"Do you have eyes on Liam?" Faith asked.

"Yes."

Kitty looked across the main concourse of Paddington Station and saw Liam seated on a bench, watching the crowd from behind a copy of *The Times*. It was midafternoon. The place was busy, but not as packed as it would become during the evening rush. Still, Kitty felt her heartbeat quicken at the sight of all the people rushing around. She took a moment to calm herself with a few deep breaths.

"Who we lookin' for again?" she asked. "Man in a gray suit?"

"Middle-aged, gray suit, carrying a black briefcase," Faith said.

"It's London," Kitty replied. "'Alf the men at this railway station 'ave suits an' briefcases."

"Don't sound so glum, Kitty! You'll ferret him out, like you always do."

"Kitty," Liam interjected. "I've got eyes on our man."

All three of them were sharing the same radio frequency, which made things go faster, but it meant Kitty had to hear the crinkling of Liam's newspaper from time to time. It wasn't loud, but it was very annoying.

Kitty scanned the crowd again. "Where?"

"Just entered the concourse. To your left."

Kitty glanced to her left and saw the target: an average-looking man with graying hair, and a gray suit to match. He carried a black briefcase, which had a scuff mark on one corner.

Kitty waited until the man had moved several paces ahead of her, and then she followed, weaving through the crowd to keep up. She did her best to slide past people the way Mrs. Singh had taught her, but it wasn't exactly a perfected art. At one point, she bumped into someone in passing. Kitty blushed awkwardly and stammered an apology as she kept going.

"Kitty, are you running into people again?" Liam asked.

"You know me—graceful as a swan," Kitty grumbled back.

She followed the man in gray to the ticket window and hung back in the crowd, close enough to watch but not so close as to be noticed. The man set his case down and fished some coins out of his pocket to pay for a ticket. There was another man at the window next to his, examining a train schedule. This fellow wore a black suit and a bowler hat.

Kitty looked down and saw what she knew to expect: the man in gray had set his briefcase down next to an identical briefcase belonging to the man in black. As she watched, the man in black picked up the man in gray's case and headed for the far side of the concourse.

"Got 'im," Kitty whispered into her bracelet.

"I see him," Liam confirmed.

He got up, tucked his newspaper under his arm, and began walking parallel to the man in black, getting between him and the entrance. Kitty hung back for a few seconds, and then followed their target.

"Remember," Faith said, "we need the case. Doesn't matter if he gets away, but we need those files."

Kitty followed the man in black across the concourse, struggling to keep up. He had quickened his pace, and Kitty didn't want to look like she was chasing him.

The man glanced back in her direction, and Kitty felt a shudder in her chest. Had she been seen? Did he know she was following her? Would he look for Liam next?

Calm, she reminded herself. *Don't look suspicious. You're just an ordinary person walking to your train.*

The man didn't seem to notice her, and he kept walking, but even so Kitty adjusted her path slightly so she wasn't following quite so directly. When the man looked over his shoulder the same way again, there was no Kitty behind him to be seen. The man in black gripped the briefcase more tightly and headed for Platform Number One, where a train was waiting to depart. Kitty followed. Glancing back at Liam, she saw that he had moved in closer.

"What's happening?" Faith asked.

"Fella's headed to Platform One," Liam reported. "I think he's making for the train."

"Kitty, follow him on the train," Faith said. "He gets off again, Liam, you go after him."

"Roger," Liam said.

"Aye," Kitty agreed.

Kitty kept her eyes locked on the man in black. He had slowed down and was looking at his train schedule again. Kitty slowed her pace too, to keep from passing him. As she watched, she saw another man, this one in a blue suit, walk past the man in black. For a moment Kitty's view was blocked by the jostling crowd. Then the man in black was on his way again.

Kitty saw that Liam was already past her, closing in on their target. He looked back at her. "Kitty, what are you doing?" he whispered. "Follow him!"

Kitty hesitated. The man in black still had his black case in hand. Everything was going according to plan: see who made the handoff, follow him on the train until he got off, see where he took the stolen files. Easy.

Except that there was no scuff mark on the case anymore.

The apprehension of a broken pattern nagged at Kitty, and she looked in the opposite direction, toward the man in blue. He had a black case too, with polished brass corners. Kitty's eyes flicked to one particular corner—and snagged on a familiar scuff mark that wasn't supposed to be important, but that she had remembered anyway.

Without a word, she turned and began to follow the man in blue.

It took Liam a minute to realize that she had broken away from their pursuit. "Kitty? What are you doing?" he demanded again. "He's getting on the train. He's getting away!"

"What's going on?" Faith asked.

"It's not 'im," Kitty hissed into her microphone. "It's not bloody 'im!"

"What?" Faith exclaimed. "You mean . . . ?"

"There were a second 'andoff!"

Kitty felt excited and nervous and angry all at once. There wasn't supposed to be a second handoff. No one had said anything about a second bloody handoff! But Kitty knew her mission: follow the case. So she did.

The man in blue returned to the concourse, went outside into the street, and walked down the block with an air of confident ease. He thought he'd shaken them.

Kitty followed at a distance, even more cautious now that she didn't have as large a crowd to hide in. Once, the man in blue looked back, but Kitty was ready for him. By the time he turned, she was busy admiring the contents of a shop window.

The man in blue resumed his walk, and a moment later, he ducked down an alleyway. Kitty scampered the remaining distance and hesitated at the mouth of the alley. She was going in alone now. No backup. That probably wasn't a good idea. She had left Liam behind in the train station, and Faith was hiding with the radio equipment in a van down the block.

Well, here goes nothing.

Kitty turned the corner and saw two men waiting for her in the alleyway. One was the fellow in blue. The other was Mr. Pryce.

Kitty exhaled and relaxed. If Mr. Pryce was there, it meant the test was over.

Pryce clapped his hands twice and gave her a delighted smile. "Well done, Miss Granger!" he exclaimed. "I thought we had you that time. You're a clever one and no mistake."

Kitty bobbed her head. "Thank you, sir. I didn't expect the second 'andoff."

"And why would you?" Mr. Pryce asked. "That was the point. You can never be entirely sure what's going to happen out in the field. One must learn to adapt quickly, to think on one's feet. But you stuck to your mission and followed the briefcase. Mrs. Singh will be very proud."

"D'you think so, sir?"

"Without a doubt," Mr. Pryce said. "It was her idea to try the second handoff. I didn't think you were ready for that kind of a challenge, but she insisted. She told me, 'Pryce, you bloody fool, Kitty's made more progress in one month than most people do in six. She can do it.' And by Jove, she was right."

Kitty grinned, delighted by the praise. She had worked so hard these past weeks, but she always felt like she was getting more things wrong than right. It was heartening to hear she was doing a better job than she'd thought. Although . . . what if this was the exception? What if she did badly next time?

Kitty gritted her teeth to silence the nagging voice of self-doubt. She was making progress. She could do this.

Mr. Pryce looked at his watch and a smile crossed his face. "Will you look at that? A successful exercise all wrapped up just in time for tea."

CHAPTER II

Kitty drove back to the Orchestra with Mr. Pryce and Mr. Gregson, the fellow in blue. They arrived a few minutes ahead of the other team. They were met in the office by Mrs. Singh, who was lounging elegantly in a chair, waiting for them. There was mischief in her eyes.

"Welcome back, Pryce," she called. "How did it go?"

"I'm pleased to report that our Miss Granger passed with flying colors," Mr. Pryce said.

Mrs. Singh smirked at him and sipped her tea. "Even the second handoff?"

"Yes, my dear. She spotted Gregson and followed him right back to me."

"I didn't even notice her following until we were halfway down the block," Gregson added.

"Splendid." Mrs. Singh got up and approached them, still smirking in triumph. "That's a bottle of champagne you owe me, Pryce."

"And tickets to the theatre to go with it, I'm sure," Mr. Pryce agreed with a grin.

Mrs. Singh put a hand on Kitty's shoulder and looked down at her, brimming with pride. "Well done, Kitty," she said softly. "Very well done."

"Thank you, missis."

At that moment, Debby rushed into the room, followed closely by Verity.

"Is Pryce back?" she asked breathlessly. "Oh, good." She waved a piece of widely spaced typewritten paper, which had a scrawl of pencil writing in between the lines of text. "I've cracked it, sir!"

Mr. Pryce turned to her. "Ah! You mean those messages we intercepted?"

Debby held up the paper for Mr. Pryce's inspection. "Just broke the encryption."

"I helped!" Verity declared.

Mr. Pryce looked pleased. "What do they say?"

"A lot of it's very ambiguous, but I think each message was coordinating some kind of meeting," Debby explained. She ran her finger along one of the pencil-written lines. "See, for each one there's a time and a day, and then some random-looking words that I think are code for locations. We managed to figure two of them out and they're both London docks."

Mr. Pryce nodded. "That's good. Make a list of the times and locations and I'll have some people give them a look."

"There's one other thing," Debby added. "The docks are used by Sheffield Imports, Ltd. And we all remember our old friends at Sheffield Imports, don't we?"

The others nodded.

Kitty raised a hand. "I don't," she said.

Debby chuckled. "I was being rhetorical, Kitty."

"Sheffield's a front company for a smuggling operation," Verity explained. "We had a run-in with them in Belfast last year."

Mr. Pryce and Mrs. Singh were looking at each other with almost identical expressions.

"Sheffield," Mr. Pryce said. "You don't think . . . ?"

"But it has to be . . ." Mrs. Singh replied.

"Smythe!" they both exclaimed.

"By Jove, we've got him!" Mr. Pryce cried gleefully.

Kitty cleared her throat to get everyone's attention. In a hesitant voice, she asked, "Who's Smythe?"

"Sir Richard Smythe," Mr. Pryce answered with a grimace. The disdain rolled off his tongue like he wanted to spit at this Smythe person, only the man wasn't there to be spat at. "He's a rotten fellow. Linked to murder, bribery, and who knows what else." Mr. Pryce turned to Verity and Debby. "Put together a plan for investigation. I need hard evidence before I can go to my superiors."

"Yes, sir," Debby said.

Mr. Pryce turned to Kitty. "In the meantime, Miss Granger, would you care to join Mrs. Singh and me for tea?"

⸎

In Mr. Pryce's cozy, wood-paneled office, Kitty settled into her chair next to Mrs. Singh and watched as Mr. Pryce laid out the pieces of a porcelain tea service on the top of his desk. It was all quite neat and fancy, and Mr. Pryce took great care as he measured out the tea from a little blue pot. Kitty appreciated that. It was very calm. Most of the time, meals were chaos: spoons clanging against bowls and cups, forks scratching loudly across the tops of plates. There was none of that here, and that was nice.

"Now then, Kitty," Mr. Pryce said, as he filled the three cups with boiling water, "Mrs. Singh and I would like to discuss your future here at the Orchestra."

"Future?" Kitty looked from one to the other in confusion. "'Ave I done somethin' wrong?"

"On the contrary!" Mr. Pryce exclaimed. "Your progress over the past month has been quite remarkable, and we are considering a change in direction."

"How would you like to become a field agent?" Mrs. Singh asked.

Kitty blinked. "A field agent? Like you an' Mr. Pryce?"

"Like us, yes," Mrs. Singh replied, "or like Verity."

Kitty didn't know how to respond. The idea of working in the field had simply seemed outside the realm of possibility for her, so she had never even considered it.

"Most of our agents are older, since it can be dangerous work," Mr. Pryce explained. "However, there are certain circumstances in which a young woman such as yourself can go about unnoticed, whereas a chap like me would stand out like a sore thumb."

"You really think I can do it?" Kitty asked.

Mr. Pryce nodded. "We've thrown a lot of new things at you these past few weeks, Miss Granger, and each time you've risen to the challenge, no matter how difficult. You just keep at it until you have it figured out. I've rarely seen such tenacity before, and never in someone so young. That sort of determination is just what we need."

"Thank you, sir."

Kitty suddenly felt very awkward. She wasn't used to getting compliments, and never for her habit of fixating on things. Most of the time when she repeated things over and over again, she was criticized. But now she was dedicated? How people made these distinctions constantly baffled her.

"It will take hard work and lots of training," Mrs. Singh

said, "but if you're willing to make the effort, we are confident you will make an excellent field agent."

"I'll do me best," Kitty said solemnly.

"That means we will be mixing some hand-to-hand combat and firearms training into your studies," Mrs. Singh said. "Do you think you're up to it?"

Kitty hesitated. Guns were frightening, and she hadn't been in a fistfight since she was nine.

"I'm 'appy to learn, missis," she finally replied, trying to look and sound more confident than she felt.

"Good," Mrs. Singh said. "We'll do our best to avoid putting you in any real danger, but one can never know. You'll need to be ready for anything."

"Then I will be," Kitty promised. She paused and sipped her tea as she considered this turn of events. "Um . . . ?"

"Yes, Miss Granger?" Mr. Pryce asked.

Kitty took another sip of tea before she worked up the courage to speak again. "With all this new training an' responsibility . . ."

"Out with it," Mrs. Singh told her.

"Might there be a pay raise in it?" Kitty asked.

To her surprise, she was answered with a hearty laugh from Mr. Pryce, and a more genteel chuckle from Mrs. Singh.

"I'm certain we can arrange that," Mrs. Singh assured her, "provided that you continue to excel at your studies."

CHAPTER 12

Combat training began with several weeks of exercise and not a single weapon in sight, which confused Kitty at first. But under Mrs. Singh's tutelage, she soon understood the reason. Running laps, performing agonizing pushups, lifting herself on bars, and enduring countless other trials was transformative. By the time the martial arts training started, Kitty felt stronger and more energetic than she ever had in her life.

She hadn't been encouraged to exercise since she was a child. Even before the end of primary school, Kitty had been told to be demure, to walk and not run, to be quiet and not cause a fuss. Suddenly that was all gone. No restrictions.

"Run as fast as you can, Kitty," Mrs. Singh would say as she looked at a watch.

"Run as long as you can, Kitty."

"Where do you get all that energy, Kitty?"

And the more she exercised, the better she felt. It was like there was a coiled spring lurking inside her, tightening again and again with each moment of stress that she experienced. It had grown so tight by now that she'd often feared it might snap. As she ran in circles around the Orchestra's gymnasium, Kitty felt the tightness lessen bit by bit. Each push-up, each sit-up, each pull-up exhausted her body but soothed her mind.

At the same time, though, she was put through a rigorous course in unarmed combat, weapons training, and even what Mrs. Singh called "evasion." This was a strange practice that paired blocks and dodges in combat with stealth training outside of it. It was all connected, Mrs. Singh explained. The same awareness of one's surroundings and control of movement that aided in hiding and sneaking were invaluable once a fight started.

"Know your ground," Mrs. Singh would say. "Know it better than the enemy."

Kitty did her best to learn, but it was hard. She was used to seeing everything at once, but she wasn't used to sorting out exactly what was important at any given moment. She'd fixate on Mrs. Singh's footwork when she was supposed to be watching her hands. Or she'd focus her attention on the baton Mrs. Singh was swinging, when she was supposed to be tracking Mrs. Singh's eyes, to see where they were looking. Each time Kitty got it wrong, she felt the spring inside her tighten.

That tension only worsened during Kitty's firearms training with Saul. The problem wasn't Saul himself; the gruff armaments master gave her precise instructions that were easy to follow. Learning basic handling and maintenance—cleaning the weapons, disassembling them and putting them back together—that was all fine. Even pleasant, in fact: an interesting, detailed task with a clear procedure and a definite conclusion. She could have done it for hours, if Saul had allowed it.

The problem was the shooting. It was loud, jolting, and intrusive. Even with protective earmuffs, the noise made Kitty wince, and she hated how the gun jerked in her hands when she fired.

Gradually, she learned to steel herself against it, if only for a few moments at a time. She kept her focus on the target and tried to ignore the chaos that accompanied each shot. The noise and vibrations were just things that happened. She knew they were coming. They couldn't hurt her.

She was a lousy shot, though, and the pace of improvement was agonizingly slow. Still, with each day, each chorus of tiny explosions clutched in her hands, the wide scattering of bullet holes in the paper target got closer and closer together.

"Excellent work, Miss Granger," Saul told her as he examined the target one morning.

Kitty looked at the target, very confused. Better than usual perhaps, but her shots were still all over place, and none of them had landed in the center.

"But I missed, sir," she protested.

Saul chuckled. "You missed the bullseye, but all of your shots hit the target. I do believe that's a first for you, and not something to be taken lightly."

"If you say so, sir," Kitty replied, frowning. "Just feels like I won't ever be any good at it. Not like you or Mrs. Singh. I 'spect you could hit it dead center every time you tried, sir."

"The only way to be good at a thing is by being bad at it over and over again until you improve," Saul reminded her as he replaced the bullet-riddled paper with a fresh one and then pressed a button to send the target back to its place across the shooting range. "You don't like guns, do you?"

"No, sir," Kitty admitted. It felt like the wrong thing to say to the person who was teaching her how to use them.

"Are you afraid of them?"

Kitty hesitated but finally confessed, "Yes, sir, I'm dead scared of 'em."

Saul nodded. "Sensible. Firearms are dangerous. I'd rather train someone with a healthy fear of them than some damn fool with more confidence than brains."

"Every time I pick one up, I'm afraid it'll explode in me hand," Kitty admitted.

"Well, you needn't fear that, as long as you remember your training, act responsibly, and keep your weapon properly maintained."

"I'll do me best, sir," Kitty assured him.

"Also remember that any time you carry a gun, you are responsible for what it does," Saul added sternly. "Don't aim it unless you're prepared to shoot, don't shoot at anything but your target, and don't pull the trigger unless you have to. A weapon is a responsibility. Treat it as such."

Kitty nodded. "I imagine you've got loads of experience with guns."

"More than my fair share," Saul agreed.

"You fought in the war?"

"I did. I was in France in 1940, then North Africa, then Sicily." For a moment, Saul's expression darkened. "Wish it had been Czechoslovakia in '38, though—show Hitler we were willing to stand by the Czechs. Or Abyssinia in '35, to put an end to Mussolini's empire-building. But that didn't happen. No one wanted a war, and we thought we could buy peace with other people's freedom."

Kitty was astonished. "You think we shoulda gone to war sooner? But me da says the war were 'orrible!"

"Horrible beyond imagining," Saul replied, with a distant look in his eyes. "And maybe it could've been stopped if someone had stood up to Hitler sooner. See, Miss Granger, dictators are just schoolyard bullies at heart. You can't buy them off by giving in to their demands, that only encourages them."

"What *do* you do, then?" Kitty asked. "Punch 'em in the nose?"

She'd done that once as a child, to a boy who'd pulled her hair and called her names. Well, and a few times after that, when other bullies had mistaken her meekness for weakness. For some reason she was always the one who got into trouble, though, so eventually she resorted to running away instead of standing up for herself. Never seemed fair, but there it was.

Saul chuckled. "Dictators, like bullies, have a kind of low cunning. They start with the easiest targets, and work their way up. The way to stop them is when you see one picking on a little fella, you get your mates together, march straight up to them, and say 'You leave him alone, or you'll have to deal with the rest of us.' Nine times out of ten, the bully will back down, and he'll think twice about picking on someone again."

"What if 'e don't back down?" Kitty asked, already guessing the answer. Saul seemed the kind of man who didn't mind a bit of fisticuffs if it was in a good cause.

"Well . . ." Saul grinned and folded his arms. "Then you've got your mates with you, so you'll probably win. But whether you win or lose, better to take a stand than do nothing."

Kitty nodded. "I'll keep that in mind, sir."

One day, during her lunch hour, Kitty stole away to the garage where the mechanics maintained the Orchestra's cars and equipment. It was a large concrete room that smelled strongly of petrol and motor oil, and at first Kitty had been intimidated by it. The smell reminded her of Ivan's hideout, and it was full of sudden loud noises.

But lunchtime was better, quieter. Most of the mechanics were out. Today, Kitty arrived with a thermos of hot tea, two cups, and a plan. She hovered just inside the doorway, looking for Tommy. She'd rather not speak to anyone else at the moment. A couple of other mechanics were still working on a bullet-riddled truck, and if they saw her alone they might ask questions.

After a few seconds, Kitty saw Tommy slide out from underneath a light blue Austin Mini that was missing both of its doors as well as its engine. The doors were nowhere to be seen, but the engine was waiting on a nearby table.

"Tommy!" Kitty called, holding up the thermos for him to see. It felt like a silly thing to do once she'd done it, but Tommy answered with a wave and a smile.

"'Ello Kitty," Tommy said as Kitty approached. "Not waitin' on a car, are ya? Don't recall seein' your name on the list."

"Oh, no, nothin' like that," Kitty assured him. She held up the thermos. "I just thought you might like a cuppa is all."

"Wouldn't say no," Tommy said happily. He wiped his hands on an oily rag as Kitty opened the thermos and filled the two cups with tea. "Very decent of ya."

Kitty took one of the cups, and raised it to Tommy's in a silent toast. After they'd enjoyed a few sips, she coughed awkwardly and confessed, "Well, to be honest, I was wonderin' if you might teach me a bit about car maintenance. I mean, it's not part of me trainin', but I'm curious to learn."

"You wanna learn how to fix cars?" Tommy asked, sounding bewildered.

"Well . . . yeah." Tommy's confusion made Kitty confused in turn. "Would it be a problem?"

Tommy shrugged. "No, it's just, girls ain't usually interested in cars, are they?"

Kitty sipped her tea while she decided how to word her response. Then she replied, "I think you'll find, Tommy, that girls can be interested in all sorts of things, only we don't talk about 'em 'cause people keep tellin' us we're not s'posed to like 'em."

"Never thought about it that way," Tommy said, nodding. "Makes sense, I s'pose."

"So you'll teach me about cars an' engines, then?"

Tommy grinned. "Sure. It'll be fun. Honestly, I wish more folks round here cared 'ow their cars actually *work*. Like Verity for instance. The girl treats everythin' she drives like it's a bloody sports car! I keep tellin' 'er to respect the limitations of the vehicle. She don't listen. No one does. All them agents think they can run their cars ragged, then bring 'em back 'ere an' we'll fix 'em up like it's nothin'. I tell ya, Kitty, it's a bloody nightmare, is what it is."

In a way, Kitty felt she knew what he meant. If something seemed simple on the outside, people took it for granted. All the complexity under the surface, all the work that went into making something behave properly, went unnoticed. "Well, if I ever end up drivin' one of your cars, I promise to—um—respect it," Kitty vowed. "An' if I do break one, I'll fix it meself!"

Tommy laughed. "Just so long as it don't become a trend. If all the agents started fixin' their own cars, I'd be out of a job!"

He motioned for her to join him next to the engine block. "For today, don't touch anythin' or you'll get oil all over ya. I'll see if I can find a spare coverall in your size by tomorrow."

"Sounds grand," said Kitty, already feeling more at ease than she did during most of her training sessions.

Tommy grabbed a wrench from his toolbox and motioned to the engine. "Now then, I'm gonna take this bloody thing apart. You just watch an' learn, yeah?"

Kitty grinned and gave Tommy a salute. "Aye, aye, sir!"

It was barely eleven and Kitty was already short of breath and tense with frustration. She was training with Mrs. Singh using wooden batons, learning to block and swing in a rapidly changing sequence. Each time she got a maneuver wrong, she was rewarded with a smack to her arm. It didn't hurt exactly, but it stung, and the impact of each blow compounded in her mind.

Today was especially bad. The clicking in her head went round and round constantly, making her remember each failed move and each strike she received. She knew she was doing it wrong, and thinking about *that* soon demanded more of her attention that what she was doing. She wanted to scream and give up, and maybe to throw to baton at something, and just the effort of keeping all those impulses in check overwhelmed her ability to think.

She was repaid for her distraction by a sharp tap to the ribs. Kitty winced and darted backward. She raised her baton defensively, trying not to twitch with the nervous energy coursing through her. Mrs. Singh slowly advanced, watching her carefully. Kitty shivered. What was going to come next? A swing from above? A punch from Mrs. Singh's empty hand? A kick to the leg, to remind Kitty that her stance was bad?

Kitty bared her teeth. It was all she could do not to snarl, which would have made her feel better but would have looked impossibly strange. She knew her stance was bad, but Mrs. Singh wasn't giving her any time to adapt! And Kitty knew that was the point, but knowing and doing were two different things! She couldn't think! How was she expected to learn if she couldn't think?

Can't think! Can't think! Can't think!

Mrs. Singh darted forward past Kitty's clumsy defense and kicked Kitty's foot out from under her. Kitty tumbled to the ground in a heap, trying not to lose her senses.

Get up! Get up! Get up! Get up!

"You were too slow that time," Mrs. Singh said, her tone strict but not unkind. "Your instincts are good, but your form is sloppy."

You're doing it wrong! You're doing it wrong! You're doing it wrong!

Kitty didn't want to have a fit in front of Mrs. Singh. She'd worked so hard to keep herself in check these past months, but the turmoil inside her was finally getting out of control.

"I know, missis, I know," Kitty grumbled.

"Let's try again. On your feet."

Kitty pulled herself into a crouch, hunched over as she struggled to keep her thoughts coherent. "Just a moment. Please. I just need a moment to catch me breath."

Mrs. Singh raised her baton and advanced again. "Out there you won't get a moment, Kitty! Out there you won't have time to catch your breath!"

It was the last straw. It was like a latch was thrown inside Kitty's head, and the stress flooded out into her. She bounded to her feet, snarling and baring her teeth. She couldn't have a moment of peace? Fine! Who needed peace? Peace was over-rated. It was better just to be wild, just to be loud, just to let it all go and—

"*I KNOW!*" Kitty screamed as she lunged at Mrs. Singh, swinging her baton with all her might.

Suddenly she found herself stopped mid-strike, with Mrs. Singh's baton braced against her shoulder to hold her in place. It was confusing, but in that moment Kitty managed to snatch control of herself again. Her body went rigid and numb, and she saw her baton extended over Mrs. Singh's head, caught effortlessly in Mrs. Singh's empty hand. The blow had been intercepted almost as soon as it had been swung.

Kitty was enveloped in a haze of fear. She'd bloody well lost her mind for a moment. Mrs. Singh would be furious, surely. Just like Kitty's father had been when Kitty had her fits as a child.

But Mrs. Singh gave Kitty a sympathetic look and released her. "In the field you won't get a moment to catch your breath," Mrs. Singh repeated, "which is why you can take one now."

Kitty exhaled, and with it her body collapsed. She sat on the training mat and held her head in her hands.

"I'm sorry, Mrs. Singh," she moaned. "I didn't mean to go mad like that, honest. I just . . ."

Mrs. Singh sat next to her. "You were hurt and you got angry."

"Somethin' like that, yeah," Kitty said.

"You get angry sometimes, don't you?"

The question made Kitty frown. *Angry* wasn't quite right. More like . . . overwhelmed. Sometimes things got too loud. The world started looming over her, and when it did she just had an urge to lose herself. She wanted to shout, or throw things, or hit something, even herself. Anything to make the noise go away and make the record in her head stop skipping.

Well, Mrs. Singh would expect an answer, and Kitty couldn't very well start explaining about the world being loud and confusing. Getting angry in a fight was something other people could understand, so she might as well go along with that.

"Sometimes, yes," she replied, her voice soft and hesitant. "Don't think ill of me for it, I beg you! I don't often lose me temper, honest!"

Mrs. Singh raised an eyebrow. "Kitty, what's the matter?"

"I'll keep me wits out in the field, I promise," Kitty insisted. "It won't 'appen again! Please don't dismiss me!"

"Ah." Mrs. Singh nodded. "No, Kitty, I'm not going to stop your training just because of one angry outburst during a sparring lesson. But it is good that I know about this. You will need to learn to keep your anger under control when you're out on a mission. Can you do that for me?"

"Yes, missis. It won't be no problem."

"Good." Mrs. Singh looked Kitty in the eyes. Her expression was very stern, but there was a hint of worry there too. "I suppose this is a lesson in itself. I know it's easy to lose your temper in a fight, especially if you're afraid or things are going badly."

"Maybe a little," Kitty agreed.

"You cannot let that happen," Mrs. Singh replied. "Never. In a fight, you must always keep your head, do you understand? You must always be aware of your surroundings, and you must be able to *act* on what you see, not simply *react* to what is happening around you."

"I . . . I'm not sure if I understand, missis."

"Kitty, do you remember when you were grabbed by Ivan's men?"

Kitty shivered at the memory and hugged herself. "I'll never forget that."

"If you are ever attacked by enemy agents while on a mission, it will be like that," Mrs. Singh said. "I am teaching you the skills to protect yourself and escape, but you will have to keep a clear head in order to use them. Let me be very serious about this, Kitty. Out in the field, nine times out of ten if you have to fight someone, it'll be a man who is bigger and stronger than you and who will not think twice about killing you."

Cold fear began to ache in Kitty's stomach. She had always known this sort of work might be dangerous, but she had never put much thought into just what that meant.

Mrs. Singh must have noticed Kitty's distress, because she took Kitty's hand and said, "I promise that Pryce and I will do everything in our power to avoid putting you in immediate danger. We certainly won't send you to chase down Russian assassins. But there may be times when we give you an assignment that we believe to be safe, and we turn out to be wrong. In that situation, you will need to be able to protect yourself. And Kitty . . ."

"Yes?"

"Let me be clear about something else. If you *are* ever in danger, your priority is getting yourself back safely. Finish the mission if you can, but it's more important to get out alive. We can always form a new plan. But we can't get a new Kitty, can we?"

"No, I s'pose not," Kitty agreed, laughing softly at the joke. It helped relieve some of the fear. But only some of it.

Mrs. Singh turned serious again. "Remember, if you're fighting someone bigger and stronger than you, there is no such thing as 'fair play.' The notion of a fair fight was invented by someone who knew they were going to win. So you do anything you have to do to get out, just like I've taught you. Go for your enemy's face, go for his eyes, kick him between the legs. You probably won't be able to punch as hard as him, so use your knees and elbows to make up the difference."

Kitty nodded to show that she understood. They were all techniques that Mrs. Singh had shown her before, only now the reason for learning them was becoming much clearer.

"If you can get your hands on a weapon, then you use it," Mrs. Singh continued. "Anything ready to hand: a rock, a pipe, anything. You grab it, you hit your enemy in the head, and you run."

"I understand," Kitty said.

"If you have to run, what do you do then?"

"Uh, evade detection, get to a safe place, notify HQ. Right?"

"That's right," Mrs. Singh said.

Kitty smiled, pleased that she had remembered correctly. "And then 'tis back home for tea and biscuits, wot?" she added, mimicking Mrs. Singh's Mayfair accent.

The moment the words left her mouth, she felt foolish.

Mrs. Singh gave her an astonished stare. "What was that?"

"Sorry, missis!" Kitty exclaimed. She put a hand over her mouth, but the damage had already been done. "I didn't mean to, only . . ."

"That was supposed to be me, wasn't it?" Mrs. Singh asked. "That's what I sound like."

Kitty cringed. "Yes, missis. I'm so sorry! I know it's rude!"

"That was actually quite good," Mrs. Singh said. "Do it again."

"What?" Kitty didn't believe her ears.

"Let me hear you do it again."

It took Kitty a few moments to summon up her courage. Was Mrs. Singh playing a game with her now? Surely she'd been insulted. When Kitty had mimicked people as a child, it had made her father furious.

"I say," Kitty said hesitantly, "aren't we all having a grand time down at the Royal Ascot this evening? My word, but hasn't Princess Margaret got a lovely hat?"

Now it was Mrs. Singh's turn to cover her mouth with her hand, as she snickered with genuine amusement. "Well, we shall have to work on your phrasing, but I am impressed. Can you do Pryce?"

"Uh . . ." Kitty cleared her throat and did her best approximation of Pryce's calm, genial voice. "Goodness, Mrs. Singh, I fear the Russians have made off with our state secrets, and also my very valuable bowler hat." Kitty winced as soon as she had spoken.

Mrs. Singh laughed again. "Now that was very good. You're something of a mimic, aren't you?"

"I s'pose so," Kitty mumbled. "Used to do it all the time. Only me da hated it, so I stopped."

"Damn foolish of him, I say." Mrs. Singh was quiet for a little while, mulling something over. "I tell you what, Kitty. Are you willing to practice it? To try learning specific accents?"

"If you think I should," Kitty said, surprised. "Would that be 'elpful?"

"Helpful doesn't even come close," Mrs. Singh said. "To be a spy, you have to convince people that you're someone you are not. Looking the part and *sounding* the part is the first big hurdle, and I think you might have an unexpected edge in that. If I give you some language tapes, will you practice with them and try to learn the accents?"

"'Course!" Kitty exclaimed. "You mean it might be useful for somethin'?"

"It could be extremely useful, depending on how many accents you can do it with, and how well you can keep it up." Mrs. Singh stood and offered Kitty a hand. "But enough talk of that. Are you ready for another round of sparring?"

Kitty sprang to her feet, determined to keep her composure this time.

"I'm ready for ten rounds, if that's what it takes!"

CHAPTER 13

"Right," Faith said to Kitty, waving a ballpoint pen under her nose. "You're in the room, something important is happening that you need recorded, what do you do?"

Kitty took the pen and turned it over between her fingers, trying to remember the instructions.

"Um, three clicks to turn the recorder on," she said, as she did it. *Click. Click. Click.* Recorder on. "Let it play." She held the pen up to her mouth and whispered. "'Ello, 'ello? Can you 'ear me, me?"

Faith smirked at her. "Just do the job, no messing about."

"Three more clicks to turn it off," Kitty finished. *Click. Click. Click.* Recorder off.

She handed the pen back to Faith, who fiddled with it and played back the message. It was a little muffled, but it came through clear enough.

"Just like that," Faith said. "Remember, there's not much tape in the pen because it's so small. If you need to record a long conversation . . . ?"

"I use the larger one in me makeup case."

"You got it!" Faith said.

"Pen's nice an' all, but when do I get one of them pocket flamethrowers?" Kitty teased.

Faith made a face and huffed softly. "I'm not allowed to experiment with them anymore. I was *so* bloody close, Kitty! Not my fault the thing blew up on the testing ground."

"Could make it a pocket grenade," Kitty suggested.

"Ooo! That is a thought," Faith agreed. She grabbed for a pencil and paper. "Note to self: thermite cigarette lighter."

As Faith began scribbling a chaotic collection of words and designs on the scrap paper, Tommy raced into the workshop.

"The Old Man's on his way!" he exclaimed. "We need the package!"

Kitty blinked a couple of times. The name didn't mean anything to her, but at its mention, Faith practically dropped everything she was holding and started rummaging around her table.

"Oh hell," Faith muttered. "Thought I had more time." After some frantic searching, she produced a little wooden tea chest from the bottom of a crate on the floor. "Got it! Where's the tea?"

Liam appeared in the doorway beside Tommy, carrying a porcelain tea service on a tray. The little cups rattled in their saucers, and Kitty heard water sloshing around in the teapot.

"Tea's ready!" Liam reported. "Water's piping hot."

Faith raced across the workshop and plopped the tea chest onto the tray. "Where are they?"

"Just arrived," Tommy said. He glanced at his wristwatch. "Saw 'em come down in the lift on me way over. They'll be in Pryce's office by now."

"What's goin' on?" Kitty asked, as she joined the others.

"Mr. Pryce is getting a visit from the Old Man," Faith explained. "Big mission, apparently. Private meeting, even Mrs. Singh's not allowed in. We're going to deliver Mr. Pryce a nice pot of tea while they chat."

That sounded reasonable, and very kind too, so Kitty nodded. "Who's the Old Man?" she asked.

"Pryce's boss," Tommy replied. "See, we all work for Pryce, Pryce works for the Old Man, and the Old Man works for the Minister. Old Man's a really important toff. Oxford fella, from what I hear. Been doin' spy work since before the War."

"Right, I'll take the tea over to the office," said Liam. "Back in a jiffy."

"No, no, no!" Faith shook her head. "Can't have *you* bring it in. Kitty should do it."

"Me?" Kitty asked, as Faith took the tray from Liam and placed it in her hands. "Why me?"

"Um, because your sunny personality is much better than Liam's," Faith said quickly. She gave Kitty a gentle push toward the door. "Now go on, take this to Pryce's office quick as you can, and then come right back here. Got it?"

"Fine," Kitty answered.

Something about all of this nagged at her as she went into the hallway, but it wasn't coherent enough to puzzle out. Faith and the boys weren't acting suspicious per se, but Kitty rather felt like she *ought* to find it suspicious. That was the odd part. Still, nothing to be done but to get the delivery over with.

She hurried along to Mr. Pryce's office and tapped at the door with her foot. It wasn't the most genteel way of knocking, but with her hands full she didn't have much of a choice. There was a long silence and suddenly Kitty was afraid she hadn't been heard. She drew back her foot to give another kick and the door suddenly opened, revealing the bewildered face of Mr. Pryce.

"Kitty? Goodness me, what are you doing?" he exclaimed.

Kitty slowly lowered her foot to the ground. "Um, I've brought some tea, sir. They said you 'ad company, so . . ."

"Oh." Mr. Pryce absorbed this and then smiled. "Well, that's very good of you, Kitty. Thank you."

"No trouble, sir. Just wantin' to be of use," Kitty said.

She glanced past Mr. Pryce and into the office. It was hard to see clearly since the door was only half open, but she caught sight of two more men inside. One was a stiff-backed military man around Mr. Pryce's age. He had a very severe face and the eyes to match, a seemingly permanent grimace, and a neat little mustache that was so expertly groomed it made Kitty uncomfortable to look at it. Hair wasn't supposed to be that precise, so Kitty immediately disliked him.

The second man was much older. He had soft white hair and a full beard, and he looked like he should be someone's grandfather. Not exactly Father Christmas, but near enough. He sat in a far more relaxed manner than his companion, with his hands gently folded on top of a lacquered wooden cane. Both of the men wore very expensive suits, though their clothes were much more subdued than Mr. Pryce's rather dramatic style. They were probably from the government.

"Who's that?" Kitty asked, completely forgetting herself in her curiosity.

"Colleagues, Miss Granger," Pryce said as he took the tray from her. "And since it seems no one told you already, this is a closed meeting and we are not to be disturbed."

"Yes, sir."

Kitty looked down and began fiddling with her fingertips. Had she done something wrong? She'd been asked to bring the tea, and she'd brought the tea. Mr. Pryce liked tea. Everyone liked tea. Why did it suddenly feel like she wasn't supposed to have done this?

Noticing her distress, Mr. Pryce gave a quick smile. "Thank

you for the tea, Miss Granger. It's appreciated."

Mr. Pryce backed away into the office and pushed the door shut. Kitty stared at it for a few moments, trying to process everything in her head. All of this really was starting to feel strange. Why had she been the one sent to bring the tea? Why had Pryce been surprised about it? Had he not asked for it?

"Bollocks," Kitty muttered under her breath. She'd been put up to something by the others and she didn't know what. With her luck it would be a bloody prank and she'd be fired for it!

Kitty ran back to the workshop and saw Faith, Liam, and Tommy sitting around a radio receiver. Tommy and Liam were sharing a set of headphones and listening to the transmission, while Faith was busy plugging a second set of headphones into the device.

"A'right, what's this all about?" Kitty demanded.

Faith answered with another question: "Pryce took the tray?"

Kitty sat in the empty seat next to Faith and gave her a severe look. "Yes 'e did. An' I know you three are up to somethin'."

"Did 'e suspect anythin'?" Tommy asked.

"Suspect?" Kitty exclaimed. "Suspect what? What did you just 'ave me do?"

"We put a radio bug in the tea chest," Faith answered.

"You what?!"

"Shhh! Not so loud!" Faith put a finger to her lips. "We're technically breaking the law. I think."

"You think?"

"Look," Faith said, "this is a real hush-hush meeting. Pryce wasn't even told about it until last night. That's what Debby said, at least."

Kitty frowned. "Seems odd."

"Aye, real odd," Tommy said. "Plus, even Mrs. Singh ain't allowed to sit in on it. Usually she's there for all the meetings with the Old Man. It's suspicious is what it is."

"Honestly, Mrs. Singh'll thank us once we tell her what they're talking about," Liam insisted.

"Ehhh," Faith said. "Let's not rush to tell Mrs. Singh, all right? Not unless we know it's something of real significance."

Someone in the doorway coughed. "Let's not rush to tell Mrs. Singh *what* exactly?" Mrs. Singh asked.

Kitty spun in her chair, and the others did the same. Mrs. Singh was leaning against the doorframe, watching them with a suspicious look in her eyes. She strode across the workshop toward them, her arms folded, like a teacher who had caught her students on the verge of releasing frogs into the classroom.

"Mrs. Singh!" Faith exclaimed. "We . . . um . . ."

"Didn't see you there, ma'am," Liam said, fumbling over his words.

"I came looking for Kitty," Mrs. Singh said. "I have an assignment for her. But this is much more interesting."

"It's nothing—" Liam began.

A glance at Mrs. Singh's stance told Kitty she wasn't having any of it. That was a trick Kitty had been forced to learn: often she couldn't read emotions on someone's face, but she could sometimes *feel* their mood by how they carried themselves and the tone of their voice. When Mrs. Singh was like this, excuses would just make her more curious and more annoyed with them.

"I gave Mr. Pryce a tea chest with a radio bug inside it so we could listen to 'is conversation with the Old Man," Kitty burst out.

Everyone looked at her, and Faith covered her face with her hands. Kitty winced. She had just done something very foolish, hadn't she? But Mrs. Singh wasn't going to believe their excuses, so what else could they have done? She'd learn the truth eventually.

"Pryce is meeting with the Old Man? You mean now?" Mrs. Singh asked. It seemed she'd had no idea it was happening. Then the other part of the statement caught up with her. "Wait a moment, you *bugged his office*?" she demanded. "Have you lost your minds?"

Faith shot Kitty a glare before she made her case to Mrs. Singh. "Look, to be fair, I put the bug inside the chest and it was Liam's idea."

"It was not!" Liam cried. "It was your bloody idea, Faith!"

Kitty's mind was turning in circles as she tried to think of a way out of this mess. The record was spinning so fast it felt like her brain was about to catch on fire, but everything started lining up correctly.

Mrs. Singh should have been in the meeting.

Mrs. Singh wasn't in the meeting.

Mrs. Singh didn't even know about the meeting.

Mrs. Singh was in the same boat as the rest of them.

"So you didn't know Mr. Pryce an' the Old Man had this meetin'?" Kitty asked Mrs. Singh.

Mrs. Singh hesitated. "I did not."

"But you're supposed to be there for all the meetin's?"

"That's the policy, yes," Mrs. Singh replied. She narrowed her eyes at Kitty. "What are you getting at?"

Kitty grabbed one of the pairs of headphones and held them out to Mrs. Singh. "Maybe you'd like to take a listen along with the rest of us, missis."

Mrs. Singh's eyes narrowed even further, but a smile slowly spread across her lips. "You are full of surprises, Miss Granger," she said, and she held one of the headphones up to her ear.

Kitty didn't answer. It had taken all her reserves of confidence to make the case so forcefully, and she suddenly found it preferable not to speak. Fortunately, everyone was too interested in the radio to pry. Faith plugged a third set into the receiver and shared it with Kitty. People were already speaking on the other end, but the conversation seemed to be the trailing end of pleasantries as the tea was being poured.

"Splendid little place you have here, Pryce," said one soft voice that probably belonged to the Old Man.

"Thank you, sir," Mr. Pryce replied. "We do our best to keep up appearances." There was a pause and the sounds of spoons stirring in cups, followed by the almost inaudible slurp of three people sipping tea at once. "Ah, that's better, isn't it?"

A third voice chimed in, sounding gruff and irritable. "You can stop being all smiles and charm, Pryce," he said. "You want to know why we're here."

Mr. Pryce chuckled. "Indeed. More specifically, I want to know why *you're* here, Gascoigne. Why can't Mrs. Singh be part of this meeting, but you can?"

There was venom in his tone. Even through the crackle of the radio, Kitty could tell he and Gascoigne didn't like each other.

"Who's that Gascoigne bloke?" Kitty asked.

Mrs. Singh was frowning. "Another intelligence officer, like Pryce. He runs his own spy network, all ex-Army chaps. His methods are a little more *direct* than ours, and a lot less subtle." Under her breath she muttered, "Bloody Gascoigne of all people . . . ?"

Kitty turned her attention back to the conversation on the radio.

"Gentlemen," said the Old Man in a soothing tone, "let us not fall to recrimination. You both are valuable assets to the Ministry, and I need you to set aside this foolishness and carry out your duty. For England."

"Yes, of course, sir," Mr. Pryce replied quickly. "On that note, this meeting . . ."

"Yes?"

Mr. Pryce sounded rather hopeful. "Do I take it to mean that you've reviewed my surveillance request?"

There was an awkward silence.

"Do I have your permission to investigate Smythe?" Mr. Pryce asked. The hope in his voice diminished slightly.

More silence.

Mr. Pryce spoke again, and this time his confidence had faded entirely, replaced by a kind of grim realization.

"This meeting isn't about Smythe, is it?"

"No," the Old Man said. "Pryce, I want you to listen to me very carefully. Stay away from Sir Richard Smythe. He is off limits to you."

"But sir!" Mr. Pryce protested.

"After that disastrous operation in Belfast, you should consider yourself fortunate," the Old Man cautioned him. "There is no evidence tying Smythe to any of the illicit dealings your report accuses him of, and I cannot sanction action taken against a respected Member of Parliament without evidence. It simply isn't done, Pryce. He's one of us."

"One of us?" Mr. Pryce repeated, almost spitting out the words. "Sir, he's a bloody—"

Gascoigne's voice roared over the radio. "A what, Pryce?

A patriot? An Englishman? A Conservative?" He scoffed. "Someone far better than your miserable lot of foreigners and socialists."

"*I'm* a Conservative, Gascoigne," Mr. Pryce retorted. "*You're* a Conservative. Smythe is a fascist and you know it. And don't you dare talk about my agents in that condescending tone. They are as brave and loyal and hardworking as any of your lads. And if you think you can walk into my office and insult them . . ."

The anger in Mr. Pryce's voice was startling. Kitty had always known him to be calm and jovial, but from his tone she imagined him looking red with anger, bounding out of his chair to wave a finger under Gascoigne's nose.

The Old Man coughed just loudly enough for the microphone to pick it up.

"Settle down, Pryce," he said. "We're all friends here."

"Indeed, sir." Mr. Pryce sounded skeptical, but he didn't argue. "With respect, if you aren't here to discuss my proposal to investigate Smythe, why are you here?"

"We have a new assignment for you," the Old Man said. "It's top priority, and I've assured the Minister that you are the best man for the job. Gascoigne's men did the preliminary work, which is why he's here. But I felt that your agents were better suited to the task than his. I want all your people working on this right away."

Kitty heard some papers rustling. It sounded like someone was opening a folder. There was a lengthy silence and then Mr. Pryce spoke again, his voice twisted with a mixture of astonishment and outrage.

"The Anti-Apartheid Movement?" he exclaimed. "You want my agents to infiltrate *The Anti-Apartheid Movement*? Sir, is this a joke?"

"It's a serious operation, Pryce, and I expect you to address it as such." The Old Man's tone remained gentle and calm, but Kitty heard a sharp needle of irritation poking around inside it.

"Now I see why you didn't want Mrs. Singh here," Mr. Pryce said. "She'd give you a bloody earful over this nonsense! But I assure you, I can do that just as well in her absence. Of all the ridiculous assignments—"

"I told you he'd be difficult," Gascoigne said. "You should leave it with my men. Or better still: close down Pryce's farce of a spy network and give me his resources. I'll ferret out the traitors, just you watch."

"Easy, Gascoigne," the Old Man answered. "We all have our part to play in the defense of Britain."

"Sir, this is absurd!" Mr. Pryce protested. "The members of the Anti-Apartheid Movement are peaceful activists. By contrast, I have evidence that Sir Richard Smythe is smuggling weapons into London—"

"Circumstantial evidence," Gascoigne countered with a snide and dismissive tone. "*Flimsy* circumstantial evidence."

Mr. Pryce ignored him. "—and you want me to waste resources spying on human rights activists? Has the world gone mad?"

"We have reason to believe that the Soviets are responsible for the Anti-Apartheid Movement," the Old Man answered. He still sounded calm, but Kitty noticed the needle of anger grow into something more like a knife. The Old Man was getting impatient with Mr. Pryce.

"Respectfully, sir, I think you'll find that *apartheid* is responsible for it! And as I've said before, the best way to stop the spread of Soviet influence is by taking a firm stand against injustice."

"That is a matter for the government to decide, not us," the Old Man replied.

"Don't start whining about injustice, Pryce," Gascoigne said. "You sound like a Labour MP on election night."

Mr. Pryce's answered him angrily, "As long as we sit by and let corrupt regimes deprive their citizens of basic rights, we hand a propaganda coup to the enemy! Giftwrapped for Christmas, no less!"

The Old Man coughed, and that alone was enough to silence both of them. "Settle down, boys," he said. "The real fight's out there, not here in the office."

"Indeed, sir," Mr. Pryce conceded, and was echoed by Gascoigne.

The Old Man continued, "You have your assignment, Pryce. I expect you to carry it out. Gascoigne will fill you in on everything his men know already. And I should not have to repeat myself, but stay away from Sir Richard Smythe. The Minister's already warned me off him."

"Why should the Minister care?" Mr. Pryce asked. "Smythe is in the opposition."

The Old Man laughed and sounded quite astonished. "Can you imagine the headlines, Pryce? 'Labour Government Spies On Conservative Member of Parliament.' Oh no, that wouldn't do at all."

"I see what you mean, sir," Mr. Pryce said.

"So no harassing Smythe."

Kitty heard chairs scraping against the floor. The meeting was over. Gascoigne and the Old Man were leaving. She quickly took off the headphones and put them down on the table. The others did the same. They all stared at each other, uncertain what to say.

Mrs. Singh looked like she wanted to strangle someone. Her hands were clenched into fists. "Of all the bloody nerve," she muttered.

Faith looked grim. "Is that all true, Mrs. Singh?" she asked. "We're gonna start spying on people protesting apartheid?"

"Not if I have anything to say about it," Mrs. Singh replied, springing out of her chair.

"My uncle's a member of the movement," Tommy said, staring into the distance, horrified. "Are we gonna spy on 'im too?"

Mrs. Singh shook her head, still seething with anger. "No, we are not. We do not spy on innocent people."

"But the Old Man," Liam said hesitantly, "I mean, he gave orders, didn't he?"

"He gave *Pryce* orders. No one has said anything about it to the rest of us, have they?" Mrs. Singh flashed a wicked smile. Then she beckoned to Kitty. "In the meantime, Kitty, come with me. I need to tell you about your new assignment. Something tells me it's now more important than ever."

CHAPTER 14

Mr. Pryce was waiting for them in his office, stewing over a cup of tea. Kitty saw anger in the lines around his eyes, but he put on a cheerful smile as she and Mrs. Singh entered the room.

"Mrs. Singh and Miss Granger! Just the two people I wanted to see. Have a seat. I'd offer you tea, but I fear I'm out of fresh cups."

Kitty sat in one of the chairs and glanced at the tea service, in particular at the tea chest. The bug was still there. Were the other Young Bloods going to listen in?

Mrs. Singh looked at the tea chest too. She picked up the tray and said, "Why don't you get started on the briefing, Pryce? I'll clean this up."

"Generous of you, my dear, but there's no need for that," Pryce assured her.

"There is," Mrs. Singh answered.

Mr. Pryce sighed. "Did Faith and Liam bug my office again? I warned them last time."

"I take responsibility for it," Mrs. Singh said, "and I'll make certain it doesn't happen again. But consider, Pryce: a last-minute visit from the Old Man and Gascoigne, and I'm not invited? That kind of thing worries the rank and file."

"Under the circumstances, I can't blame them," Mr. Pryce admitted. "But make it clear to them both: not again, ever, or there will be serious consequences. The Old Man and I could have been talking about anything. State secrets, perhaps."

"Thankfully, it was just Gascoigne being an ass as usual," Mrs. Singh said, as she carried the tea tray out of the office.

Mr. Pryce now removed two folders from a drawer in his desk and set them in front of Kitty. He opened the top one. Inside was a typewritten dossier with a man's photograph pinned to it. The man was middle-aged, with graying temples and a jaw that jutted out like he wanted it to look more impressive than it actually was. Kitty skimmed the first page of the dossier and immediately recognized the name.

Sir Richard Smythe.

Kitty quickly flipped through the following pages, taking in every detail. She didn't understand a lot of it, but she knew that it was all important so she did her best to absorb all of it, even the parts that made no sense to her.

"This is Sir Richard Smythe," Mr. Pryce said. "Member of Parliament for Lower West Wickham, and an utterly despicable man. We've been following him for the better part of three years."

"What's 'e done?" Kitty asked.

"My investigation has been able to tie Smythe to at least half a dozen acts of murder, extortion, blackmail, and bribery, and he has some uncomfortably close ties to 'friendly dictatorships' around the world. Unfortunately, the evidence is almost entirely circumstantial—based on common associates, unverifiable eye witnesses, and other unreliable methodologies." Mr. Pryce sighed. "To be honest, I'd probably dismiss the evidence myself if there wasn't so damn much of it. Pardon my language."

"I'm from the East End, sir," Kitty reminded him. "Swearin' don't bother me."

"Of course." Mr. Pryce returned to the matter of Smythe. "On top of everything else, Smythe is a fascist."

"I thought 'e were a Conservative," Kitty said, rereading the file. She'd never heard of a Fascist Party MP. It was probably illegal, or at least it ought to be.

"Officially yes," Mr. Pryce said, "but in his younger days, dear Sir Richard was a disciple of Oswald Mosley."

Kitty knew the name, but she was astonished to hear it. "What? Best friends with Hitler and Mussolini, that Oswald Mosley?"

"That's the one," Mr. Pryce confirmed. "Sir Richard was a teenager in the '30s, when Mosley was playing would-be dictator with his British Union of Fascists. Apparently, he followed Mosley around like a dog and absorbed as much right-wing drivel as he could. The man was a card-carrying Blackshirt until the mid-thirties."

Kitty grimaced. The war had been well before her time, but her father had told her stories about it. He'd had plenty of choice words to say about the "bloody Germans" he'd fought, but some of his harshest sentiments were reserved for Mosley and the British Union of Fascists. As Kitty saw it, fascism was for sore losers who wanted to blame someone else for their own failures, petty men who started wars other people had to fight.

"Then 'ow's 'e a Member of Parliament now?" Kitty asked.

"After '36, Smythe's family forbade him from being publicly associated with Mosley, and they pulled on the right strings to get any record of his fascist associations suppressed," explained Mr. Pryce. "But there's evidence that the two of them corresponded and met privately up until a few years ago.

It seems they had a falling out when Mosley came back into politics in '59."

"Why?"

"Sir Richard had already been a member of the Conservative Party for more than ten years at that point," Mr. Pryce answered. "He still shared Mosley's ideology, but he'd managed to tailor it to the party line. I suspect but can't prove that Sir Richard is trying to shift Conservative politics further to the right, gradually converting the party to fascism from the inside."

As he said this, the door opened and Mrs. Singh joined them again. She wrinkled her nose at the mention of Smythe.

"*Suspect*," she scoffed, folding her arms. "We all know he's doing it."

"Knowing and proving are two different things, Mrs. Singh," said Mr. Pryce. "I can't arrest a man just because I 'know' he's guilty." He turned back to Kitty. "Anyway, when Mosley came back, he ran for Parliament as his own party, the Union Movement. He was utterly trounced, and Labour won the election. Rumor is, Sir Richard believed that the Conservatives would have won if Mosley had just kept out of it."

"After that, the two of them parted ways on very bad terms," Mrs. Singh said. "As far as we can tell, they haven't spoken since. Not that it matters. Mosley is old news. Smythe is the dangerous one now. He's not a major figure in the party, but he has some influence. Over the past ten years, he's arranged for dozens of his fellow covert fascists to stand for election as Conservatives, and about twelve of them are currently in Parliament. And that's just the ones we know about. It's possible he's lured sitting MPs over to his camp as well. He plans to turn the Conservatives into a modern-day British Union of Fascists."

"He can try," Mr. Pryce interjected. "Speaking as a Conservative, I think the party has too much sense to let that happen. At any rate, politics aren't our concern, espionage is—and we have a whole list of conspiracies and crimes that Sir Richard might be involved in."

"You said 'e murdered someone?" Kitty asked.

Mr. Pryce gave her a nod. "Last year we connected him to the murder of a Northern Irish politician who was trying to resolve the conflict between the Catholics and the Protestants. Smythe wants Britain to become uniformly Anglo Protestant, so inflaming sectarian violence in Northern Ireland plays right into his hand. It 'justifies' men like him repressing the Irish Catholics." Pryce grimaced. "I saw Sir Richard and the assassin plotting together with my own eyes, but I didn't get any tangible proof, so my superiors dismissed it. And now, it seems that some of Sir Richard's associates are smuggling weapons into London, and we don't know why."

"But I thought . . ." Kitty began. She had heard the Old Man tell Mr. Pryce to stay away from Smythe.

Mr. Pryce answered her unspoken question. "After the debacle in Northern Ireland, my superiors warned me off investigating Smythe in any official capacity, so instead we're looking into one of Sir Richard's main associates. That brings us to your mission."

Mr. Pryce moved Smythe's file to the side and opened the next folder. It was another dossier, this time for an older man with a balding head and a wide gray mustache.

"This is Henry Lowell, Earl of Chiswick," Mr. Pryce said. "He's a member of the House of Lords and close friends with Sir Richard Smythe. Ideologically, he's somewhere to the right of Francisco Franco."

Kitty shivered. Hard to imagine someone more hardline than the Spanish dictator.

"Given free rein," Mr. Pryce went on, "he'd gladly close down the House of Commons, divert all power to the hereditary lords, and deport anyone not Anglo Protestant while he's at it. Of course, that's not politically acceptable language so in public he just talks about a return to tradition and 'keeping Britain British.' But it's clear where his sentiments lie."

"You can see why he and Smythe are such good friends," Mrs. Singh added. *"Britain for the Britons* was one of Smythe's actual campaign slogans. His policies are just a slightly dressed-up version of Lowell's reactionism."

Kitty waited a moment for some things to line up in her head before she spoke. "You think that if there's anyone who'd be workin' with Smythe, it'll be Lord Lowell, aye? So you're gonna investigate 'im and hope it leads you to evidence against Smythe. Once you get the evidence, you take it to the Old Man an' then 'e's got to let you go after 'em both."

"Very good, Miss Granger," Mr. Pryce said with a smile.

"So I'm to . . . what?" Kitty asked. "'Ow do I investigate a lord?"

Mrs. Singh chuckled. "I like the enthusiasm, Kitty, but you won't be doing it singlehandedly. In fact, the investigation into Lowell has been going on for nearly a year now. We were watching him before then, but after the mess in Northern Ireland, Lowell's become our only real option. Anyone lower down is too insignificant to make a difference."

"At the moment, Lowell is being watched by Verity Chase," Mr. Pryce said.

"So that's where she's been!" Kitty exclaimed, far more loudly than she meant to. It had been a mystery bothering her for weeks.

"Indeed. Two years ago, Miss Chase arranged a chance meeting with Lord Lowell's daughter, Diana. She's maintained the link since then, and she recently made contact while the family was abroad."

"Monaco?" Kitty asked.

Mr. Pryce looked astonished. "How did you know?"

"On me first day, Verity told Debby she'd been in Monaco. I were just guessin'."

"On your first day?" Mrs. Singh asked. "Honestly, Kitty, the things you remember."

"Well, we're going to put that memory of yours to work," Mr. Pryce said. "For the past few weeks, Verity has been Diana's guest at the Lowells' country estate, keeping an eye on Lord Lowell. As far as she can tell, he doesn't suspect her. Periodically, most of the family will go traveling somewhere, like a weekend in France or a trip to the seaside. Lowell always remains behind, and Verity believes he's using those times to meet with Smythe and others."

Mrs. Singh spoke next. "Verity has searched Lowell's office and the other rooms of the house. She hasn't found anything incriminating, but she hasn't been able to get into Lowell's safe yet. Verity also believes that there's a hidden room somewhere in the house, but she can't locate it. That's where you come in."

"Me?" Kitty asked.

"We want to put your powers of perception to work," Mr. Pryce explained. "Verity has already mentioned to Diana that her cousin, Kate, will be visiting England on her way to see family in India and would like to stay in the countryside for a few days. The Lowells have agreed, so all that remains is to get you familiar with your cover identity and then send you out. By the way, how is your Canadian accent?"

"Canadian . . . ?" Kitty blinked a couple of times to summon up the particular structures of the accent. "Not too bad, sir," she said, speaking like she'd heard on the recordings. "Except I sometimes get it confused with the American."

"Ah, that's very good," Mr. Pryce said. He picked up the third folder and handed it to her. "Keep practicing, and in the meantime, this is your cover identity. Read it, memorize it, learn it until you know it better than you know yourself. Understood?"

"Yes, sir." Kitty looked over the documents inside. "Kate Greenwood of Ottawa? That's me?"

"Yes," Mr. Pryce answered. "You are Kate Greenwood. Verity is your cousin, Vera Cunningham."

"Since it's your first assignment, we thought that using the same initials would make it easier to remember," Mrs. Singh added.

"Yes, probably," Kitty agreed. An uncomfortable thought struck her. "What am I to tell me da?"

"We'll say I'm going on a business trip and need my trusted secretary to accompany me," said Mrs. Singh. "Sound plausible to you?"

"Oh, definitely, missis." Kitty exhaled, glad that her father wouldn't have cause for worry. "When do I leave?"

"Verity and the Lowells are in Scotland at the moment," Mr. Pryce said. "They're due back soon. Verity will meet you in London next Thursday and drive you up to the Lowell estate. Your work should only take a few days, but if you and Verity feel that you need to stay longer, we will give you a number to call. Ask for your aunt Mildred and say that you're having such a lovely time that you'd like to put off the trip to India for a few more days."

Kitty nodded. "An' are you me aunt Mildred, sir? Is that your code name?"

Mr. Pryce's smile drooped a bit, while Mrs. Singh covered her mouth with a hand to stifle a laugh.

"Yes, Kitty, I suppose I am technically your aunt Mildred," Mr. Pryce said, "but you're not to mention that to anyone outside this room. Security, you understand."

"Yes, Aunt Mildred," Kitty replied, very pleased that she was getting the hang of all this code name business.

CHAPTER 15

For the next week, Kitty devoted almost every waking hour to memorizing her cover and perfecting her new accent. She couldn't take any of the materials home, of course, but when she wasn't at work she played silent word games in her head to make sure that she was getting the pronunciation right—even though Mrs. Singh insisted that she already sounded authentic enough to fool the Lowells. Maybe that was true, but there were always these little quirks that Kitty felt she was missing. It became another one of her fixations. Every day Kitty identified more inconsistencies between her accent and the recordings, and set to work getting them right.

All the while, she imagined just what sort of person Kate Greenwood would be. The file had all the factual information Kitty needed—date of birth, mother and father, home address, habits and hobbies—but turning all of that into a real person was Kitty's responsibility. She had to think and act like this new person, which seemed daunting at first, until she realized that she had sort of been doing that all her life. Whenever she pretended that she wasn't overwhelmed by a crowd, or hid a fixation, or stayed outwardly calm in the midst of panic, it was like putting on a cover identity. She was pretending to be someone else, someone without her eccentricities. If she could do that convincingly, she could do this.

Kate Greenwood was a mostly quiet girl, she decided. That was the easiest thing for Kitty to demonstrate anyway. She liked listening to conversations, not necessarily participating in them. Once people knew that, they wouldn't find it odd that she wasn't very talkative. Of course, that meant she had to suppress her urge to get excited about things, since that would be interpreted as an eagerness to talk. She'd have to be careful about that.

On Thursday, Kitty went to work as usual, and transformed into her new self. It wasn't the most dramatic change in the world, but her new identity came with a set of posh dresses, jewelry, and a new curled hairstyle, compliments of Mrs. Singh. Mrs. Singh had also shown her how to pass herself off as a rich Canadian, including the necessary table etiquette. It was all very strange, but it involved following patterns, which Kitty understood and could commit to memory.

Patterns were very useful.

Just after lunch, she got a final briefing from Mr. Pryce and Mrs. Singh and a final test of her cover, although at that point she had rehearsed being Kate Greenwood so many times, it felt like she was starting to know the cover better than herself. Mr. Pryce seemed pleased with the result, but Mrs. Singh was more cautious. Although she didn't say anything specific, Kitty sensed she was troubled and didn't understand why. Didn't Mrs. Singh trust her to do the job? They wouldn't be sending her otherwise.

After leaving the office, Kitty paused outside the door and heard Mrs. Singh say, "I don't like this. She's not ready."

"She *is* ready," Mr. Pryce replied. "She knows her cover

backwards and forwards. She's a quick learner, our Miss Granger."

"It's one thing to know her cover. It's another to maintain it under pressure." Mrs. Singh sounded very worried. "We're doing this too quickly. She needs more time to prepare."

"There isn't any more time," Mr. Pryce answered. "You've seen the reports. Weapons and explosives are being smuggled into London, and I know Smythe's involved. Lowell is our only way to draw a link between them."

"Why even bother with Smythe?" Mrs. Singh asked. "We should be putting all efforts into finding those weapons!"

Mr. Pryce grumbled, obviously perturbed. "Gregson's on it, but who knows if he can find them in time? For all we know, Smythe has them already. And even if we do find them, what then? Smythe gets away *again*. I cannot keep chasing this man, Mrs. Singh. Innocent people are dead because I didn't stop him in Belfast, and who knows how bad this is going to get."

"I know, Pryce." Mrs. Singh gave a gentle sigh. "But I don't feel right putting Kitty in danger like this. She doesn't have Verity's experience in the field."

"It's an easy assignment," Mr. Pryce insisted. "Lord Lowell won't even pay her any attention. The only person to win over is Diana, and Verity will handle that. But if there really is a hidden room in the house where Lowell's meeting with Smythe, we have to find it, and Kitty is the agent with the best chance of doing that."

There was a long and very uncomfortable silence.

"I know," Mrs. Singh finally said. "But I don't like it all the same."

In the hallway, Kitty frowned at the conversation. It hurt to realize that Mrs. Singh didn't think she could accomplish the mission, and even Mr. Pryce sounded uncertain, acting on desperation instead of confidence. That stung Kitty. All her life, people had doubted her, but she had begun to think that things would be different at the Orchestra.

It seemed that wasn't so. No matter how hard she worked, she was still just Kitty Granger, the girl who couldn't be trusted to do things properly.

Well, she would show them. She'd find whatever Lord Lowell was hiding and drag it out into the light if it killed her.

Kitty was still angry at what she had overheard as she went to meet Verity at Piccadilly Circus. She waited with her suitcase beside the fountain south of the intersection and talked softly to herself to calm her temper. She didn't really understand why she was being sent out if they didn't trust her to accomplish the mission, but that didn't matter. People often did things she didn't understand. The solution was to keep calm and get the job done.

She had taken a taxi and arrived punctually, so she was only left to wait a few minutes before a bright red convertible pulled up alongside her. In the driver's seat was Verity, looking extremely fancy in a bob hairdo and a boldly colored mod dress. She looked ready for a party rather than a drive to the country. Verity pulled her sunglasses down onto her nose and grinned at Kitty.

"I say!" she exclaimed. "Going my way?"

"Veri—Vera!" Kitty remembered to use Verity's cover name. She assumed no one would be watching them in London, but it was a worthwhile precaution.

Verity leaned over and pushed the passenger door open. "Hello, coz," she said as Kitty climbed into the car. "How was your flight?"

"Long," Kitty replied. She had been told that a flight across the Atlantic was several hours, which was very long in her mind.

"Did you enjoy your sight-seeing in London?"

"Oh gosh, it was just wonderful, Vera," Kitty said. "I could simply look at it for hours."

She was very aware of speaking in the strange accent. The practice over the past week had served her well. She was mentally sounding out the syllables of each word even before she spoke them. In her head, she conjured up the shape and feel of them. This one rounded, that one short. *Remember to speak your h's, Kitty. Don't go shrill on the vowels, Kitty.*

It actually worked quite well. As Verity drove toward the outskirts of London, they chatted away about fake topics invented for their fake identities, and Kitty never once slipped up. She felt proud of herself, which wasn't a common thing. But she was doing a good job, and that was what mattered.

As they left the city and its suburbs and drove out into the countryside, Verity's mood shifted and became much more businesslike.

"What's the matter?" Kitty asked softly.

Verity looked surprised. "Oh, nothing. We don't have to keep up the pretense until we arrive, so I thought I should fill you in on some details. I've already checked the car to be sure it isn't bugged. We can speak freely."

"Bugged? Do they suspect you?"

"Not a chance," Verity assured her. "Lord Lowell assumes I'm just one of his daughter's flighty friends. But I always give the car a once-over just to be safe."

"Mr. Pryce said you needed me to find a secret room," Kitty said, hoping to prompt a more thorough explanation. Mr. Pryce and Mrs. Singh hadn't been able to tell her much beyond that, since Verity's ability to communicate back to base was limited.

"So, long story made short, Lord Lowell has been having meetings with people at the country house," Verity explained. "It's disguised as parties and shooting weekends and such, but I know the point is to meet with his fellow conspirators. They probably think it's harder to be noticed in the country than in London."

"Conspirators? Then he *is* up to something?"

"Oh, no doubt," Verity said. "They have dinner and drinks and that sort of thing, but at some point in the evening they all disappear—no sign of them in the house, but their cars remain in the driveway. That tells me there's a hidden room. I've been trying to find it, but I'm stumped, and if I search too thoroughly, someone will notice."

Kitty nodded. "That's what you need me for."

"Mrs. Singh told me you have a talent for finding hidden things." Verity grinned. "Now's your chance to prove it."

"Do me best," Kitty replied. She winced as she lapsed into her old accent. "I'll do my best, Cousin Vera. Promise."

"Attagirl!" Verity nudged Kitty with her elbow and gave her a smile. "Oh, and while you're at it, if you come across Lowell's safe combination, do let me know. I haven't been able to find the numbers, and I don't have the tools to crack the damn thing."

"Does Mr. Pryce know you need tools?" Kitty said, surprised. "He could've sent some with me."

Verity shook her head. "If it was a key lock, I'd simply pick it, but a combination safe has to be drilled open. Couldn't pack anything that would look suspicious if somebody decided to rummage through my bags, and a drill doesn't exactly disappear into the lining of a suitcase."

Kitty pondered this. "Could disguise it as a hair dryer, though, couldn't you?"

Verity raised an eyebrow. "That's a thought. But you'd still have to do something about the noise when you used it. I'll have a chat with Faith about it when we get back to London. For now, it's the combination or nothing."

"How am I supposed to find the combination?" Kitty asked.

Verity shrugged. "No idea—just keep your eyes and ears open in case you stumble on any clues. But your primary mission is finding that hidden room. The safe is where Lowell has most of his private documents, but the room is where he and his associates actually meet. If we find it, we can bug it before their next meeting."

"You make it sound so easy," Kitty said.

Verity snorted. "Easy? Not at all . . . but I think between the two of us we can manage. Right?"

"Right!" Kitty answered.

⁜

It was a lengthy drive out to Lord Lowell's estate, but Kitty rather enjoyed cruising through the English countryside with Verity. She had never been outside of the city before, so the view was incredible to her. Half the time she was too busy staring at all the grass and trees to pay attention to much else.

After a couple of hours, they passed through a little village and turned off the main road. A stone country house overlooked them from the top of a hill. As Verity drove through the front gates and up to the door, Kitty sank back in her seat. She felt dwarfed by the place, which was odd since there were many much larger buildings in London. It was just that out here, everything else was small. The house was the biggest and most imposing building for miles. And it was the home of the local lord, who probably didn't care to be reminded that the time for aristocracy had passed half a century ago.

Verity looked into Kitty's eyes and asked, "You ready?"

"Um, yes," Kitty answered, making sure she believed herself when she said it. There was a job to do and she was going to do it. No use getting cold feet now.

An elderly man in a black coat and gray trousers appeared at the top of the front steps. Verity waved to him enthusiastically, and the man approached them with a stiff and purposeful gait.

"Hello, Stokes!" Verity called as she climbed out of the car. "Told you I wouldn't be long."

Stokes nodded slightly. "Yes, Miss Cunningham."

Verity swung her hand to indicate Kitty. "This is my unfortunate cousin Kate. Miss Greenwood to you."

"Indeed, miss."

"Kate, this is Lord Lowell's butler, Mr. Stokes. He's an absolute dear."

Stokes gave no reaction to the compliment, but he said, "Thank you, miss."

Kitty bobbed her head at Stokes. "Very pleased to meet you, I'm sure."

"Is Diana in?" Verity asked him.

"Yes, miss. I believe Lady Diana is playing tennis with Miss Phyllis and Miss Ivy. His Lordship is in the library and not to be disturbed, but I shall tell him of your arrival when he emerges."

Verity laughed. "Well that's fine, Stokes. I'm not here to see him, am I?" She took Kitty by the hand. "Come on, I'll introduce you to the girls. Stokes, take Kate's bags up to her room, will you?"

"Certainly, miss," Stokes answered.

Kitty glanced up at the house and took a deep breath. This was it. Her first mission. Everything she had trained for had led to this moment.

What if she made a mistake? What if someone got killed? What if the mission was ruined and it was all her fault?

Before fear could paralyze her, Kitty clenched her teeth and took a deep breath through her nose.

She was going to do this. Lives were at stake. People were counting on her. All her life, everyone had assumed she was a lost cause, too odd to amount to anything. Well, the Orchestra believed in her—even if Mrs. Singh and Mr. Pryce had their doubts—and she wasn't going to let them down.

"Lead on," she said to Verity.

CHAPTER 16

Kitty followed Verity around the side of the house, gripping her handbag tightly. She cast a glance back at the car as Stokes directed another servant to unload the suitcase. Kitty felt an instinctive aversion to having her things handled by strangers, especially strangers she was supposed to be spying on. What if they got curious and searched her luggage?

She felt a surge of panic at the thought, but it slowly subsided. There was nothing incriminating in her luggage so there was no need to worry. This was just her private nature asserting itself, and she would have to push her way through that. She couldn't do anything suspicious.

They passed through some gardens running along the side of the hill and finally reached the back lawn, which stretched off into the distance. Kitty's head turned in all directions as her eyes tried to take in everything. There was just so much to pay attention to: flowers, trees, birds, and the house itself, with its countless windows and little nooks and crannies. The size of the house bothered her. How was she supposed to find a secret room in this place? It probably had a hundred rooms, and she couldn't search them all without someone noticing!

A tennis court sat to one side of the lawn, a few feet away from the house. Two girls dressed in white were serving a ball back and forth, while a third lounged in a chair, drinking a glass of lemonade. One was blonde, the next a brunette, and the one in the chair was a redhead, like they were a matched set. They were all about Verity's age, and they seemed to be having a marvelous time, laughing and applauding whenever someone scored a point.

"I drive down to London for an afternoon, and you all start playing tennis without me?" Verity exclaimed as she and Kitty approached. "What treachery is this?"

The other girls stopped the match and turned to her. The blonde girl grinned from ear to ear, and the other two quickly copied her. In fact, all their movements were unnervingly coordinated. The hairs on the back of Kitty's neck stood on end.

"There you are, Vera!" called the blonde. She spoke with a very posh voice, and her diction was so flawless it made Kitty shiver. "We looked *everywhere* for you this morning. You know we cannot play doubles without you!"

Verity sighed and pushed Kitty forward. "I told you last night I was going to pick up my cousin. You agreed she could stay for a few days before she leaves for India."

"Oh, of course!" the blonde said. "Was that today? Silly of me, I quite forgot." She approached Kitty and held out a hand. "Hello! You must be Kate."

"Must I?" Kitty asked awkwardly. It was meant as a joke, but it just sounded stupid when she said it, and Kitty tried to hide her own embarrassment with a laugh.

The blonde didn't seem to care. She grabbed Kitty's hand and said, "Vera has told me all about you! I'm Diana Lowell." She waved her hand at the house and grounds. "Welcome to the old homestead."

"Very pleased to meet you," Kitty said. "Vera's letter said

she was staying with some simply wonderful friends, and since I was stopping off in England anyway . . . I hope you don't mind."

"Not at all," Diana promised. "The more, the merrier, as they say. Any friend of Vera's is a friend of mine. Now then, meet the girls." Diana's friends had joined them, and she put a hand on each of their shoulders as she introduced them. "This is Phyllis and this is Ivy." The brunette and the redhead respectively. "They're making a summer of it."

"Hello," Kitty said, offering her hand to each of the other two girls.

"Well aren't you simply darling?" said Phyllis. She shared a grin with Ivy and said, "Poor girl looks like we're going to eat her."

"Don't be horrid," Diana admonished. She took Kitty by the arm and led her to one of the chairs facing the tennis court. "You're going to have a splendid time while you're here, I promise. And you must tell me all about Canada."

"Oh, certainly." Kitty tried to summon up some of the incidental facts she had memorized for her cover. Suddenly nothing was coming to her. Instead, she tried deflection. "Have you ever been to Canada?" she asked.

Diana looked amazed at the question. She snickered. "Oh God, no!" She looked at the other girls. "Honestly, who goes to *Canada*? If I wanted to see a backwater, I'd simply visit Wales!"

Phyllis and Ivy started laughing, echoing Diana. Again, there was that timing. Diana did something, and the other two followed her. Kitty glanced at Verity, who gave her a momentary look of sympathy before joining the laughter. Not wanting to look out of place, Kitty chuckled nervously.

"You're right," she said. "It's, um, very boring! I would never go if I wasn't born there."

Diana giggled and gave Kitty a shove. It wasn't exactly hard nor exactly mean, but it didn't feel genuinely playful either. "That's the spirit!" she exclaimed. "Vera said you were a good sport. Now you sit down and watch as we play a proper game of doubles." Diana snapped her fingers. "Vera, darling, grab a racquet. You're with me."

Verity looked down at her clothes. "I'm not dressed for it. Can I change?"

"Certainly not!" Diana replied. "I've been absolutely dying for a proper game of doubles all day, and you're not getting off that easily. Play in what you're wearing."

Kitty saw frustration flash across Verity's face, but Verity suppressed it. She smiled demurely, took of her shoes, and handed them to Kitty, before joining the other girls on the tennis court.

"You know, if I get grass stains on this dress . . ." she began.

"Oh, shut up. I'll buy you a new dress," Diana answered, like that was all that mattered.

Verity took her position on the court beside Diana. She gave her racquet a twirl around her fingers and swung it back and forth to test the weight. The movement immediately drew Kitty's gaze to Verity's fingers, which were lively and dexterous as they moved. It made Kitty think of her own fingers, and she looked down at her hands. Were they as agile as Verity's hands? Was that important for spying, or just for playing tennis?

It took Kitty a moment to realize that she'd become distracted. The laughter and shouting of the other girls snapped her out of it, and she looked up at the match. She quickly folded her hands in her lap and hoped that no one had noticed her odd behavior. This was a new place full of new people and being in the field on a real mission was a very new experience. It was all starting to make her feel anxious, and that meant trouble.

Keep your head together, she reminded herself. *You're not Kitty Granger, you're Kate Greenwood, and Kate Greenwood doesn't get distracted.*

She lay back in the chair and watched the other girls play. It was actually quite exciting. Kitty had never seen a proper tennis match before, and never one on grass. There was a lot of running back and forth, because the ball never bounced very high if it hit the ground, so everyone was sent racing to intercept each volley that came over the net. A few times the ball would hit the lawn and bounce, and someone would catch it with a daring dash and a flick of the wrist—but more often those attempts failed, and the ball rolled to a stop a couple of feet away, taunting the poor player who had missed the swing.

Kitty expected Verity to be the star of the game, since Verity seemed to be awfully good at a lot of things. Instead, she proved to be a capable player, but not noticeably better than anyone else—least of all Diana, who shone the most. Kitty wondered if that was by design. Diana seemed to fume and pout whenever a set went against her. Were the others letting her win to humor her?

After a little while, the girls stopped for a break. Diana walked to a nearby table, where there was a pitcher of lemonade and some glasses on a tray. She filled a glass for herself without waiting on the others, and took a drink. Her face immediately went sour.

"Oh, Lord, it's warm! Ew, ew!" Diana exclaimed.

Verity tried some and made a face. "Well, yes. How long has it been out?"

"Well I don't know! A few hours?" Diana frowned. "It won't do. Someone will have to go and tell Cook to make some more." She looked around with an angry expression. "Oh drat, where is the maid? Probably doing housework or something useless. The junior maid is on her day off, or else she'd be here to take care of it, the lazy twit . . ." She began calling toward the house, "Susan! Susan, get out here, you're needed!"

Kitty glanced at the other girls. Verity was trying not to look annoyed, while Phyllis and Ivy gave each other nervous glances. Kitty felt very uncomfortable too, with all the anger rolling off of their hostess. It did seem like a very silly thing to get so upset about.

"Don't be cross," Verity said. "Look, I'll just go to the kitchen and sort it all out."

Diana pointed a stern finger at her. "You stay right where you are, Vera. We're in the middle of a match, and I'm not losing my partner over some lemonade." She turned to the house again and shouted, "SUSAN!"

An idea came to Kitty. It was a long shot, but any opportunity to explore the house on her own would be useful. She didn't know where to start looking for Lowell's hidden room, so if she could eliminate even part of the house now . . .

"I'll do it," she said, giving Diana a sweet smile. She had practiced doing that to prepare for the role. "I'm not playing, so I may as well make myself useful."

Diana fixed her with an astonished stare, and for a moment, Kitty feared she had done something wrong. Then Diana's expression changed dramatically, but Kitty couldn't read whether she was angry or pleased.

"Well!" Diana exclaimed. "That is the first good idea I've heard in ages. Your cousin can stay as long as she likes, Vera, if she's willing to fetch and carry."

"Good old Kate, always happy to help," Verity said. She took Kitty aside and pointed toward the glass French doors nearest to them. "Look, the kitchen is easy to find. Go straight through those doors into the house, turn right at the first hallway and follow it past *Lord Lowell's study.*" She emphasized those words just slightly. "The stairway to the kitchen is just beyond. No need to rush; we'll be here for hours, if Diana has anything to say about it."

"Right," Kitty said.

She waited until the game had resumed before going to the French doors and slipping inside. She found herself in a little parlor looking out on the lawn. It was very elegant and filled with all sorts of expensive furniture and decorations, like a small ivory statue on an end table and several portraits that glowered down at her. They were probably long-dead members of the Lowell family, and Kitty felt like they were watching her and knew what she was up to.

Kitty did a quick circuit of the parlor just in case anything stood out to her, but she didn't expect to find anything there. Verity would've covered this ground already, and a public room like the parlor wasn't a good place for the entrance to a secret chamber. The floorboards all felt equally solid beneath her feet, though it was hard to be certain through the carpet. The wallpaper all matched, and none of the wood looked out of place. Short of tugging on every book and wall fixture in search of a trigger-point for a hidden door, that was about all that she could do.

Next Kitty hurried into the hallway and followed it toward the middle of the house. Her eyes darted all around, taking in as many small details as possible, until her head swam from the overabundance of information. Nothing stood out as suspicious. It was frustrating, but at least it meant she wouldn't have to search this part of the house again later.

Lord Lowell's office was farther down the hallway. Kitty tried the door and found it unlocked, so she crept inside. The room was dark and somber, and it looked very old. The parlor had been updated with modern furnishings to help drag the old manor house into the 20th century, but aside from a telephone on the desk, Lowell's office looked like it hadn't been changed in a hundred years.

The big desk, right in the middle of the room, was very tidy, and the papers on it were placed into neat stacks. A crystal vase of cut flowers sat on a nearby table, and the flowers tickled Kitty's nose. She sniffled to keep from sneezing.

Kitty flipped through the papers: mostly accounts and other bits of bureaucracy that seemed to have no connection to the Orchestra's investigation. After a quick search of the desk's surface, Kitty adjusted everything back to exactly how it was, right down to the unpleasantly off-center placement of one of the pens. It made her cringe to look at, which was how she knew she had replaced it properly after her search.

The desk drawers were locked and there was no time to pick them. This was just a preliminary examination. She would have to do more searching later. Very conscious of the time, Kitty examined the walls, but nothing revealed itself to her. No inconsistencies in the wallpaper, no bumps or depressions in the paneling, no mysteriously uneven sections of the floor. The secret room wasn't here either.

But there might be something else. Verity had talked about a safe, and that reminded Kitty of her discovery in Ivan's hideout. Behind one of the paintings she found Lowell's safe.

It was big and heavy and imposing to look at. It had a combination dial, as Verity had said, so there was no hope of picking it open.

Kitty pushed the painting back in place and frowned. There might be something useful inside, but how were they supposed to find the combination?

A floorboard creaked out in the hallway, barely audible from where Kitty stood. Her heart began pounding, and she froze in place. Was she about to be discovered?

She scurried to the wall on one side of the door, where she could be shielded from view when the door opened. She made herself as small and unassuming as possible, and waited.

Her eyes fell on the heavy curtains gathered at either side of the window. A thought started building itself in her head. She could hide behind those curtains. They were wide and thick enough to mask a human shape. Should she move over there now, or—

The door opened and a man walked in. It was Lord Lowell, looking almost the same as in his file photograph. Kitty's breath caught in her throat and she pressed herself against the wall. Lowell had a newspaper tucked under one arm, and he went straight for his desk, giving the door a push to close it behind him.

You have to go, Kitty told herself. *Get out of here or else he'll see you!*

As Lowell passed, Kitty stepped sideways and caught the door with her hand. Her fingers fumbled against the wood, and for a moment it felt like she was going to lose her grip. Her heartbeats thudded painfully, and she recognized the onset of panic.

Get out! Get out! Get out!

Kitty scrambled around the door and back into the hallway. She doubled over and gasped for air. Panic washed over her and it was all she could do to keep on her feet.

From inside the office, she heard Lowell call out, "Is someone there?"

Lord Lowell must have heard her. She was going to be discovered. She had bungled the mission and now everything was ruined!

Stupid, stupid, stupid Kitty!

No. Through the miasma of self-recrimination, Kitty's better judgment forced its way into her mind.

He didn't see you. Look innocent.

Kitty hastily backtracked toward the parlor and then started walking down the hallway again, trying to look like there was nothing suspicious about her. Just as she got back to the office, Lord Lowell flung the door open and stepped out in front of her. Kitty stopped short and looked startled, which was probably the sincerest emotion she had shown since arriving at the estate.

"Oh goodness!" she exclaimed.

Her voice quivered with fear, which was very real to her, but was understandable under the circumstances. She drew back from Lowell and gasped. That gave her a moment to steady her nerves and push away the fog of panic in her brain. As Lowell stared at her, Kitty exhaled dramatically and felt some small measure of tension leave her. She wanted to inhale and exhale over and over again for the better part of an hour to make it all go away, but that wasn't an option.

"I do beg your pardon, sir, you gave me such a fright!" she said, as she did everything in her power to look like she was relaxing after an unexpected shock. She had no idea if it worked.

"Who the devil are you?" Lowell demanded. "What are you doing in my house?"

Kitty gasped. "Oh no! Diana didn't tell you?"

To her relief, this had an immediate effect on Lowell. "Oh, you're one of Diana's friends, are you?"

Kitty put on her best sweet smile and said, "Yes, sir, I'm Kate. Vera's cousin? Diana said I could stay for a few days."

"Ah, yes." Lowell glanced back into the office with a look of concern on his face, but then he turned his attention back to Kitty. "Diana mentioned something about it. I didn't realize you were arriving today."

"I'm so sorry, Lord Lowell. I hope it's no trouble."

"No, no, not at all." Lowell sounded gruff and annoyed, but at least his suspicion was fading. "Canadian, are you?"

"Yes, that's right. I'm from Ottawa." Kitty gave him a big shrug. "I guess the accent gives it away."

Lowell chuckled. "Not an easy thing to hide. Welcome to the old estate. Do forgive my . . . brusqueness."

"Oh, not at all, sir!" Kitty replied. "I didn't mean to startle you. Diana sent me to get some fresh lemonade from the kitchen, and I'm a little bit lost."

Lowell pointed down the hallway. "Last door on the right. Take the stairs down." He started to return to his office, then paused. "Diana will tell you, but dinner is at eight. Do not be late."

"No, sir. I'll be prompt, I promise."

Lowell nodded. "Good," he said, and left Kitty in peace.

CHAPTER 17

After the close call in Lord Lowell's office, Kitty kept a low profile for the rest of the evening. That was fine, because being in Diana's company gave her access to most of the ground floor and upstairs rooms. The girls traipsed all over the house, partly because Diana seemed to enjoy showing it off to a new guest and partly because she was too restless to stay in one place for long.

Kitty kept her eyes peeled for clues. At first she'd wondered if there might simply be an unused room somewhere, a room everyone knew about but thought abandoned, which was really Lowell's secret meeting place. But one of the girls would surely have mentioned a vacant room. Diana seemed to love telling stories about which famous people had slept in which bedrooms, which ancestor had added which design touches, and which poor souls had died in unexpected parts of the house.

So a completely hidden area seemed more likely. Kitty quickly drew up a mental blueprint, then tried to figure out if there were any conspicuous inconsistencies between one side of a wall and the other. As far as she could tell, there were no large unaccounted-for spaces between rooms. And she couldn't go around knocking on the walls to hear if any of them were hollow. At least not while the other girls were around.

Dinner was served in an opulent dining room. Lord Lowell joined them and sat at the head of the table, but he spent most of the meal reading some papers and pretty much ignored his daughter and her friends. Occasionally he exchanged a few words with his wife, Lady Constance, but neither of them seemed too interested in conversing with the young people. It seemed like the family dinner was more a matter of tradition than an occasion for actual socializing. As soon as the meal was done, Lowell vanished into his office and wasn't seen again for the rest of the evening.

The girls retired to a sitting room and spent the evening listening to music on the record player while they chatted and played cards. Kitty did her best to be pleasant and social, but the strain of all these people was beginning to wear on her. Soon, she was flicking her fingers under the table so much it threatened to become noticeable.

Finally she excused herself from the game and lay down on one of the sofas. She stared at the ceiling and pretended to be enthralled by the music. It actually wasn't that far from the truth, and gradually Kitty found herself ignoring the people and things around her as her mind started the long process of unwinding from the day's events.

"Penny Lane is in my ears and in my eyes . . ." she mumbled to herself, singing along to the music under her breath. When she was younger, she had sung aloud to things without hesitation, but her parents had scolded her so much that the joy had gone out of it for her. Now she kept the singing mostly in her head so no one would notice. Still, the repetitive sound was soothing, and it helped her cycle through what she had already learned, and what she needed to do next.

She didn't notice the world drifting away until Verity leaned over her from behind the sofa. "Watcha doing?" she asked Kitty.

Kitty's instinct was to jerk away from the sudden disturbance, and she gripped one of the cushions with her hand to keep from doing it. It took a lot of effort, but she answered Verity with a bright smile and even managed to make eye contact, despite everything whirring around in her head.

"Just enjoying the music, coz," she replied.

Verity smirked at her. "You're hiding."

"No law against that."

Kitty glanced at the other girls, but none of them had taken any notice of her. Ivy and Phyllis were still playing cards, and Diana was smoking a cigarette while she read a magazine.

Verity went around the sofa and sat on the floor in front of Kitty. "See anything interesting on your trip to the kitchen this afternoon?" she asked softly. It was an innocuous question, but there was little chance of being overheard.

"Nothing stood out to me in the parlor, the hallway, or the office," Kitty whispered back. "I'll need more time to look at the rest of the house properly."

Verity replied with a little nod. "Wait a couple of days. There'll be plenty of time for exploring over the weekend."

"All right," Kitty said.

"Remember, you're here to have a good time," Verity said knowingly.

"What are you two gossiping about?" Diana called to them.

Kitty froze. Had she heard what they were saying?

As Kitty's mind started spinning into panic, Verity laughed and called back to Diana, "Nothing important. Kitty was telling me about a schoolmate she fancies." She gave Kitty a nudge. "Not very interesting from the sounds of him."

Kitty inhaled and exhaled a few times to calm herself.

They hadn't been overheard. Everything was fine.

"Oh goodness!" Diana exclaimed. "Tell me all about him!"

"Um . . . well . . ."

It took Kitty a second to conjure up her fictional crush in her head. It was on the fly, so the details were more or less pulled at random from whatever was going through her head at the moment, but it was enough to be believable if she had to go into details.

"His name is Richard," she said. "He's very handsome and wears spectacles, which I like very much. And his father works for the government."

Diana laughed. "His name is Richard? Oh, that's very funny! My godfather's name Richard."

Kitty winced. Diana must be talking about Smythe. And that was probably where Kitty had summoned the name from too. She had read Smythe's and Lowell's files so many times over the past few days, their names were rummaging around in the cluttered storage bin of her mind. It was a miracle she hadn't said "Henry" instead.

"Oh really?" she asked. "What a coincidence!"

She kept smiling innocently. Inside, she felt like a fool, and she caught Verity giving her a wide-eyed, warning look.

Diana snickered. "Pssh! Don't be stupid. It's a frightfully common name."

"Sorry," Kitty said sheepishly.

Kitty saw Verity give her another pointed look. The message was clear enough: keep your wits and don't make any references that might sound suspicious.

"Well, if your boy has spectacles he's obviously very plain and I don't want to hear about him," Diana continued. "Let's talk about something else."

She said this with great finality, which was unfortunate because there was no other topic of conversation at hand, and an awkward silence drifted over them.

"Someone talk about *something*!" Diana demanded irritably. "Here, I'll start—"

"Your name is very pretty," Kitty interrupted. She had thought of something to say, and hadn't been able to stop herself even when Diana started speaking. "It suits you," she added quickly.

Diana seemed annoyed at Kitty's rudeness, but it was softened over by the compliment. "Why thank you. Nice of someone to notice." Diana struck a pose and tossed her hair back. "I was named for Diana Mitford, you know."

"Really?" Kitty asked. At first, the name didn't mean anything to her, but she pretended to be very impressed.

"Well, Lady Mosley, I should say," Diana amended.

And that was the missing piece. Diana was named for Oswald Mosley's wife, because Mosley was friends with Lowell as well as Smythe.

Kitty rummaged around in her head a bit more and a few ideas started to line up. Diana's age meant that she had been christened shortly after the war, when there would certainly have been a dark shadow over Mosley's reputation. That meant that not only had Lord Lowell not minded about Mosley's fascism, he actually saw nothing wrong with it. And that in turn meant . . .

Her train of thought was interrupted by Diana.

"Such a glamorous lady. It's quite right that I was named after her."

Kitty decided it was best if she nodded in agreement, so she did, very enthusiastically. "I can see that. You're very glamorous indeed, Diana. I wish I was more like you. Oh, if you don't mind me saying so."

She made a point of acting like it might be presumptuous to give a compliment, which only pleased Diana all the more. "I don't mind at all. It's only natural to want to be like me. Everyone else does."

Ivy and Phyllis hurriedly offered some jumbled statements of agreement. Kitty got the sense that platitudes of that nature were commonplace in Diana's circle.

Diana turned to Verity and said, "It seems your cousin has good taste, Vera. I'm glad you brought her."

"Kate is just a darling," Verity agreed.

"I see that. I hope you can stay longer than the weekend," Diana said.

The offer sounded sincere, but Kitty had learned not to trust polite words offered in the moment. She didn't understand why a person would say something like that without meaning it, but people often did.

Diana's cigarette was almost burned down, so she stubbed it out in an ashtray and lit a new one. The smell immediately wrinkled Kitty's nose, and she shuddered. Tobacco had such an awful stench. Pungent things got on Kitty's nerves. It had been tolerable when Diana was on the other side of the room. Now it was overpowering.

"Cigarette?" Diana asked, holding her silver case out to the rest of them.

Verity and the others reached for their own cigarettes eagerly, and passed the lighter around between them. When it came to be Kitty's turn, she just stared at the row of white sticks and tried not to look sick.

"Um, no thank you," she said quietly.

Diana looked surprised and annoyed. "What's the matter? Don't smoke?"

"No," Kitty said.

"So, you start now," Diana replied, thrusting the cigarette case at Kitty's face. "It'll do you good."

The stench of tobacco filled Kitty's nose. She felt dizzy and her stomach began to turn. "No, thank you," she said. "I'd rather not."

Diana laughed at her. "God, you're an odd one, aren't you? I offer you something and you turn it down. That's just rude, you know. When people offer you things, you're meant to take them and say thank you."

"I'm sorry, I just . . ." Kitty stammered.

"Bet you're a teetotaler too, aren't you?"

Any trace of niceness was gone now. The starkness of the change confused Kitty, and it frightened her. Consciously, she knew what it meant: Diana's niceness was fake, a fabrication to get what she wanted from people. This was the real her. But Kitty didn't *understand* someone acting that way. It was difficult enough having one face to share with the world, let alone two.

Verity leaned forward and got between them. "She's just a kid, Di. Ease off, will you?"

"Well, it's spoiled my mood." Diana huffed in annoyance and took a drag of her cigarette.

"Don't fuss," Verity said gently. "Let's have a drink, and it'll all be fine." She put a hand on Kitty's shoulder. "Kate, why don't you go to bed? It's getting late for you, and you've had a long day."

Kitty nodded. She needed to leave the room. That was the important thing. She had upset Diana, and that was going to cause a problem if she stayed. It wasn't an unusual situation for her to be in, but the circumstances were unfamiliar. She hadn't done or said anything wrong, she was certain of it. She had just turned down a cigarette. How could that possibly be so upsetting to someone?

Still, she didn't complain. She got up, waved to the other girls, and hurried out of the sitting room. As she made her way upstairs to her room, she ran over things in her head, trying to make sense of them.

Diana was rich. Her father was a lord. This house was her castle and the girls were her court, like something out of an old book. If she wanted something, she got it. Her father probably gave her anything she asked for, and her friends seemed to go along with all her whims—perhaps because her family was more powerful than theirs—so she wasn't used to being refused. Being refused made her question whether she really was in charge. That made her angry. It forced her to consider that maybe the world wasn't as she imagined it. Rather than accept that possibility and move on, she had an angry outburst to force everyone around her to do what she wanted again, preserving the illusion of control.

Kitty smiled as she reached the top of the stairs, pleased at having pieced the strange encounter together. The incident was suddenly less confusing and therefore less frightening. Most important, it had given her a better sense of how to manage Diana—and managing Diana was the key to getting access to Lord Lowell.

CHAPTER 18

Now that Kitty understood what she was dealing with, the next few days passed far more pleasantly than the first one.

She knew that the best way to avoid conflict was to placate. It felt wrong to do that, and several times Kitty had to bite her tongue to avoid saying something terse in reply to an unreasonable demand or a casual insult, but she set her mind to it, and she managed to keep quiet and smile pleasantly even while being mocked for being so quiet. The insults never lasted long. They seemed reflexive more than conscious.

Kitty figured that spies had to put up with all sorts of unpleasant things to get the job done.

In the lulls between the commands and the cruel words, she was actually having fun. Ever since she'd left school and started working at the shop, she'd barely spent any time in the company of her peers. Everyone at the Orchestra was very nice, but during working hours they were all focused on the job. And come the evening, Kitty had to rush off home. This was the first time she had been properly social in what felt like forever.

Of course, it was tiring too, and Kitty found solace in a few scattered moments of staring silently into the distance, or focusing on something innocuous in front of her. Today, Saturday, it was a glass of soda. The five girls had gone down to the local village to take in the country sights, and now they were at a little restaurant, enjoying some fizzy drinks and pastries.

"Oh, God!" Diana whispered. "Did you see what she's wearing?"

For a moment, Kitty thought they were talking about her. She looked up in alarm and then glanced at her dress. Like all the clothes she had brought, it was much nicer than anything she actually owned. No, it couldn't be that.

"What are we talking about?" she asked.

Phyllis nodded toward the waitress who'd delivered their food and drinks. "Her. Honestly, she's not even bothering to look nice."

"I wouldn't be caught dead out of the house looking like that," Ivy agreed.

Kitty stole another glance. The girl was normal. Normal look, normal clothes. Nothing expensive, because who would wear something fancy to wait tables? She looked tired, but of course she did: managing all the customers in this restaurant must be hard work. It was the only place in town aside from the pub. Probably a family-run business.

The girl was about Kitty's age, which made Kitty think of herself. They were both very ordinary—only ordinary wasn't allowed. That was the girl's crime. Her cheap clothes, her lack of glamor, struck Diana's coterie as evidence of inferiority.

"Oh, I don't know," Kitty began. "I think she looks rather—"

She was interrupted by a kick under the table from Verity, and quickly stopped talking. No contradicting the other girls. All that mattered was the mission.

"Such a boring little town," Diana grumbled, gazing out of the window at the rustic buildings outside. "I cannot stand being here."

"It's only a few more weeks," Verity said.

"And then we go to Paris!" Ivy exclaimed. "That will be such fun!"

"Maybe." Diana scowled. "Daddy says Paris might not be in the cards just now."

Kitty perked up at this. A change in plans was noteworthy, even if it might not mean anything. She glanced at Verity and saw that her partner had the same idea.

"Why not?" Kitty asked.

Diana shrugged angrily. "He didn't say. Just 'might not happen.' Probably something to do with his business. He always puts that first."

She sounded genuinely hurt—more than merely annoyed at being denied a holiday.

"Doesn't Parliament recess for the summer in a couple of weeks?" Verity asked.

"Probably," Diana said. "But he always has work to do. I expect that Daddy thinks the government is more important than me." She gave a high-voice laugh, a blatant attempt to hide how she really felt.

The wheels in Kitty's head started turning again. It sounded like Lord Lowell disappointing his daughter wasn't unusual. Neither Ivy nor Phyllis seemed surprised by it. Maybe Diana's cruelty wasn't just born from indulgence, but also from her father's neglect. He certainly hadn't paid much attention to any of them over the last few days.

Kitty suddenly thought about her own father. He was often overbearing, but at least he showed an interest in her well-being. Lowell just didn't seem to care. Everything was more important than his daughter. He showered her with luxuries, and then refused to acknowledge her. That couldn't be good for anyone.

"So here we are, in the country, being bored." Diana cast her gaze toward Kitty. "Looks like you came at just the wrong time, Kate. Nothing going on here."

Kitty was immediately conciliatory. It was her instinctive defense when people around her were angry and shifted their attention onto her.

"Oh, I don't know. I'm having such a lovely time, just us five. I think your countryside is very charming."

She shoved the straw into her mouth and took a long drink so that she wouldn't have to say anything else. The resentment radiating off of Diana was very unpleasant, but there was an aura of fear around Ivy and Phyllis that was even worse. They were scared, probably that Diana would vent her frustration at them.

"Well, you're Canadian. What do you know?" Diana grumbled.

Verity leaned forward and put her hand on Diana's arm. "Oh, dash it all, forget the countryside. Let's all go to London! It'll be fun! I know this marvelous discotheque in Mayfair . . ."

Kitty noticed Ivy and Phyllis shaking their heads, signaling for Verity to stop talking. Diana's scowl grew worse.

"Daddy has expressly forbidden me to visit London, and if I can't go, none of you can."

"We wouldn't go without you!" Ivy assured her.

Verity frowned and looked confused. "Did he say why?"

"He never does," Diana answered. "Probably afraid I shall have a good time and embarrass him. Honestly, I'm drunk in Biarritz *once*, and you'd think I'd disgraced the whole family!"

Kitty saw the muscles around Verity's eyes tighten for a moment. She was thinking about something, deducing something. Then Verity put on an encouraging smile and patted Diana's hand.

"Forget it. We'll just have fun here," she said. "Boring old countryside or not. Besides, we're going to the seaside next week. Better than London. The city's far too hot this time of year anyway."

Diana shrugged, not exactly agreeing or disagreeing.

As the girls returned to their drinks and sweets, Verity exchanged a look with Kitty. Kitty wasn't completely sure what she was supposed to take away from it, but Verity was definitely onto something.

On the walk back to the manor, Kitty trailed behind the others while they chatted away. The long conversation in the restaurant, compounded by the cloud of angry emotions that had overshadowed the meal, had made the record player in her head skip. It was hard to concentrate, which might become a problem if it got worse.

Kitty held her hands behind her back and brushed her fingertips together as she gazed off across the countryside. Anyone would think she was just taking in the sights or maybe watching the birds, when in fact she just needed something unimportant to occupy her eyes while her brain sorted things out.

A planned trip abroad being canceled? Diana forbidden from traveling to London? Lowell's distraction? It might all be nothing, or it might add up to validate Mr. Pryce's suspicions. Still, Kitty didn't actually have enough information to make any deductions. Mrs. Singh had cautioned her against conjecturing without facts to go on.

Instead, she turned her mind to the problem of the hidden room. Verity believed it existed, so Kitty assumed that it did. Where, then, would it be? She'd already ruled out the two main floors. The attic, perhaps? But that was where the servants' quarters were. Even good servants would get curious if their employer was always rushing to the top floor.

The only place the room could be was underground, where there would be no tell-tale signs of its existence.

As Kitty pondered this, she saw Verity slip away from the others and fall into step beside her. Kitty blinked a couple of times to get her whirling thoughts together.

"I think the hidden room is in the basement," she said quietly, forgetting to let Verity speak first.

Verity paused with her mouth half open, interrupted a moment away from saying something. "Oh," she said, sounding surprised. "You think so? I assumed there would be some sort of hidden passage near Lowell's office."

"I can't find any space large enough for it on the main floors," Kitty explained. "The basement is the only possible place. Question is where exactly."

Verity considered the problem. "Below stairs is the servants' domain. Lowell can go down there if he chooses, but not without attracting attention. And if he's meeting with people in secret, they can't go wandering through the servants' hall . . ." Her eyebrows arched suddenly and she gasped. "Oh God, I'm a bloody idiot. Why didn't I think of it?"

"What?" Kitty asked.

"It must be in the wine cellar." Verity looked almost angry. Kitty decided she must be frustrated with herself. "It's deep underground, and Lowell can go there whenever he wants. I've been down there briefly, and absolutely nothing stood out to me as suspicious, but . . ."

"I should take a look," Kitty said, hoping she sounded

decisive. "I shall go late at night, when everyone else is in bed. If I'm seen, I'll just pretend I'm going to the kitchen for a glass of milk."

Verity frowned. "It's risky. If you're caught wandering the halls and claim you're going to the kitchen, that's one thing. But if you're found in the wine cellar 'looking for some milk,' there will be trouble."

Kitty felt her face twist into a sour expression. Things never lined up easily when they needed to.

"What were *you* doing in the wine cellar when you went?" she asked Verity.

"I went with Diana to steal a bottle of wine," Verity answered matter-of-factly. Her eyes widened. "That's it. That's how we get you down there."

"I steal some wine?" Kitty asked, bewildered. Getting caught stealing seemed almost as bad as getting caught spying.

"I suspect Lord Lowell's used to Diana and her friends raiding the wine cellar. He'll forgive Diana just about anything, so as long as *she* gives you the order to go down there, we're in the clear."

"Then how do we get Diana to send me?"

Verity grinned. "That's the easy part. I'll just wait until it's late and Diana starts bemoaning something, and I'll say 'Why don't we crack open a bottle of wine to make up for not being in London?' Diana will agree, of course, and then you can jump in and volunteer before Ivy or Phyllis does."

As she absorbed this, Kitty took a breath and exhaled to steady herself. "All right, it's a plan."

CHAPTER 19

It wasn't a long walk to the manor, but Kitty was feeling over-heated and annoyed by the time they got back from town. As they neared the driveway, she noticed a new car standing in front of the house. It was a very expensive-looking Aston Martin. Whoever owned it had just arrived.

Diana gasped at the sight of it and exclaimed in delight, "No! It can't be!"

"What?" Kitty asked. She looked at Verity for an explanation, but Verity seemed just as confused as Kitty.

Kitty followed Diana into the foyer, only to freeze in place. The owner of the car was standing there, handing his driving gloves to the footman and exchanging a few pleasant words with Lord Lowell.

Sir Richard Smythe turned toward them as he heard the front door open. His face lit up at the sight of Diana and he held out his arms.

"Diana! My favorite niece!" Smythe exclaimed, speaking in a tone of tenderness that such a horrible man didn't deserve to use.

Diana clapped her hands in delight and rushed to embrace her godfather. "Uncle Richard!"

Kitty immediately looked at Verity, but Verity's guarded

expression offered her no reassurance. Smythe was there. Smythe was at Lowell's house. The Orchestra already knew that the two were in league with one another, but Smythe was actually there!

"And who are all of you?" Smythe asked, casting a glance at Kitty and the other girls. "Ah! Ivy MacIntyre. How are you? Been ages."

Ivy bobbed her head at Smythe. "Oh, quite well, Sir Richard, thank you. Papa sends his best wishes."

Smythe chuckled. "You don't have to tell me, Ivy. I had lunch with your father just this morning. He didn't mention you were up here visiting Diana. And who are the rest of you?" He waved his hand at Kitty, Verity, and Phyllis. "Diana's friends, I assume."

"Of course they are, Uncle Richard," Diana said. "Who else would they be? This is Phyllis. She's a friend from school. And Vera. We met abroad. She's very stylish when she means to be. And Vera's cousin Kate. She's Canadian, but we are doing our best with her."

Kitty bristled at the implied insult, but Smythe only laughed. "Don't be silly, Diana. Stalwart fellows, those Canadians. Well, the ones who don't vote Liberal at least." He exchanged a hearty laugh with Lord Lowell. Kitty pasted on a smile, though nobody was looking very closely at her. Everyone was focused on Smythe.

"What are you doing here, uncle?" Diana demanded. She seemed far happier than Kitty had seen her in the past few days, which jarred with the facts Kitty knew about the man.

Smythe patted Diana's hand. "What? Can't a fellow visit his favorite goddaughter?"

"Parliament's still seated," Diana said. "You never miss it."

"I'm just visiting my old friend," Smythe insisted. He clapped a hand on Lowell's shoulder. "With Labour in charge, we true Englishmen have to stick together." He laughed at his own words, and again Lowell joined him. Diana giggled. Kitty forced herself to smile. This was all in fun, or at least it was supposed to be, and Kitty couldn't let on that she knew otherwise.

"Are you staying awhile?" Diana asked eagerly. "Do say you're staying!"

"I'm here through the weekend," Smythe said. "Come Monday morning, it's back to London to work."

Diana scowled. "Work. You're just like Daddy."

"England can't manage itself to suit one girl's wishes," Smythe said indulgently. That patronizing tone made Kitty want to grind her teeth. "Your father and I must keep things in order, whatever those stupid Labour ministers think."

"Leave them at the reins much longer, and they will surely drive the country to ruin," Lowell agreed. He motioned in the direction of his office. "Now then, I don't mean to deprive you of your godfather, Diana, but Richard and I have some business to discuss before dinner. You girls run along and don't disturb us, all right?"

Smythe and Lowell retreated from the foyer. As the girls passed through on their way to the sitting room, Kitty glanced down the hallway and caught a glimpse of the two men just before they disappeared into the office.

"Do you have the papers?" she heard Lowell ask.

Smythe patted the briefcase he was carrying. "Yes. Better put them in the safe."

Kitty made a note of that as Smythe closed the door behind him. So, either they weren't visiting the hidden room yet, or it really was accessed through Lowell's office. Kitty thought about the latter possibility but quickly discarded it. More likely, Smythe and Lowell would visit the secret room when there was no risk of discovery.

In the meantime, Smythe's presence meant something was definitely going on. All the more reason to work quickly and finish the mission as soon as possible.

The rest of the day passed in a blur for Kitty. She followed the other girls around, doing whatever they were doing as convincingly as she could. Half the time, she found an excuse to just sit quietly, staring into the distance or nodding while they talked. All the while, ideas were circling in her mind. Dozens of dramatic possibilities surfaced, only to be tossed away as rubbish.

Smythe had murdered people. Maybe he and Lowell were going to murder the Prime Minister. Or maybe they planned to assassinate the Queen!

Ridiculous.

Perhaps it wasn't murder after all. Maybe they were really gangsters only *pretending* to be upstanding members of Parliament. Perhaps there was a heist afoot! They were going to defraud the government, or steal the crown jewels!

An absurd idea.

No, this was about politics. Kitty thought about Smythe's words to Diana. *Your father and I must keep things in order.* Smythe was in the opposition and Lowell was a lord, so neither of them had any direct control over the government. Maybe they were plotting blackmail to force the Labour ministers to do what they wanted.

Or . . . what if they were planning to force an election and ensure that the Conservatives won? Kitty didn't understand politics very well, especially since she was too young to vote. It had never really concerned her. How was she to know what kind of scheme was plausible, and what kind would be farfetched?

She would have to ask Verity when the opportunity arose. In the meantime, she kept pondering in silence.

Smythe and Lowell emerged from seclusion in time for dinner, both looking very pleased about something. The meal was far livelier than previous evenings. Smythe was very conversational, asking Diana about what she was doing lately and making small talk with the other girls about their families. Kitty was forced to invent a number of small details about her fictional background to fill in the gaps that her file hadn't included. It wasn't difficult to do, but she had to be precise about what she said so those details remained consistent.

After dinner, Lowell and Smythe stayed in the dining room to enjoy brandy and cigars, while the girls went with Diana into the parlor. Diana was brimming with excitement at all the attention she was getting. Suddenly, her annoyance over being confined at home was gone, although Kitty suspected that the novelty of her godfather's visit would wear off soon enough.

As they listened to some music on the record player, Diana suddenly exclaimed, "I feel like a drink. Who's with me?"

"Oh, I'm absolutely dying for a glass of wine," Verity agreed.

"Yes!" Phyllis chimed in. "Let's make this a real party!"

"Are we allowed to?" Ivy asked nervously.

Diana scoffed at her. "It's my father's wine, stupid. I can have some if I want."

"So we should go ask His Lordship if he minds you raiding his cellar?" Phyllis teased.

Diana glared at her, and Phyllis turned quiet.

"No, someone will have to go sneak it," Diana admitted. "You go, Phyllis. Serves you right for being so snide."

Phyllis made a face at her. "I just lit my cigarette! Give me a few minutes!"

Kitty caught Verity glancing at her with a knowing look in her eyes. This was a perfectly innocent opportunity to visit the wine cellar.

"I'll go," she said. At first, her voice was too soft and uncertain, but she cleared her throat and repeated the offer. "I'll go, Diana. I don't mind."

"Attagirl, Kate!" Diana said. "You're a good sport. You know the stairs down to the kitchen?"

"Yes."

"Take a right at the bottom instead of going straight. The cellar is right there. Just grab something new. Daddy will be furious if he finds out we've gotten into his good wine."

Kitty bobbed her head. "I can do that. I'll—um—I'll be right back."

"Don't get caught!" Diana called after her, as Kitty hurried out of the room.

Kitty crept toward the main hallway and the kitchen stairs. The path took her past the dining room. Smythe and Lowell were still inside, talking over their brandy and cigars. Kitty paused near the doorway in case they were discussing anything important.

"See, that's always been the problem with old Mosley," Smythe said, jabbing his cigar in Lowell's direction to emphasize his words.

"*The* problem?" Lowell asked with a laugh. "Oswald's a dear friend, but even I know he's a bloody fool."

Kitty stayed put. From this angle, she had a good view of

them both, and she was fairly certain the darkness of the hallway would obscure her from view if either of them happened to glance toward the door.

"Just look at '59," Smythe continued. "He returns to Britain ready to be swept into office on a wave of anti-immigrant sentiment, and what does he do? He runs on his bloody Union Movement ticket and loses, of course."

"Foregone conclusion," Lowell agreed.

"And he was surprised when it happened again last year! You can't win in national politics by running as a minor party. The votes just aren't there. Now, the only way that fascism can save Britain from itself . . ."

Lowell waved his hand at Smythe and shushed him angrily. "Watch your words, man! We talked about this. Not in the house, not while there's company."

"Don't be such an old hen, Henry," Smythe replied. "No one's listening. Anyway, like I've always said, infiltration is the only way to fix this country. I told Mosley, you know. I said, 'Oswald, the only way we're going to get a strong man at the reins of Britain is if we have our men—good, loyal men—join the Conservatives, stand for election as Conservatives, and eventually take over the party.' Damn fool didn't listen."

Lowell said, "It was a good plan. It still would be, if it weren't taking bloody long."

"Ten years and only twelve men to show for it," Smythe agreed bitterly. "In my youth I might've had the patience to see it through, but now . . ."

Lowell nodded. "I spoke to our mutual friend the other day," he remarked, mulling over his brandy. "He said we should consider waiting, giving infiltration more time to run its course." Even as he spoke, Lowell scoffed at the idea.

"Not getting cold feet, is he?" Smythe asked.

Lowell shook his head. "No, he's with us. Just thought he should give his honest advice before—well, before it's too late to reconsider."

"Unsurprising," Smythe mused. "Left to his own devices, he'd probably stay hidden in a back room, looking at poll numbers and calculating the likelihood of winning marginal constituencies until Kingdom Come!" The two men shared a laugh at the idea. "What did you tell him?"

"That I'm tired of waiting," Lowell replied. "I'm not a young man anymore and I would like to taste the fruits of victory myself, not toil for years just to pass the torch to a new generation of fa—" He caught himself. "Nationalists."

Smythe chuckled at the euphemism. "I know exactly how you feel, Henry. Now is not the time for hesitation, it is the time for decisive action."

Lowell raised his glass. "To a better Britain risen from the ashes."

"A better Britain," Smythe echoed.

Kitty quickly hurried past the door. Her hands were trembling. She had no idea what the two of them were plotting, but it was something troubling. Probably something violent.

She hurried to the basement and turned right into the cellar to avoid being spotted by any of the servants. She found herself in a grim brick-walled room that smelled musty and stale. It was probably hundreds of years old, old enough that the lights hung from the ceiling on strings because their wires were on the outside of the walls. The room was also surprisingly squat, and even though Kitty was small, she kept glancing upward at the ceiling, certain that she was going to smack her head against it. Something about the layout made her feel uncomfortable, and she turned in circles a few times, unable to fix on exactly what it was.

She crept past the rows of wine racks, which were only partly full but had an impressive display of bottles. Well, at least they looked impressive to Kitty. She knew nothing about what made wine good or important, but just the quantity astonished her. A lot of bottles were covered in dust, which drifted into the air as Kitty passed and tickled her nose. Kitty sniffled and snorted a couple of times to make sure she didn't sneeze.

First things first: find the hidden room. Then grab a bottle of wine and get out. Diana probably wouldn't care what she picked as long as it wasn't expensive enough to be missed. Kitty made a note of one rack of bottles that looked very new and not at all dusty. She'd grab one of those on her way out.

Ah, but the cellar. Something was wrong with it, and Kitty couldn't decide what. The dimensions were off somewhere, but she was noticing it subconsciously. It was gnawing at her, making her feel anxious. Where was it?

Kitty started pacing the length of the cellar, keeping her gaze focused on the nearest wall, waiting for the troublesome irregularity to reveal itself. On her second pass, she realized something else was bothering her. It wasn't just that the room's shape was odd. There was a breeze.

Kitty held out her hands and felt the air gently flow through her fingers. It wasn't strong, but air was definitely moving from one end of the room to the other, which it shouldn't be in such an enclosed space.

Follow the breeze, find the door, she thought.

She turned until she felt the breeze flowing against her face and slowly advanced toward it. The path was taking her in the direction of the far corner. Nothing about the walls looked particularly suspicious and they all had wine racks in front of them. Kitty stopped and let her eyes dart around freely, looking for inconsistencies. She could do this. There was something hidden here, she just needed to find it.

"What are you doing down here?" someone exclaimed from the far end of the cellar.

It was Smythe.

Kitty screamed and whirled around. Smythe was standing a few paces inside the door, staring at her. His face was contorted in astonishment.

Did he suspect what she was up to? He knew, didn't he? He knew!

A flood of memories came back to Kitty. Captured by Ivan, the threats of violence, the knowledge that she was going to be tortured for information. Except then she hadn't known anything. Now she did. What she knew could put Verity and everyone else in danger.

Kitty felt the world around her start to blur in the midst of panic. Everything turned fuzzy, except for Smythe. He just loomed there, growing bigger and more frightening as the room melted into a haze. Kitty wanted to scream and run and hide.

No. Keep your head together, Kitty. He doesn't know anything.

She pressed her foot against the stone floor until it hurt. The pain and the pressure forced the haze away a little bit. She gave a very visible sigh of relief and put a hand to her chest.

Canadian accent, she reminded herself. *Canadian accent.*

"Oh my goodness, Sir Richard! I'm so sorry, you startled me."

Kitty pretended that seeing him was a relief, like she had expected it to be someone worse. Smythe had no idea that she knew the truth about him. She was just some girl, one of Diana's emptyheaded friends. He was suspicious of her presence in the cellar, but not of her as a person.

"What are you doing down here?" Smythe repeated. He approached her, looming over her, making it very clear that he was in charge and he expected an answer. It was terrifying, and yet in one way it was also reassuring: it confirmed what Kitty suspected. Smythe was trying to overawe a girl he had caught trespassing, not apprehend a spy. Kitty suspected that if her cover had been blown, he would have grabbed her without hesitation.

Kitty exhaled and blinked, knowing she looked frightened and pitiful. "I'm so sorry, sir! It was all Diana's idea, I promise!"

"Diana?"

"To steal some wine," Kitty answered, like it was the only possible explanation. "The girls felt like having a drink, so Diana said one of us should take a bottle from His Lordship's cellar." The panic was still coiled inside of her, and she let a little bit of it out as she said, "Please don't tell Lord Lowell! I don't want him to think that I'm a thief. Oh God, and don't tell Diana I told you! I don't want her to think I can't keep a secret!"

Kitty clutched her hands together piteously and looked up at Smythe with widened eyes. She guessed that a man like Smythe liked to feel as though he was in charge, so she let him.

Slowly, Smythe answered her with an understanding nod, and his expression became sympathetic. "Ah, I see."

He looked around the shelves and grabbed a newish bottle from one of the racks. He passed it to Kitty with a smile.

"I don't think His Lordship will miss this one," he told her.

Kitty clutched the wine bottle in both hands, terrified of dropping it. Her hands were still trembling. Even with the moment of danger past, all her muscles were tensed and braced to run. She tried not to show it.

"Thank you, Sir Richard," she said.

Smythe nodded. "Oh, and I wouldn't mention you seeing me down here to anyone. If Diana finds out you were caught, she'll be very cross with you. And while I won't say a word of this to His Lordship, if he should hear of it from somebody, you'll be blamed for the theft, not Diana. Just some advice."

"Understood, sir, not a word," Kitty promised.

Smythe smiled and pinched Kitty's cheek. "Good girl. Run along then."

Kitty rushed from the cellar. She got all the way to the privacy of the stairway before her whole body shuddered and she pawed at her cheek to dispel the sensation of being pinched. Being touched by anyone made Kitty cringe, but Smythe was so monstrous that it had made the intrusion much worse. The man was a killer. There was blood on his hands. Kitty wiped at her cheek again, like there was blood on it too now.

Stop it. Stop it.

Kitty took a few deep breaths to calm herself. Smythe would be along any moment. She had gotten away this time, but if she was discovered in a panic on the stairs, Smythe would start asking other questions.

Strangely, though, Smythe did not emerge. Curious, Kitty slipped back down the stairs and glanced into the cellar. Smythe was nowhere to be seen.

A smile slowly spread across Kitty's face. Smythe had used the secret door. It really was down there. She had been right.

CHAPTER 20

Kitty was forced to wait until everyone retired to bed before she could tell Verity what had happened. Verity was alarmed at first, but after some discussion they both agreed that Kitty was probably in the clear. In any case, they now knew for certain where the hidden room was located. All they needed now was an opportunity to actually access it.

On Sunday morning, everyone went to church in town. There was nothing unusual about that of course, although Kitty hadn't actually been to church regularly since her mother died. Her father was never all that enthusiastic about it, and Kitty didn't like the crowds.

The building was packed with people, and very hot. Kitty spent most of the time gazing in the direction of the vicar, pretending to be interested in the service while trying to ignore all the people around her. They were loud and sweaty and *present*, and it was horrible. She clutched her prayer book tightly and tapped her foot under the pew to stay calm. In the end, she got through it, and she was proud of herself for that.

She returned to her room afterward, while everyone else went off to freshen up for the big afternoon dinner. She was still a bit hazy from all of the people at the service. It would pass. She knew it would pass. And besides, she was getting very good at devising ways to speed up the recovery process. She doubted that her discomfort around crowds would ever go away entirely, but necessity had forced her to find ways of coping with all the noise.

At first, Kitty didn't realize what was wrong in her room, but she knew that *something* was wrong the moment she arrived. She stopped dead center and slowly turned around, holding out her hands, afraid to touch anything.

Verity, who had followed her, stopped a few steps away and leaned back to avoid being bumped by Kitty's hands.

"What is it?" Verity asked.

Kitty held a finger to her lips for silence. She needed to think. What was setting her off? Her luggage was closed and under the bed. The bed was made. Her detective novel was on the nightstand. Everything was where she had left it.

But it wasn't *how* she had left it.

Kitty went to the table. The book was slightly off-center from where she liked to put it. She had a pair of pencils that were now resting at slightly different angles. Her glass of water was just a little to the left of where it was supposed to be. She looked at the bed. The pillows were puffed a little differently than how she'd left them, and there were a few scattered wrinkles in the covers that she was certain hadn't been there before.

Don't panic. Maybe the maid turned down the bed.

That would explain the pillows and sheets, but not the rest. Kitty knelt and looked at her suitcase under the bed. She always pushed it in straight back, just a little bit under the lip of the bedframe. It felt like it was supposed to sit there. Now it was crooked, and sticking out slightly. The difference was almost unnoticeable. Certainly no one else would have cared, but Kitty did.

She glanced around the room and saw countless other little changes, from the chair to the rug to the tilt of the lampshade. They weren't right.

Someone had been in here moving things. They had tried to put them back but hadn't gotten it quite right. It wasn't the maid. The maid wouldn't have gone through her luggage.

Verity tapped her on the arm. "Is something wrong?"

Kitty's mind was whirling, ticking through possibilities. This was because of the incident with Smythe last night. It had to be. They were on to her! They had searched her room, and maybe they had planted a bug somewhere!

Calm. Calm. Calm. They don't know anything! Maybe they suspect, but they don't know.

"Vera, I think I left my handbag at church. Will you walk me down to look for it?"

Verity glanced at Kitty's handbag, which was still on her arm. She was only confused for a moment, before she nodded to show she understood.

"Of course I will," Verity said. "We should hurry if we're to make it back before dinner."

Kitty managed to hold her tongue until they reached the garden outside. That was as far as they needed to go. If someone later questioned why they hadn't walked all the way into town, that would confirm that her room had been bugged. Otherwise, they could pass this off as just an idle stroll.

"What is it?" Verity asked. "Something's wrong with your room."

"I think it was searched," Kitty explained. "Things were a little off center, or at odd angles."

"You noticed that just going into the room?" Verity sounded like she couldn't decide whether to be astonished or skeptical.

"I often notice things like that," Kitty answered timidly. It was odd, and she didn't want Verity to think she was odd.

To Kitty's surprise, Verity smiled at her. "Impressive. I have a lot of training, and I can't do that at a glance. But I suppose that's why you're here."

"Yes," Kitty said. "And we know where the hidden room is. I only need a few more minutes alone in the cellar to find exactly where the door is and how to open it. Any thoughts about when we can try?"

Verity frowned. "If they searched your room, it's because Smythe and Lowell are taking precautions about you."

"Do you think they're onto me?"

"I doubt it," Verity said. "More likely they went through your things to find anything incriminating, like a gun or spy equipment. It's the reason why we didn't bring any."

Kitty nodded.

"We're supposed to go down to the seaside on Tuesday and stay until Wednesday," Verity mused. "I wonder if Lord Lowell is coming with. The beach isn't far. If the whole family is out of the house, we could go back in the middle of the night and take a look. Then again, if Lowell's staying here, it's risky."

"I suppose we shall have to see what happens on Tuesday then," Kitty said.

"Yes," Verity agreed. "Meanwhile, we keep our heads down and our ears open." Verity glanced toward some of the trees, and a troubled look crossed her face. "I just wish I could get into Lowell's safe. There's no telling what's in the hidden room, but Lowell's safe might very well have tangible evidence of some sort, whether it's letters or accounts or a schedule . . ."

Kitty pictured the Lowell's office, with all the details she'd noticed while she was in there. An idea began to build in her head. "Actually, I—I think I can get the safe open."

"How?" Verity looked astonished at the very suggestion. "We won't be able to use proper tools. And it's too good to crack by ear."

Kitty was silent for a moment as she pondered how to explain the plan she was formulating. "Smythe put a case of documents in the safe when he arrived. He leaves tomorrow morning, so Lord Lowell will have to open the safe for him."

"You aren't suggesting that we lure them out of the room and hope they leave the safe open, are you? That is not going to happen."

"No, no, nothing like that," Kitty promised. "I just need to be there when they open it."

"*Be there?*"

"I can hide behind the curtains before they come in, and peek out while they're focused on the safe. That way, I'll get the combination, and then we can go back later and get a proper look inside when no one is around."

"The curtains? You won't be able to see the dial from there!"

"No," Kitty agreed, "but I can see which direction it's turning and how far it turns. If I know the number it starts on, I can guess each part within maybe five numbers. Then I'll just try those combinations until it works."

"Within five numbers?" Verity asked. "That's still a lot of possible combinations."

"It's a whole lot less than *all* the possible combinations," Kitty replied.

Kitty barely slept that night, she was so nervous about the next morning's operation. It was the only way to get into the safe, but it was definitely going to be risky. If she was caught, they were done for. There would be no way to play off her presence as innocent, like she had done in the cellar.

For the past few days, none of the girls had gotten up before noon, with the exception of Sunday, and even then Diana and Ivy had almost slept through Sunday service. Monday was different. Kitty heard Diana go downstairs bright and early to say goodbye to her godfather, and Verity went along with her. There was no noise from Ivy or Phyllis, so once the coast was clear, Kitty sneaked out of her room and crept downstairs. She hurried down the hallway to Lord Lowell's office and slipped inside. There was no telling how long she would have to wait in hiding, but this was the best option available.

She checked the dial on the safe first. It was set at 23. Kitty committed the number to memory and ducked behind the curtain. And then she waited.

At the start it was dull, but after about twenty minutes it had become unbearable. What had she gotten herself into? Smythe might take an hour to leave, and what if he decided to leave his papers behind when he did?

The noise of the door opening broke her out of her churning thoughts. Kitty tensed, and she gently pushed the curtain back from the wall with her fingertips, creating the tiniest possible peephole for herself. She saw Lowell cross the room toward the safe, and heard Smythe offering his farewells to Diana.

As Lowell opened the safe, she watched the movements of his hand and listened carefully.

First, a quarter turn to the right. Somewhere between the upper nineties and five. She couldn't fix it better than that.

Next, a short twist to the left. Kitty almost missed it. Oh God, what could it be? Ten? Fifteen?

Don't panic. Keep focused. What's the last number?

Finally, a very long turn, almost all the way around to the far right. Kitty flinched and blinked rapidly as she measured the scraping of the dial and the shifting position of Lowell's hand.

It had ended up somewhere around thirty.

All right, she could work with that. Call it 5-10-30. An easy sequence to remember. She would just have to try some variations on it when she had the chance.

Smythe came into the room and took the briefcase from Lowell.

"Smile, Henry," Smythe said, giving Lowell a jovial pat on the arm. "Soon we're going to do something rather wonderful."

Lowell did indeed smile. It was the expression of a man far too pleased with himself to be trusted. "Saving Britain from itself," he agreed.

Lowell closed the safe and gave the dial a firm spin to clear the number. Then he and Smythe went outside and closed the door behind them. Kitty peeked out into the office, relieved to be alone again. She only had a few moments to wait before the door opened again, and Verity poked her head in.

"Come on, let's go," Verity hissed at her.

Kitty dashed out from behind the curtains and hurried into the hallway. Verity closed the door and took Kitty's hand, leading her toward the foyer and the main staircase.

"Did you get it?" Verity asked quietly.

"Near enough," Kitty said.

"Good, we'll try tonight." As they reached the foyer, Verity whispered, "Go halfway upstairs and then come back down like you've just woken up, understand?"

Kitty nodded. They both paused at the corner of the staircase and leaned out to see where everyone was. Smythe and Lowell had gone out to the front steps and were exchanging a parting handshake. Diana was still in the foyer, hovering by the doorway and looking very disappointed at her godfather's departure. No one noticed Kitty and Verity.

Kitty scurried upstairs to the first landing, turned, and walked back down again, with a slow and shuffling pace that emphasized just how early she felt the morning was. When she reached the foyer, she saw Verity meandering in from the dining room, holding a piece of buttered toast between her fingertips.

"Morning, Kate!" Verity called, giving Kitty a wave. "Finally decided to join the rest of us?"

Kitty reached the ground floor and stifled a big yawn. "It's so early," she protested. She looked out through the front door and watched Smythe get into his car and drive away. "Oh, has Sir Richard left already? Goodness, how do you people get up at this hour?"

Kitty found it almost impossible to keep her excitement contained for the rest of the day. Luckily, no one was watching her closely. Diana and the others spent hours getting their luggage together for the upcoming seaside trip and planning out all the exciting things they were going to do while they were there. It was strange: just a few months ago, an outing like this would have been the most interesting thing Kitty could imagine.

Now it was just a feature on the landscape of her new life.

Just after midnight, Kitty met Verity in the upstairs hall, and they sneaked downstairs. Kitty's heart was pounding. They didn't dare turn on any lights, so they lit their way with an electric torch. Every shadow seemed to be a man lurching toward them as they crept past. Each portrait on the wall had Smythe's face leering down at them.

Once inside Lowell's office, Verity illuminated the safe with her torch and nodded to Kitty.

Kitty took a few long breaths to sooth her nerves, and began trying combinations. First she tried the base sequence she had remembered, although she didn't expect it to work. Those were just round numbers to keep fixed in her head.

5-10-30. Nothing.

Kitty adjusted.

4-10-30. 3-10-30. 2-10-30. 1-10-30. 99-10-30 . . .

She tried every number from 98 up to 5. Nothing. Kitty grimaced and switched to the next set of numbers. 5-9-30. 5-8-30. 5-7-30.

After almost a hundred combinations, Verity groaned softly. "This is taking forever! This was a bloody mistake. I knew it wasn't possible to guess."

"I'm doin' me best," Kitty snapped back. In her frustration, her East End accent began slipping through. Even as she spoke she kept running through the number combinations almost automatically. Her hand twisted the dial from place to place rapidly, acting on numbers her brain produced before she was even conscious of them. "I know *roughly* what it is, just not exactly, a'right?"

"Accent," Verity whispered.

Kitty didn't even stop working. "What's it matter?" she

demanded. "If they catch us 'ere doin' this, it won't matter what me bloody accent is, will it?"

"Sorry," Verity mumbled and fell silent. She clearly knew Kitty was right.

"You needn't bloody apologize, just let me work," Kitty replied. "I'll be fine talkin' posh again once we're done, but right now I can't do this *an'* be a bleedin' Canadian!"

"I'm amazed you can do that at all. How are you keeping track of which combinations you've done?"

"I just am, a'right? It's what me 'ead does."

And then the safe clicked. Both girls fell silent and stared at each other.

"You did it," Verity gasped.

"Of course I did," Kitty said, settling back into the Canadian accent. "I've a good head for numbers."

She tried to make it sound like it had been easy, but that was a lie. Her fingers were sore from the number of times she had turned the dial, and her head felt unpleasantly foggy and hot. It was like how she felt after running a few miles, only it was her brain and not her legs. But she gave Verity her most convincing smile.

"Great work!" Verity exclaimed softly. Without warning, she gave Kitty a tight hug. Kitty froze in place, startled and unsure how to respond. After a second, Verity released her and asked, "What was the combination?"

"Um, one, ten, thirty-two."

Verity's brow furrowed. "I'm a bloody fool." She smacked herself in the head. "Why didn't I think of that before?"

"I don't understand," Kitty said. "Is the number important?"

"Only to someone like Lowell or Smythe," Verity answered. She made a disgusted face. "The first of October, 1932. The founding of the British Union of Fascists. Trust a man like Lowell to use that."

They shared a mutual grimace and turned their attention to the contents of the safe. There was some money in neat stacks of bills, and lots of papers. As they moved the money out of the way, Kitty made a note of where it had been stacked and how the stacks had been placed. She would make certain there was no sign of their intrusion once they left—unlike Lowell's attempt to search her things.

Verity flipped through the paperwork hastily. "Some bonds . . . insurance documents . . . business paperwork . . ." She wrinkled her nose. "I can't tell if any of this is important. We'll have to come back later with a camera, now that we know the combination."

Kitty spotted a diary in the back of the safe, and she quickly skimmed the pages. It was a list of Lowell's daily schedule for the past year. Very quickly, certain names and entries began to repeat themselves.

"Look at this," she whispered to Verity. "Over and over again, he's meeting with someone called SRS."

"Sir Richard Smythe," Verity said, voicing Kitty's own thoughts.

"And look here, other names and initials. Tom, Jim, HMR, JEP. Are these people in on the plot too? There are dozens of them!"

Verity took a look. "Most of those are probably ordinary people he's meeting with—politicians I expect—but at least some of them must be conspirators. It seems Lowell likes to list everyone by their initials as a shorthand." She arched an eyebrow. "What about this Tuesday? What's on the schedule while his family is away?"

Kitty flipped forward until she found the date. It was a short entry, scribbled quickly in sharp, slashing letters that covered both Tuesday and Wednesday as a single entry.

SRS.

TOM.

JIM.

LONDON.

Kitty gasped in relief at the unexpected windfall. She Verity's face light up with a similar reaction.

"He's going to meet the other conspirators in London tomorrow!" Verity said. "We can sneak back at night while Lowell is out of the house. If we arrive late, the servants will all be in bed, and no one will be down there for us to walk in on. We'll have plenty of time to bug the room and search it for useful evidence."

Kitty grinned. "Until tomorrow night, then."

CHAPTER 21

Tuesday's trip to the seaside was more enjoyable than Kitty had expected. She rode in Verity's car while the others drove separately, which gave her a welcome respite from their chatter. It was also a relief not to be Kate Greenwood for a little while. She spent most of the drive gazing at the countryside, letting her mind relax.

Kitty had never been to the beach before, not a proper one anyway. Her experience with the shore was the edge of the Thames, and that was a far cry from the pleasant, sandy expanse of this holiday beach with its dark blue waves, and its boardwalk and pier stretching out into the water. It was a beautiful sight, and the hotel they were staying in was more luxurious than she had ever imagined possible.

Perhaps she just needed a better imagination. Verity and the other girls took it all in stride, and Ivy even remarked that she loved this place because it was so rustic. It astonished Kitty to hear that, but then again, these girls were used to the south of France, and cruises, and wintering abroad, and all sorts of expensive things that Kitty had never encountered before. It just served to remind her of the tremendous gulf between her and them. If they knew who she really was, they'd hate her just for being poor. And that made her angry.

It wasn't fair, but it was the world she had to live in.

Still, the day was a lot of fun. The girls went swimming and sunbathing, and looked at the shops along the pier, and had some lovely ice cream at a charming little place near the hotel. Kitty bought a camera and tried not to show how extravagant the purchase felt to her. She allowed herself to be drawn in by her surroundings, and for a few hours she even pretended that this could be her life someday, and not merely the side-effect of working undercover. How horrible that she had to pretend to be somebody else just to enjoy simple things that certain people could take for granted.

By the time evening arrived, Kitty had come back to reality. Tonight, while Lord Lowell was in London and the rest of the group was down here, she and Verity were going to sneak into the Lowell house.

"Clever of you to bring your own car," Kitty noted as Verity pulled them out onto the main road. It was after midnight, and she and Verity had just sneaked out of the hotel.

"I'm not just a pretty face, you know," Verity replied, smirking at her.

Kitty grinned back. "I know."

She rested her hands protectively on the camera in her lap. She had already made a show of using it to photograph the sights with Diana, so if it was found in her luggage later, no one would think anything about it.

Verity glanced at Kitty. "Are you nervous?"

"A little bit," Kitty admitted.

"Good. That'll keep you on your toes. But don't worry: the

only people at the house will be the servants, and they'll all have the good sense to be in bed when we get there. We'll be in and out and back to the beach long before sunrise."

Kitty nodded and settled back into her seat. It was an hour's drive to the manor, so she closed her eyes to rest them a bit longer. Despite Verity's reassurances, she feared she wouldn't be getting much sleep tonight.

***

She woke again as Verity slowed the car and parked it off the side of the road a short distance from the house, hidden from view by a small stand of trees. Kitty rubbed her eyes and grabbed the camera.

"Something's wrong," Verity whispered.

"What?"

Without answering, Verity led Kitty to the edge of the property, where they could see the house and the front driveway clearly. Some of the lights were on in the house, which was strange given that it was after midnight. Kitty realized that there were several cars in the driveway, when there shouldn't have been any at all.

"What's going on?" she asked, still in Kate Greenwood's accent.

"Something tells me the meeting isn't happening in London," Verity replied. "It's happening here."

"But it said London in the diary!"

"That must be referencing something else," Verity said.

"Are we giving up the mission?" Kitty asked.

Verity shook her head. "We've come this far. At least we can take a look. We can't bug or search the meeting room while they're here, of course, but we have the camera, so if we get a photograph of the conspirators together, even better."

Kitty nodded. She followed Verity across the grounds and through the garden. The French doors leading into the sitting room were locked, but Verity had brought her lock picks and had the door open in no time.

As they crept through the house, Kitty heard the floor-boards creak under the footsteps of people all around them. A couple were upstairs, and at least two were on the ground floor with them. Who knew if any more were downstairs?

She noticed movement at the end of the hallway before Verity did, and pulled Verity into the library just as two men dressed in black turned down the hallway toward them. Kitty waited until the men had passed before returning to the hall-way and making for the cellar stairs.

"I didn't know Lord Lowell had bodyguards," she said to Verity.

"He doesn't," said Verity grimly. "Those aren't body-guards, those are soldiers."

"Soldiers! From our army?"

"I don't know. Military-trained, though, I'd bet my life on it." Verity gave her a very intent look. "Kitty, if this goes bad, you get out of here, find a phone, and call for help. Understand?"

"Yes, but—"

"No buts. Don't worry about me. If something happens, you run."

Kitty bobbed her head and tried not to look upset. She didn't want to abandon Verity if something went wrong. The very idea made her feel horrible.

There was no one in the cellar when they reached the bot-tom of the stairs, though Kitty did spot another guard in the kitchen, stationed by the door that led outside. Lowell obviously didn't expect anyone to know about the meeting, so this level of security made it clear he was a man who took every possible precaution.

"All right, Kitty," Verity whispered. "Do whatever it is you do. Find that door and get it open."

Kitty nodded. She went to the far corner of the cellar, where she had felt the breeze the other night. It was there again. Kitty rubbed her fingertips together as she looked at the two walls, trying to figure out which one the airflow was coming from. The right side, she thought. She knelt on the ground and peered at the base of the wall behind the wine rack. There was a thin sliver of light along the very bottom, and a stronger breeze forcing its way through. That was the door.

"It's here," she said.

"Good! Now how do we get it open?" Verity asked.

Kitty stood again, pondering. There would have to be a latch or something—a mechanism that would be easy to activate, but would go unnoticed. Peering at the wall in front of her, she reached past the shelves of the rack so that she could feel the bricks. They felt real enough, and none of them moved under her touch.

"Not there," she murmured.

Then the realization hit her. The latch wouldn't be at eye level. Lowell knew it was there. It would be something he could just reach for without looking.

Kitty positioned her hands at about the level she assumed Lord Lowell's would be at and reached forward.

"What are you doing?" Verity asked.

"Shh!" Kitty hissed.

She ran her fingers along the bricks, gently pushing against each one. After a few tries, a brick gave under her hand and she heard a gentle click. The door swung outward and Kitty caught it with both hands.

Verity shot her an astonished look that turned into a grin. "You did it!"

Kitty scrunched up her face at her. "Don't sound so surprised."

Together, they pulled the door the rest of the way open. Behind it was a long tunnel lit by a string of electrical lights, just like the cellar. Kitty heard voices coming from the far end, and she led the way forward, keeping to the shadows as best as she could. If they were seen now, they were in real trouble.

After a few dozen feet, the tunnel ended in a large room with a low ceiling, built like a bunker. There was a table in the very middle, along with some desks and cabinets covered in documents, maps, and various kinds of equipment. Kitty saw a weapons rack against one wall, each shelf holding an automatic rifle. She shivered at the sight.

Four men sat around the central table, looking over a set of maps. Kitty immediately recognized Smythe and Lowell. The next man was unfamiliar to her, but he had a grim, military bearing and he wore a pistol in a shoulder holster. The fourth man Kitty did know, but he wasn't supposed to be there, and it took a few moments for her mind to reconcile that knowledge with the fact of his presence.

The Old Man tapped one of the maps and spoke in the same soft, calm voice that he'd used in Mr. Pryce's office.

"So, we are agreed. Richard will oversee the placement. James will handle security. Henry and I will set the remaining wheels in motion so that order can be restored immediately after it's done."

"Agreed," said the man called James.

"Have our supporters been notified to avoid the building this morning?" Lowell asked.

Smythe nodded. "There will be a series of convenient mishaps preventing their arrival. Illness, family concerns, traffic, a faulty alarm clock. Not that it makes too much difference. Once we are in control, the reasons why our men survived won't be important."

Kitty stared blankly ahead, still trying to understand what she was seeing.

"My God, that's James MacIntyre, Ivy's father," Verity whispered.

A wheel clicked into place in Kitty's head. Those weren't names in the diary, they were all initials. JIM. James MacIntyre. TOM . . .

"And that's the Old Man," Kitty murmured. Her voice came out hoarse and trembling.

Verity slowly shook her head, as if trying to convince herself that Kitty was wrong. "I don't know what he looks like all that well, but it can't be him," she insisted.

"It is," Kitty said. "I never forget a face."

"But he's on our side."

"I don't think so," Kitty replied.

She watched as Lowell poured four glasses of Scotch and handed them out to the men. He raised his glass into the air and proclaimed, "Gentlemen! Hail victory!"

"Hail victory!" the others echoed.

"Tomorrow will be a long day," Lowell continued. "The longest day in British history. But when the dust settles and all is done, the sun shall rise on a new England and a new Empire!"

"To England!" Smythe cried.

"To England!" came the response, and the four men drank.

Kitty shook her head to make herself come to her senses. She couldn't just stand there being stunned.

She pulled out the camera and started snapping pictures of the room. She winced as the camera shutter clicked with each photograph, but the noise was soft and the conspirators were distracted by their self-congratulation. Besides, getting proof of the conspiracy was the most important thing now. Kitty knew it was a risk she had to take.

The four men finished their drinks and stood. Verity grabbed Kitty's arm and pulled her deeper into the tunnel. "They're leaving," she whispered to Kitty. "We have to get out of here."

As the conspirators entered the tunnel, Kitty followed Verity back toward the cellar, scrambling to keep ahead of the men without making any noise. Kitty winced each time her shoes scraped against the floor. It sounded horribly loud to her, a monstrous sound that reverberated through the tunnel and would surely draw the men's attention.

As soon as she was in the cellar again, Kitty shoved the door shut.

They made for the stairs. Kitty went ahead, clutching the camera for dear life. She absolutely had to keep it safe until they could get the film back to Mr. Pryce and Mrs. Singh.

Halfway up the stairs, Kitty heard the guard in the kitchen shouting after them. "You there! Stop! Who are you?"

Kitty and Verity looked at each other. Verity was still at the bottom of the stairs. She mouthed the word, "Run!" and turned to face the guard. Kitty hesitated, torn between protecting the film and protecting her partner. She couldn't just leave Verity there, could she?

She slowly crept back up the stairs, feeling a crushing pressure of self-loathing at the thought of abandoning Verity. She couldn't just run away!

But it wasn't only the mission. Kitty was terrified. Her heart pounded against her ribs, and the familiar notes of panic swarmed inside her head. She wanted to scream and run, and it was only with great effort that she settled for just running.

At the top of the stairs, she forced herself to stop and peered back into the basement. She saw the guard grab Verity. There was a struggle, but he was quickly joined by the man called James, who subdued her with a vicious blow to the head. Verity sagged in the guard's arms, on the verge of unconsciousness.

"Well, well, what have we here?" mused the Old Man. "Security not up to snuff, Henry."

"My God!" Lowell exclaimed. "That's Diana's friend Vera. What is she doing here?"

"I think you'll find that she is an enemy agent," the Old Man replied. He sounded amused. "I did warn you that Pryce was getting curious."

Smythe grunted in annoyance. "You said he was getting curious about me, not Henry."

"It seems he doesn't tell me everything." The Old Man sighed. "Well, there's nothing for it now. James, go and deal with the problem. I want to find out how much Pryce knows."

Smythe looked at his watch. "We don't have time for this. We need to be ready by sunrise." He looked at the guard holding Verity. "Take the girl upstairs and find out what she knows. Have a couple of the boys search the grounds for her cousin. They're probably both spies."

Kitty ducked back as the guard hauled Verity's body upstairs. The conspirators remained below, but Kitty heard them head for the kitchen door, to depart the house and carry out their horrible plan. What was she to do?

Hide. Call for help.

Kitty gathered her resolve and ran for Lowell's office—and the telephone inside it.

CHAPTER 22

Kitty closed the office door carefully to avoid making any noise. She would be found eventually, so time was of the essence. She grabbed the phone and rang up the contact number Mr. Pryce had given her. Her hands were trembling so much she had to dial the number several times to get it right.

"Come on, come on," she whispered into the ringing phone, hearing the desperation in her own voice.

After what felt like an hour, someone picked up on the other end of the line. "Hello?" It was an older woman whose voice Kitty recognized—one of the agents managing the phone exchange the Orchestra used.

Kitty hesitated. Her mind was going wild with terrible thoughts. If the Old Man was in on the conspiracy, who else might be compromised? Was the exchange safe?

Stop that, Kitty! she scolded herself. Caution was one thing, but paranoia wasn't going to do her or anyone else any good.

"Hello?" the agent repeated.

"Yes!" Kitty answered, too loudly. She lowered her voice and tried again. "Hello, this is Kate Greenwood. I need to speak to my Aunt Mildred. It's urgent."

"Just a moment, Miss Greenwood. I'll see if I can find her." The agent went away and Kitty was left with stifling silence. She leaned against the desk, holding the phone to her ear and tapping her foot anxiously. Every part of her was trying to scream, except that each part wanted to scream different things and her brain wasn't even sure about itself.

Should she hide? Should she run? Should she do her job and stay on the line? Why were the curtains such an ugly shade of mustard? Why did rich people have so many paintings in their houses? How much noise would the window make if she broke it to escape? Should she photograph the contents of the safe while she was waiting?

That last idea sounded like a good one, so she got up to do it, but the phone cord wasn't long enough, and she ended up turning back and forth automatically, shifting her attention between the safe and the phone. The terror and stress had almost paralyzed her thinking, leaving her to act on momentary impulses that had no follow-through. The broken record was spinning so fast, she feared it might burst right out of her skull.

Get your head together, Kitty!

Suddenly, there was a click on the other end of the line and she heard Mrs. Singh's voice.

"Kate? It's Aunt Mildred. What is it?"

"Mrs. Singh!" Kitty exclaimed. In her panic, she lost all sense of code names and secrecy, and her Canadian accent started to slip.

There was a pause, and then Mrs. Singh asked cautiously, "Is this line secure?"

"I—I think so. It don't matter! They've got Verity!"

"What?" Mrs. Singh roared.

"They've kidnapped Verity an' I dunno what to do!"

"Who has?"

Head together. Head together. Head together.

Kitty took three deep breaths and felt some measure of the tension bleed out of her. The frantic feelings were still there, clustered inside her brain, but her muscles relaxed a little and she could think better. She had to be clear. She couldn't waste time panicking.

"Lowell and Smythe are workin' together along with a man named James MacIntyre. They're plannin' to do somethin' 'orrible tomorrow. I don't know what, but they just left the 'ouse an'—"

"And they have Verity?" Mrs. Singh asked. There was worry in her voice, even though she was trying to hide it.

"She let 'em catch 'er so I could get away and warn you," Kitty said. "An' that's not all. You need to warn Mr. Pryce about the Old Man!"

"What?" Mrs. Singh sounded truly bewildered. "What about the Old Man?"

Kitty tried to get the words out, but at first it was just a jumble. Finally, she managed to exclaim, "'E's part of the conspiracy! 'E's the fourth member!"

There was a pause. "No," Mrs. Singh murmured, the worry in her voice growing worse. "No, that is not possible."

"It is!" Kitty insisted. "I've seen 'em with me own eyes! I 'ave photos, honest!"

"Oh, no . . ." Mrs. Singh's voice trailed off.

"Missis?" Kitty asked.

"Pryce went to meet the Old Man this afternoon," Mrs. Singh said. "He hasn't come back. Bloody . . ." Suddenly, Mrs. Singh's tone became very calm. Kitty could tell it was meant to calm her in turn. "Where are you?"

"I'm in Lowell's 'ouse."

"Get out of there now. Hide."

"I can't leave Verity!" Kitty insisted.

"And I can't let them take both of you," Mrs. Singh replied. "Get out of the house and hide. I'm coming to get you."

Even though she was on the phone, Kitty shook her head like Mrs. Singh could see it. "It's not safe, missis! There's men 'ere with guns! I dunno 'ow many."

Mrs. Singh's tone was purposeful, and as hard as iron. "Watch them try to stop me."

Mrs. Singh's determination ought to have made Kitty feel safer, but it only made her panic grow worse as she remembered how far from London they were. "But we're two hours away!"

"I'll see you in forty-five minutes," Mrs. Singh said. "Get someplace safe and wait for me."

The phone clicked as Mrs. Singh hung up and the line went dead.

Get to hiding. Wait. They were easy instructions. Kitty could follow them. Clear instructions. A set sequence. She could do that.

The door to the office opened.

"What the bloody—" exclaimed the man who stood in the doorway. He was one of Lowell's guards. There was a pistol in a holster on his belt, but he hadn't drawn it. "Christ, another one of you."

The panic came back with a vengeance. Kitty backed away, only to find herself pinned against the desk. The guard advanced into the room, one hand outstretched to grab Kitty.

"You're comin' with me, girl," the guard said. "Don't run. Don't make this hard for me, or I'll shoot you. Understand?"

Kitty didn't respond. Her mouth moved, but she couldn't make words. The world turned hazy as her mind tried to find some way to process both the fear welling up inside her and the countless overwhelming details surrounding her. It was too much to absorb. The two waves of information crashed together and exploded behind her eyes.

"No!" Kitty shrieked. "No! No! No! No!"

It was too much to think about anything now. It was like when she had been taken by Ivan. Her body just reacted of its own accord. Everything was too bright, too loud, too much. It needed to stop.

Without realizing what she was doing, Kitty smashed her forehead into the guard's face. The man grunted in pain.

"You broke my nose, you little—" he exclaimed. He was silenced as Kitty's forehead struck him a second time, and then a third.

The guard shoved Kitty away from him and clutched his mouth and nose. Kitty stumbled and fell against the corner of the desk. Her side hurt from the impact, but it was hard to pay attention to the pain. It was just one of too many pieces of information assaulting her brain. The pain, the noise, the fear, the blood on the guard's face, even the lingering stench of tobacco and cologne permeating the office, all just mixed together as part of the haze. Everything was horrible and loud, and Kitty couldn't think through all the noise.

There was a sudden burst of pain across Kitty's face— shocking enough to break through the haze. Kitty swayed dizzily from the impact and touched her cheek. What had just happened?

Her answer was the guard's hand, which swung at her a second time. Terror spiked inside of Kitty's chest, but with that came a fresh burst of adrenaline. Kitty ducked away and scrambled to the other side of the desk. The guard growled at her and made another swipe with his hand. It seemed he was disoriented from his own injuries and couldn't decide whether to hit Kitty or grab for her.

Ultimately, it wouldn't matter. The man had probably a hundred pounds on Kitty, and close to a foot in height too. If this remained a struggle of blows, Kitty was going to lose.

Focus, Kitty! Focus! Remember your training!

The guard swung at Kitty again, and again she ducked away from the blow. She gritted her teeth and clawed her way through the fog in her brain. The next time the man grabbed for her, she dashed to one side of the desk. He countered, and she went the other way. Her mind was still turning in circles, but now it was searching for a way out. She needed something she could use to even out the disparity between them. An advantage that didn't depend on size or strength.

A lucky swipe caught Kitty in the shoulder and the guard grabbed her. Kitty struggled to get free, but she was hauled directly over the desk and thrown to the floor. She looked up and saw the guard reach for his pistol.

"Right, I warned you . . ." he said.

Kitty remembered Mrs. Singh's advice from so many weeks ago. She fell onto her back to get better leverage and snapped her foot up into the man's groin, putting as much force behind the kick as she could manage. The guard's eyes bulged and he gurgled in agony. He looked like he was going to be sick. For the moment, the pistol was forgotten.

Kitty scrambled to her feet as the guard spat and snarled at her. He was incoherent now, but not overcome. He grabbed for her with his bare hands, clawing like an animal. The pain made it hard for him to think. Kitty could work with that. She kicked at him again, but this time she missed his groin and her foot struck his leg. As Kitty tried to pull back for a third kick, the guard grabbed her foot and yanked hard. Kitty toppled backward onto the floor.

The guard was on top of her now. Kitty struggled to get up, but the man was huge and heavy. He shoved her against the carpet. Spittle and blood leaked from his mouth and his eyes were bloodshot. Kitty clawed at his face with her nails, drawing more blood. The guard screamed and grabbed Kitty's wrist, pinning it to the floor. His other hand encircled her throat and began to squeeze hard.

The world around them turned empty. Kitty had never been strangled before. It was strange and terrifying. Her lungs began to burn, and she heard blood pounding in her ears. Everything else became distant and quiet. She struggled, but it was no good. She just wasn't strong enough.

In each of her thundering heartbeats, Kitty heard Mrs. Singh's voice.

Get your hands on a weapon. A rock, a pipe, anything.

The floor was littered with items from the top of the desk. Kitty had one free hand, so she was going to use it. She felt around blindly, searching for anything that she could to defend herself. A pen, maybe, or a pencil. She could stab with those. Her hand brushed against some ink and paper, but no pen. Nothing useful, and the world around her was growing more and more hollow as her lungs continued to burn.

Her fingers closed around something round and solid. A paperweight. As good as a rock.

Kitty looked her attacker dead in the eyes and smashed the paperweight into the side of his head. The man shudder from the impact and his eyes got wider with confusion. But still, his hand stayed firm around Kitty's throat.

Kitty hit him a second time and the guard collapsed into a senseless pile. Kitty yanked his hand away from her neck and gasped for air. She lay there for a few moments, just remembering what it was like to breathe.

Get up. You have to get up. More people will come because of the noise.

Kitty wriggled out from underneath the unconscious guard and grabbed the top of the desk, using it to haul herself upright. Her head swam and she knew that she was swaying like a reed in the wind. It took several more gasping breaths to steady herself, and nothing could stop the pounding of her heart.

She had almost died.

Get out of the house. Go to the window. Get out of the house. Go to the window. Get out of the house.

The command repeated over and over inside her mind. Kitty stumbled to the window and shoved it open. She thought of the camera and turned back.

There were voices and footsteps in the hallway. Men were coming.

She saw the camera on the floor, among the mess. The lens looked broken, but the case was intact. The film might still be recoverable. Kitty grabbed the camera and, without really thinking about what she was doing, dove out the window. It was a drop of a couple of feet, and the landing was painful since she wasn't properly prepared for it. Still, nothing was broken.

Kitty crawled along the side of the house, trying to stay below the sightline from the ground-floor windows. Any minute now, the men would arrive in Lowell's office, see the open window, and know she had gone outside. She had to get away before they spotted her. She would run across the grounds to the car. Then she could drive—she'd never driven a car, but she knew enough now from spending time in the garage with Tommy. She could manage . . .

Where would she drive to? To the seaside hotel to get their luggage? As if that mattered anymore. It was all ordinary, expendable stuff, and their cover was already blown. Should she drive back to the Orchestra? Hope that she met Mrs. Singh along the way?

Hope that Verity was still alive by the time Mrs. Singh arrived?

Kitty closed her eyes tightly, fighting tears of pain, fear, and frustration. She couldn't just run away. Verity was in danger. Who knew what sort of awful things would happen to her when the guards tried to make her talk? If Kitty ran away, any harm that came to Verity would feel like her fault, and she couldn't live with that.

She looked along the wall of the house and saw that the library window was still dark. No one was inside that room. That was her way back in.

CHAPTER 23

The library windows were locked, so Kitty broke a pane of glass with the camera. The noise was louder than she had intended, or at least it sounded that way to her. No time to worry about that, though. With her free hand she reached inside to undo the latch. A piece of glass cut the top of her arm as she did so, and she winced. Thankfully, it was a shallow cut and away from the arteries. She wasn't going to bleed out from it, but it reminded her that she needed to be careful.

Kitty opened the window and crawled inside. She crept to the hallway door and opened it a crack. The noise of tramping boots filled the house. She couldn't pinpoint how many men there were, but it was several. Enough of them that their movements must've covered the sound of the breaking window glass, which was one silver lining.

From the direction of the upstairs landing, she heard a man shouting, "You two! Keep working on the girl. Make sure she talks. The other one's outside somewhere. Bashed Jenkins's head in."

Another voice joined him, and Kitty heard footsteps descending the stairs. "Is she armed?"

"Dunno," said the first voice. "Left Jenkins's gun, so I assume not. Take her alive if you can, bring her back for interrogation. If she puts up too much of a fight, do what you have to."

Kitty bit her lip to keep from making any noise as the men reached the ground floor and walked past the library. She waited until their footsteps receded. Through the library window, she saw electric torch beams waving back and forth out on the lawn. Most of the men were outside searching for her, and Verity was upstairs.

All right, Kitty. You can do this. One, two, three, go!

She stayed where she was, frozen in place. Her feet refused to obey her.

It was the fear. It was paralyzing her. Kitty scowled with all her might, so that she felt the muscles in her cheeks and jaw straining to make the expression. A small measure of sense came back to her. The haze receded a little. The fear was still there and so was the skipping record, but her hands and feet started to obey her again.

One, two, three, go!

Kitty opened the door and ran for the stairs. She didn't stop until she reached the landing, where she dropped to her knees and looked down into the foyer. There was nobody behind her. She listened for the sounds of people. Nothing. She was alone.

A muffled scream came from the upstairs hall. It was Verity.

Kitty scurried up the remaining steps and into the hallway. Moving as quietly as she could, she advanced on the noise. The scream quickly stopped, but it was replaced by voices. Straining her ears, Kitty followed them to a guest bedroom near the side of the house.

"What was your mission?" a man said from inside.

"I don't have a mission!" answered Verity's voice.

"Stop with the lies, girl. What were you doing snooping on the meeting tonight?"

"I don't know anything about all of that," Verity insisted. "My name is Vera Cunningham—"

Her voice died amid a loud smacking noise. Kitty winced at the sound and touched her cheek reflexively.

"I know that name ain't real," the man said, "but I don't care. What I care is that you're a spy, and you're going to tell me everything about your mission, or else these pretty little hands of yours won't be good for much after tonight."

"Please!" Verity cried. "My name is Vera Cunningham. I'm a *thief*! I was here to rob the house! I thought it would be empty tonight!"

Her terror sounded real, but even so she was channeling it through another cover, protecting the mission. Kitty was impressed—amazed, in fact. But it wasn't enough. The lie wouldn't stop Lowell's men.

"That's how it's gonna be, eh? Get the pliers, Tom." There was a pause, and Kitty thought she heard chuckling. Then the man spoke again. "This is gonna be fun, girl. You know 'This Little Piggy,' do ya?"

Kitty knew she had to do something. She looked around for any sort of solution. She couldn't take the room by force, even if the men didn't have guns. What could she do?

There was an old grandfather clock between her and the stairs. Maybe she could knock it over and the noise would bring the men out of the room. But if she did that, there was no way she could get to a hiding place before she was seen.

Her gaze fell on a porcelain vase on a small nearby table. The vase looked fragile, and it was small enough to throw. That was something.

She grabbed the vase and crouched behind the table, hoping she'd be concealed in the dim light of the hallway. She threw the vase against the wall a little ways down the hallway, near enough to be heard, but hopefully far enough away that the men would leave the room to investigate.

"You hear that?" asked one of the men.

"Aye." There came the click of a pistol hammer being cocked. "The other girl might be in the house."

The door slowly opened and one of the men looked out. He turned both ways, and Kitty made herself as small as possible to keep hidden.

"Cover me," the man said to his partner. "That came from near the stairs."

The man stepped out into the hallway, with his pistol ready and aimed. As he advanced toward the staircase, the other man ventured out, holding his own gun.

"Do you see anything?" he called.

"There's a broken vase here," his partner answered. "Looks like someone knocked it over. Must be the other girl. Probably ran when she did." The man reached the staircase and leaned over the railing. "Don't see anyone. Odd."

The other man followed him for a few steps, leaving a small gap open by the door. "This isn't good."

"Don't make no difference. They'll find her sooner or later."

As the men called to one another, Kitty crept around the table and tried to calculate how long it would take her to get inside the room and lock the door. It was going to be a near thing. One of the men was still very close indeed. If he noticed her before she got the door shut, she wouldn't be able to keep him out.

She glanced down at the camera in her hand and an idea came to her. The poor thing deserved a medal after what it was being put through tonight. She gripped the strap and let the camera dangle from her hand.

As Kitty neared the door, the man in front of her seemed to sense her approach. That was not a surprise, but even so, as he lifted his head and turned toward her, Kitty's chest clenched with fear. Fortunately, she was well acquainted with this primal reaction, and she had anticipated it. She didn't freeze, and as the man turned toward her, she swung the camera overhand and smacked him in the face with it.

The man cried out and stumbled away. His companion turned and shouted. Now they both knew Kitty was there. Kitty dashed into the room and shoved the door shut behind her.

Lock it!

Kitty threw the bolt to secure the door and looked around. Her eyes turned toward Verity, who was tied to a chair by a length of cord taken from the curtains. She had a bloody nose, and bruises were forming on the side of her face, where the men had hit her.

Verity looked at Kitty in shock. "What are you doing here?" she cried. "You were supposed to get away!"

"I weren't gonna leave you," Kitty answered.

She heard pounding on the door. The men were trying to break it down. Kitty hurried over to Verity and untied her. Verity leapt to her feet and shoved the chair under the doorknob, wedging it shut.

"That should hold them for a little bit," she said. Then she hugged Kitty. "Thank you," she whispered.

Normally Kitty disliked being touched, especially unexpectedly. But with Verity it didn't feel as intrusive. Even in the middle of a crisis, there was a calm about Verity that made Kitty feel more at ease. She didn't pull away, and after a moment she gave Verity a pat on the back.

"Kitty Granger don't abandon 'er friends," she whispered.

With a sigh, Verity pulled away and sat down on the edge of the bed. She wiped the blood from her face with the back of her hand. "Now we're in a bit of a pickle," she said to Kitty. "They will get the door open eventually."

"I got a call through to Mrs. Singh," Kitty said, trying to stay hopeful. "Said she'd be 'ere in forty-five minutes."

Verity laughed, and it wasn't a happy sound. "Forty-five minutes? From London?" Then she shrugged. "Well, if anyone can do it, she can. When did you talk to her?"

"Maybe 'alf an hour ago," Kitty ventured. It was hard to say. Ever since they'd been discovered, Kitty's sense of time had grown shaky. That was on account of the haze caused by her overwhelmed senses, and it had only gotten worse after the fight in Lowell's office.

There was a loud crash from the door. The men outside were starting to throw their weight against it. The door and the chair shook from the impact.

"I'm not sure the door will hold much longer," Verity said.

Kitty nodded. "Then we gotta get outta this room." She went to the window and looked out. It was still dark outside and it was difficult to gauge just how far down the ground was. "Think we could make a rope with them sheets?" she asked Verity.

Verity frowned and rummaged through the bedsheets, yanking on the fabric to test its strength. "Maybe," she said. "We won't be able to tear them, so we'll have to tie them end on end. They probably still won't reach all the way to the ground.

If we get it wrong, it's a long drop onto pavement. And even if that works, the men out there are sure to hear us."

Kitty noticed that the window wasn't latched. She opened it and leaned out. A small ledge jutted out from the stonework below the window. It was decorative, but it would certainly hold her weight.

She looked at the window of the next room. It wasn't far, and maybe it was unlatched just like this one. And the wall was rough, with deep gaps between the stones and more decorative stonework that could serve as handholds. The bedroom windows didn't slide up, they swung outward, so she wouldn't need any leverage to get it open if it was already unlocked.

"What if we climb along to the next room?" she asked Verity.

Verity's expression grew very uncertain. She took a look for herself and acknowledged, "It might work. And then what?"

"If we can, we sneak downstairs an' get back to the car."

Verity still looked doubtful, but she said, "Fine. Let's try it. Better than waiting around for the door to break down."

Kitty led the way. She slid out feet first and waited until she felt her toes reach the ledge. Once they were planted firmly, she took a deep breath and started climbing. It was sort of an awkward sideways slide, moving her feet inch by inch while her fingers groped for handholds. Feeling her way along in the darkness was a special kind of agony, as she balanced the sensations of her toes trying to keep their foothold, her fingers searching for safe purchase, and her ears and eyes straining to detect anything at all that might help her.

Finally, Kitty reached the next room, opened the window, and climbed inside. Then she turned and helped Verity in after her. Verity was moving gingerly. Her injuries weren't superficial, and from the way she stood, Kitty gathered that she'd been hit in the side and stomach too.

Even so, Verity wore a determined look as she grabbed a candle holder from the mantelpiece and held it like a club.

"Whatcha doin'?" Kitty whispered.

"We're only one room down," Verity whispered back. "Those men are going to see us as soon as we open the door. I don't think we can run for it, so if we have to fight, we're going to fight properly."

Kitty felt herself trembling at the idea. She had experienced more violence in this one night than in the entire rest of her life. She'd almost been killed! And now she had to realize that it wasn't over, not yet. It wouldn't be over for a while.

What had Smythe said? *The longest day in British history.* It already felt like it.

She set her face to show that she was equally determined, and unplugged the bedside lamp. It was big and heavy. It might work.

"You're going to use that?" Verity asked.

"Do me best," Kitty replied.

Verity sighed. "All right." She went to the door and slowly turned the knob. "Don't attack unless they see us. If they do see us, attack before they do."

"Got it."

Kitty followed Verity into the hallway. Only one of the men was still there, glaring at the door to the empty bedroom, and occasionally throwing his weight against it. *Where's the other man?* Kitty wondered, as she and Verity made for the stairs.

She gasped as the missing guard appeared at the top of the staircase, holding a fire ax in his hand.

"Right, I've got the ax!" he called to his partner. "Let's

break the damn thing . . ." His words trailed away as he spotted Kitty and Verity. "Christ! They're here!"

The other man turned and saw them too. "Get 'em!"

Kitty's mind spun in circles as she anticipated what was going to happen next. Both of the men had guns and would likely draw them now. That meant running wasn't an option, but if they got into close quarters fast enough, the guns wouldn't be a problem. Then again, that meant getting into close quarters in the first place.

Kitty's eyes flicked toward the ax. That was the biggest danger. Not only did the men have the advantage of size and strength, the ax gave one of them reach and deadly force. The ax had to go first.

"Go left!" Kitty shouted at Verity as she raised the lamp above her head and charged the man holding the ax. He hadn't expected a fight in the hallway, so he was still gripping the weapon high on the handle, just below the head. That would make it hard for him to swing.

The guard shifted his grip, steadied haft with his other hand, and started to swing. There was a confused look on his face at the sight of Kitty running at him and not away from him, but the confusion only slowed him down. It did not stop him.

As Kitty closed the distance she roared as loudly as she could and threw the lamp with all her might at the man's face. The man raised his hands to block the throw, and the ax came with them. The lamp's body smacked him in the chest, and the ax blade became caught in the lampshade as the man struggled to knock it away. It was a tiny opening at best, and Kitty knew better than to squander it.

She knew she had to strike. First, something had to be done about the man's height. As the guard struggled to free the ax from the lamp, Kitty kicked him in the shins again and again until the man finally stumbled and cried in pain.

Hobbling in place, he took one hand off the ax handle and reached for his injured shin.

Next, the ax. With the man bent over, Kitty grabbed his arm and bit him on the wrist as hard as her jaws could manage. It was surprisingly easy, especially given how badly her head was spinning from the fear and the noise. Just a simple set of motions: wrist, teeth, bite. Simple was good. Simple was easy. Simple was going to keep her alive.

The man screamed again and dropped the ax. He let go of his shin and grabbed Kitty by the scruff of the neck, trying to yank her away from his arm. Kitty kept her jaws locked on tight until the guard threw her against the wall. The jarring impact made Kitty gasp, and she had to let go. The guard clutched his wrist and howled curses at her.

Act. Act. Act, Kitty thought. She had to keep attacking. Even hurt and disarmed, the man had every advantage over her. The only way to beat him was to make him react to her, not the other way around.

Simple was good. *Keep it simple.*

Kitty rushed back at him and kicked him in the shins again, this time going for both legs. The man lurched forward and almost fell. He managed to grab Kitty's arms, and slammed her against the wall again. Kitty saw one hand ball into a fist and draw back to punch her in the face.

Kitty couldn't hit anywhere near as hard, and she knew it, but she did have another weapon at her disposal. She curled her fingertips and clawed at the man's face. It was a chaotic mess of blows that didn't aim for anything in particular, but she left marks across the man's cheeks, forehead, and nose. She kept going until the man finally knocked her away with a savage blow to the side of her head.

Kitty hit the ground and lay there as the world spun in circles. Her heart was pounding and there was a cloud of noise hovering over her.

She looked up and saw Verity struggling against the second guard. Verity was a much better fighter and she'd already gotten in several good hits with her candlestick, not to mention her elbows and knees. But she had been struck too. Blood was streaming from her nose, and she looked exhausted from the fight. The guard loomed over her, undeterred.

Kitty gritted her teeth and pulled herself onto her knees. She looked over her shoulder. The man behind her sagged against the wall, trying to catch his breath. When he saw her rise, he cursed loudly and fumbled for his pistol. Kitty knew he was going to shoot her and be done with it.

Her gaze fell on the shards of the vase she had broken as a distraction—now scattered on the floor within arm's reach. She grabbed the largest chunk of porcelain and threw it at the man's face. This time she hit him dead in the nose. The man grunted and cursed some more, his gun forgotten for a moment.

It was just long enough. Kitty forced herself to her feet. It was a strange experience. Her body felt impossibly light, like she could just float away from all of this. She didn't even register the pain anymore, even though she knew that everything hurt. But even feeling light as a feather, her limbs were sluggish and fought her as she made them move.

Kitty lowered her head and charged just as the man yanked his weapon free of its holster. His hand was still injured from the bite, and he struggled to bring the gun to bear. Before he could finish aiming Kitty drove her shoulder into the man's stomach and tipped him backward a half step.

There wasn't much force behind the charge, but the guard was already off balance. As he stumbled, he collided with the grandfather clock that stood in the upper hall. It bonged loudly from the impact, and the man dropped onto the floor, stunned and swooning.

Kitty saw the man and saw the clock and her mind made an instantaneous connection. Her hands reacted before her thoughts did. She grabbed the clock and heaved it away from the wall with every ounce of strength she had. It tipped over and fell onto the guard in a mass of wood and brass.

No time to stop. Check on Verity. No time to stop. Check on Verity.

Kitty gasped for breath as she turned toward the other fight happening a few feet away. Verity had gotten some more good hits in, but she was on her knees now, struggling to get up while the remaining guard pinned her down with one arm. And she'd been disarmed: the candlestick lay on the ground beyond her reach. She had neither leverage nor ability to maneuver. The fight had finally been distilled into one of raw strength, and her enemy had all the cards there. The man reached for his gun.

Gun.

Kitty snatched up the pistol belonging to the man she had just taken down. Her hands were trembling, but she didn't drop it. She tried to remember her training. She hated using firearms. They were loud and heavy and they shook when she shot them. None of that mattered now. Only Verity mattered.

Safety.

Her eyes looked at the gun's safety catch. It was already off.

Hammer.

She pulled back on the slide, cocking the hammer.

Aim.

She leveled the pistol at the guard. He was still in the middle of drawing his own weapon. His attention was only on Verity. He wasn't in a hurry. He thought he had time.

Or maybe it was just that the whole world was moving so slowly. Kitty felt her heartbeats coming at one a minute. That was just her brain, though. She couldn't allow herself to be confused by it.

Fire.

Kitty's finger squeezed the trigger.

CHAPTER 24

Kitty found herself looking straight ahead, over the smoking barrel of the pistol. For a second, she wasn't even certain what had happened; she must have blanked out.

Then everything came back to her.

Her first thought was of Verity. She looked down and saw her on the ground, leaning against the wall and gasping for air. Verity looked at Kitty in utter amazement, tinged with the shadow of recent terror. Slowly a relieved smile crossed her lips, but the look in her eyes remained the same.

"My God," Verity whispered. "You just saved my bloody life."

Kitty remembered the man who had been attacking Verity. She looked for him next. He was on the ground too, with three bullet holes in his chest.

"I shot 'im," she said. She had never shot anyone before. She had no idea what she should think or how she should feel about it. She just felt numb. The noise alone had overpowered her senses.

Verity got to her feet and went to Kitty. She placed her hand on Kitty's and gently forced the gun down. Kitty hadn't really thought about the fact that she was still aiming it, but at Verity's touch she relaxed her arm and let it fall.

"Is 'e dead?" Kitty asked.

Verity looked at the guard. "That's about as dead a man as I've seen, yeah."

The pistol tumbled out of Kitty's hand. Verity just managed to grab it before it hit the floor. Kitty covered her mouth and gasped.

"I killed someone!" she squeaked. She suddenly felt very small and wretched.

Verity got in front of her, blocking her view of the dead man. She took Kitty's face in her hands and gazed into her eyes.

"Kitty, listen to me," she said softly. "You had to do it. He was going to kill me, and then he was going to kill you. You saved both our lives."

"But . . . but 'e's dead!"

There was a disconnect inside her brain. The twin understandings that she had killed the man and saved their lives weren't meeting up. She was having trouble reconciling that the one had led to the other.

"He beat me for information and he was going to murder the both of us," Verity said. "He doesn't deserve your guilt, Kitty."

She pulled Kitty into her arms and held her close. Kitty was shaking and her eyes stung. She was terrified and everything was horrible except for Verity. Verity was different. She was like a blanket drowning out all the terrible things in the world.

Very slowly, the noise died away until it was a faint crackle, and the record in Kitty's head slowed and stopped skipping. She was still trembling, but her senses were returning to her.

"Bloody hell!" someone shouted from downstairs. "Were those gunshots?"

"Damn well were!" someone else replied.

"We have to get out of here," Verity whispered.

She let go of Kitty and snatched up the pistol. Kitty didn't want her to let go, but she didn't fight. Verity was right. They had to escape. She clung to Verity's hand as they crept to the edge of the landing and looked down. The guards from outside had returned to the house. Now they were swarming around in the foyer. Two of them were already making their way up the stairs.

"There!" one man shouted. "I see them!"

Verity grabbed Kitty and pushed her back as gunfire erupted from the staircase. Bullets flew past them, splintering the edge of the wall and spraying the air with plaster.

"Kitty, I'm going to do something very rash," Verity said. "If I don't make it, you have to reach the car and get back to headquarters, understood?"

"No, I'm not leavin' you again!" Kitty insisted.

"There isn't any choice, Kitty!" Verity cried.

Gunfire erupted from the foyer, and suddenly the men were shouting in confusion. Kitty winced, expecting them to spring on her and Verity any moment, but the attack never came. Instead, there was more gunfire from the foyer, and then a long silence.

Kitty looked at Verity, who looked back with equal confusion. In the silence, they heard Mrs. Singh shouting frantically.

"Kitty? Verity? Where are you?"

"Mrs. Singh?" Kitty gasped. She and Verity dashed to the landing and looked down. The men on the stairs were dead, and so were the ones in the foyer.

Cautiously, the two girls began descending the stairs. As they neared the lower landing, Kitty saw Mrs. Singh standing in the hallway, looking in all directions. She was dressed in black with her hair tucked under a cap to keep it out of the way. A Walther PPK pistol was in her hand, held at the ready with her finger beside the trigger. Agent Gregson was standing next to her, similarly dressed and holding a submachine gun against his shoulder.

"Mrs. Singh!" Kitty exclaimed.

Mrs. Singh and Gregson spun around at the noise and aimed their weapons. Recognizing the two girls, Mrs. Singh lowered her pistol, and Gregson just gave them a nod and went back to covering the hallway.

Kitty raced the rest of the way down the stairs with Verity close on her heels. Her heart was pounding still, but this time with excitement and relief. Mrs. Singh's eyes were lit with fire and worry. She looked like a lioness prepared to destroy anyone and anything that got between her and her cubs.

"Thank goodness you're here," Verity gasped. "I don't think we'd have lasted much longer."

"We came as quickly as we could," Mrs. Singh said.

"A lot bloody faster than you're supposed to on the A12," Gregson added.

Mrs. Singh ignored him, focusing on Kitty and Verity. "Is there anyone else in the house?"

Kitty counted the bodies, shuddered, and then shook her head. "Don't think so, missis," she answered. "There's two more upstairs, and they're not movin' neither. 'Tween them and this lot, I'm pretty sure that's everyone Lowell an' Smythe left behind."

"Gregson, do a sweep of the house to be sure," Mrs. Singh said.

Gregson nodded and slipped off down the hallway.

"What about Lowell's servants?" Mrs. Singh asked.

Kitty shrugged. She didn't know.

Verity answered, "Given what we overheard, and the level of security we found here, I'm absolutely certain Lowell gave them the night off. The men were talking treason at the meeting. Something tells me Lowell isn't foolish enough to trust even his butler with that kind of information, let alone the cook and the housemaids."

Mrs. Singh nodded. "That makes sense. Now, you'd better tell me what's going on here."

"Better still," Verity said, "we can show you."

✦

They led Mrs. Singh to the cellar and the secret room. On the way, Mrs. Singh stopped to check the kitchen and the other downstairs rooms for more of Lowell's men, but everything was empty. It seemed that they were safe for the moment. The question was, how safe were they for the long term?

Once inside the hidden room, Mrs. Singh gave a whistle. "My word, this is something. When your report mentioned a hidden room, Verity, I assumed it would be a glorified cupboard. But this . . ."

"I know," Verity agreed. "Everything about this mission is beyond what I had expected."

Mrs. Singh looked at Kitty. "You said you saw a meeting attended by Smythe, Lowell, James MacIntyre, and . . ." She hesitated. "And the Old Man."

"They was all sittin' 'round the table," Kitty said. "An' I swear on me life it were 'im, missis. I don't forget faces!"

She felt the need to reiterate that point, since she knew the claim was going to be dismissed as impossible.

"Calm down, Kitty, I'm not doubting you," Mrs. Singh assured her. "Normally I would be skeptical, but given that Pryce never returned from his meeting with the Old Man today, I'm inclined to believe you. You said you had photographs?"

Kitty offered her the camera, hoping that the film inside hadn't been damaged after its many mishaps.

Mrs. Singh took it and nodded. "Good. We'll have these developed as soon as we get back to the Orchestra. In the meantime, let's search the room to see if we can figure out what those bastards are up to."

"They said somethin' about MPs not comin' in to work today," Kitty ventured.

"Hmm." Mrs. Singh frowned. "An assassination, maybe?"

"Masked gunmen in Parliament?" Verity suggested.

Mrs. Singh thought about it and shook her head. "You can't take over the government just by shooting some MPs," she said. "Enough would get away, and then you'd have a state of emergency on your hands. Even Smythe and Lowell aren't stupid enough to do that, and certainly not the Old Man."

The three of them scattered around the room and started searching through the files. The conspirators had taken a lot of the evidence with them, but they'd left behind a few lists and registers. There were names that didn't mean anything to Kitty but piqued Mrs. Singh's interest. Verity found a ledger of arms sales. Totaled up, it amounted to enough equipment to support a small army. There was also a financial list of some sort, with large sums of money listed alongside serial numbers of some kind. Bank accounts perhaps? Bribes?

Then, as Kitty opened another folder and started flipping through the photographs inside, her breath caught in her throat.

Some were snapshots of crates full of weapons and explosives; others showed those same crates being offloaded from ships and small smuggling boats. Kitty came to a photograph of Mr. Pryce, taken at the same location as one of the arms deals. It was the same place, but the background was very slightly different. The pictures had been taken on different days.

But why had Mr. Pryce been photographed at all?

"Mrs. Singh, look at this," Kitty said.

Mrs. Singh and Verity both joined her.

Verity gasped at the photograph. "You don't think Pryce is in on it too, do you?" She sounded very worried at the idea.

Mrs. Singh immediately shook her head. "I've known Pryce for almost twenty years," she said flatly. "He would sooner die than turn traitor, and there is no way he would ever work with fascists. But this"—she waved the photograph in her hand— "is meant to make it look like he's connected. They probably planted someone to covertly take pictures when Pryce went to inspect the sites Debby found. That's the Old Man's work, obviously."

Kitty shuffled through the rest of the photos. There were more pictures of Mr. Pryce, and a few of other members of the Orchestra, all adults and mostly agents from a working-class background. The photographs didn't show anything actually incriminating, but taken alongside other pictures of clandestine meetings and smuggled weapons, they could be interpreted to suggest a connection.

At the bottom of the pile, she found a collection of notes. Skimming them told her everything.

"Oh God!" she exclaimed. "Missis, this is s'posed to be a report to MI5 from one of the Old Man's agents. It says Mr. Pryce is in contact with . . . the Soviets? That can't be possible!"

"What else does it say?" Mrs. Singh asked.

Kitty skimmed the rest and summarized. "There's talk 'bout weapons bein' smuggled in, an' a plot to start a Communist uprisin' among the factory workers an' West Indians in London . . . an' Liverpool, an' Birmingham, an' Manchester. It says Mr. Pryce's network is really Communist spies. But that's not true, is it? I don't understand."

Mrs. Singh scowled. "Oh, *I* understand," she said. "They're planning to stage a terrorist attack against Parliament, and then they're going to blame it on Pryce and his 'foreigners and socialists.' If they can spark panic about an impending Red revolution, they can justify martial law across the country."

"It's diabolical," Verity said, aghast.

"Question is," said Mrs. Singh grimly, "how is the attack going to come?"

"I think I know," Verity replied. She unrolled a long piece of drafting paper she had found. It was a blueprint of the Palace of Westminster. On the basement level, directly below the House of Commons, X's had been drawn in thick pencil.

Kitty's thoughts spun around for a moment and a series of terrible imaginings lined up. Parliament. Basement. Explosives. Missing MPs.

Gunmen might not be able to kill all of the government ministers at once, but a bomb in the basement could.

"They're gonna bloody blow up Parliament!" she exclaimed.

CHAPTER 25

Gregson met them back in the foyer a few minutes later. Kitty was carrying an armful of documents, including the map of Parliament and the folder of observation materials about the Orchestra.

"The house is clear, ma'am," Gregson told Mrs. Singh. "Find anything downstairs?"

"A buffet of evidence," Mrs. Singh replied. "Smythe and Lowell are plotting to blow up Parliament, and stage a coup during the chaos."

Gregson blinked a couple of times, trying not to look dumbstruck. Finally, he said, "What a bloody inconvenience, ma'am."

"My thoughts exactly," Mrs. Singh said. "We're heading back to headquarters to get some more agents and deal with the conspiracy before it can cause any more trouble. Can you take care of this mess?" She motioned toward the bodies on the floor.

Kitty glanced at the bodies and flinched. She quickly looked away, feeling sick to her stomach. It was unsettling to hear Mrs. Singh speak of the corpses as just another detail to be managed. Of course, just a few minutes ago those same men had wanted to kill her and Verity, but their deaths were still horrible to contemplate.

Gregson nodded. "Not a problem, ma'am. I'll call one of our MI5 contacts. Let them deal with it."

"Is that safe? I would prefer not to have the girls dragged into this."

"My lads know to keep their questions about our involvement to a minimum," Gregson said.

"Good." Mrs. Singh turned to Kitty and Verity. "Are any of your belongings still in the house?"

"No," Verity answered. "Everything is at our hotel in Wolton-on-Sea. It's a little town about an hour down the road. Do you think we should go back there? Resume our cover?"

Mrs. Singh pointed to the bruises across Verity's face. "In your current state? No, better to make a clean break now before there are any awkward questions—and before Lowell rejoins his family, knowing who you are. Gregson, after you're finished here, pop down to Wolton and retrieve their things. Take Verity's car."

"It's parked behind some trees beyond the gate," Verity said. She rummaged in her pocket and produced the car key for Gregson. "Rooms sixteen and eighteen at the Seaview Hotel."

"Got it," Gregson told her.

Verity frowned. "Just a moment." She opened the drawer of a desk against the foyer wall and pulled out a pen and a piece of blank writing paper. *"Dearest Diana,"* she said aloud as she wrote the words, *"I finally read the letter that came for me this morning.* She'll just think she wasn't listening when I received it. Happens all the time with her. *My mother has taken deathly ill, so I must go home. Going to drive through the night. I've taken Kate with me, as she is my responsibility and not yours. Didn't want to wake you since it's some godawful hour. See you next time in Monaco.*

Love and kisses, Vera." She ended the letter with a little flourish of the pen. "There, that ought to assuage her."

"You don't think she'll believe it, do you?" Kitty asked. It sounded like a very flimsy pretense.

"Could go either way," Verity admitted, "but hopefully she'll chalk up the timing to bad luck. She'll be very distracted tomorrow anyway." Verity folded the letter and passed it to Gregson. "Diana's in room fifteen. Just slip it under the door while you're there."

"Not worried about leaving something with handwriting, Miss?" Gregson asked, as he tucked the letter into his pocket.

Verity grinned. "I always use a different hand for each cover. A bit to keep track of, but it's fun!"

Mrs. Singh make a skeptical noise in her throat. "Hmm. Even so, I think you'd better retire Vera Cunningham for the foreseeable future."

"A pity," Verity mused. "I was really starting to like this hairstyle."

Mrs. Singh check her watch. "Sun will be up soon. Gregson, we shall leave you to it. Come on, girls, we need to get back to London."

Within minutes, Kitty was sitting in the back of Mrs. Singh's car, staring out of the window as they sped through the countryside. The creeping light of dawn was just beginning to appear along the horizon. Kitty wanted to sleep, but she was too exhausted to manage it, so she just stared at the passing landscape and said nothing. In the front seat, Mrs. Singh and

Verity were talking, planning. Kitty wasn't paying attention to their words. Probably she should have been, since she was still a part of the operation, but it was all she could do to keep herself together.

Her mind kept cycling through everything that had happened, replaying all the worst parts of the night like a grotesque film reflected in the glass of the window. She thought about everything that she might have done wrong. She thought about everything new that could go wrong from here.

She thought about how she had shot a man. That kept cycling the most, finding its way into the middle of her other thoughts no matter how hard she tried to push it away. She was a murderer. She'd murdered someone. She was a spy. Spies murdered people. She was a murderer either way.

Stop it, Kitty! Stop thinking about that!

But she couldn't stop. It just sat there in her head, overpowering everything else. This was who she was now: a person who spied, and lied, and killed. And it didn't matter that she was spying, lying, and killing in the service of her country, to keep innocent people safe. Even in a good cause, she had to carry the weight of what she had done.

In the films, spies drank martinis, and shot people without remorse, and had a clever retort for every occasion.

Real life wasn't like the films.

Automatically, Kitty's fingertips were tapping each other, jumping from finger to finger in an endless sequence that was irregular the first few times through, and then repeated like a pattern. That relieved some of the pressure inside her mind. But it couldn't fix everything.

Bloody hell, she needed a crossword, or a good scream, but neither of those was available at the moment.

She almost didn't notice when they neared the city. It took her a few minutes even to register that the sun was coming up properly. She had lost most of the drive to her cyclical thoughts. That was fine, though. It had given her a chance to process. Her surface-level consciousness had gone blank, but her brain had kept working. It was sorting the problems out so that she could think about other things, important things, like the rest of the mission.

They reached London a little after sunup. Parliament didn't sit for several hours, and Smythe surely wouldn't blow it up before the ministers he wanted to kill were there, so that meant they had a little time. It meant they could properly plan their next course of action.

Kitty had snapped out of her trance by the time the car pulled up to the Orchestra's headquarters. She stretched her neck and looked around. The muscles in her back and arms were sore from the fighting, and also from sitting for so long. As they pulled into the parking lot, Kitty felt a sense of unease come over her. Something was wrong.

She saw two men standing along the wall, smoking cigarettes while they guarded the entrance. The men had guns, both topped with silencers. Kitty didn't recognize either of them, and she knew most of the faces in the Orchestra.

"Look out!" she shouted.

Mrs. Singh spotted the man and cursed. She spun the car around and hit the accelerator. The car lurched forward and rolled behind a large van that was parked to one side. It offered a little momentary cover, but that wouldn't mean much.

"Out of the car and stay flat on the ground," Mrs. Singh whispered.

Kitty did as she was ordered. She crawled onto the pavement and lay there, her heart pounding. She saw the two men approaching. They couldn't see her from that angle, but she watched their boots as they got closer and closer. Verity dropped to the ground beside Kitty and put an arm over her protectively. It made Kitty feel a little safer, but she knew it wouldn't matter once the men reached them.

Inside the car, she saw Mrs. Singh screw a silencer onto her own gun and crawl out on the other side. Mrs. Singh edged forward along the far side of the car, and Kitty lost sight of her behind the rear wheel. Suddenly a shadow fell over Kitty and she looked up at the two men, who had just come around the side of the van.

"What've we got here?" one of the men asked, glaring down at her.

"Oh, 'ello," Kitty said awkwardly. "I'm Kitty."

Both of the men looked confused. "What?"

Kitty heard the sharp rattle of a silenced weapon firing. One of the men collapsed, followed by his companion. As they lay the pavement, looking even more confused at what had just happened, Kitty put a hand over her mouth to keep herself from screaming at the sight.

Mrs. Singh came around the car, her pistol aimed at the bodies. Verity's hand covered Kitty's eyes for a moment. At first, Kitty didn't understand why, until she heard the noise of the gun again.

Mrs. Singh was making sure the men were dead.

Kitty forced herself to take long, deep breaths as she and Verity got up again. She was trying not to panic. Strangely, a sensation of calm had come over her. Maybe the trauma of the night had finally battered her good judgment into pieces.

"I'm sorry you had to see that, Kitty," Mrs. Singh said.

"No, I understand, missis," Kitty replied, through chattering teeth. Her whole body was trembling. "You saved me life."

"What are those men doing here?" Verity asked. From her nervous tone, Kitty knew she already suspected the truth.

"The Old Man's sent 'em to kill the Orchestra," Kitty said quietly.

Mrs. Singh nodded. "I suspect once it's done, they'll doctor it up as a raid by the security services. They're probably inside planting more 'evidence' against us already."

Mrs. Singh stepped around them and opened a panel underneath the glove box. Inside were two more pistols and four magazines of ammunition. For a moment, Kitty feared Mrs. Singh was going to give her one, but Mrs. Singh just shoved the magazines into her pockets and closed the compartment.

"You two should stay with the car," Mrs. Singh told them. "This is going to get rather messy, and you've been through enough already."

"You can't go in there alone!" Verity exclaimed. "You have no idea what you're walking into!" She opened the compartment and grabbed the two extra pistols. She handed one to Kitty, who shivered as her fingers touched the weapon. "We're going with you. Someone has to watch your back in there!"

Mrs. Singh looked at Kitty. Her expression softened as she read the fear in Kitty's face. "What about you, Kitty? You can wait for us here."

Kitty clenched her jaw tightly, trying to work up whatever reserves of strength she had left. Verity was right: Mrs. Singh needed someone to watch her back, and Verity did too. The pressure along her teeth and the tightness in her jaw muscles helped shove a small bit of the terror and confusion out of her mind. The rest she forced down someplace deep, where she hoped it would stay until all of this was done.

"I'm goin' with you too, missis," Kitty said firmly.

Mrs. Singh looked as if she had misgivings, but she said, "Fine. Both of you stay close to me, and keep to cover. Don't shoot unless you have to, or I say so." She looked into Kitty's eyes and said gently, "I'm sorry, Kitty. This was not how your first assignment was meant to turn out."

"I'll be fine, missis. I promise."

"No one is ever 'fine' after their first time, Kitty," Mrs. Singh replied. "So when this is all finished, we are going to sit down and talk about everything, do you understand?"

Kitty bobbed her head. It was much easier than speaking at the moment.

Mrs. Singh led them inside the building, to the front office. They were met by another unfamiliar man dressed in street clothes, like the men in the parking lot. He raised his gun the moment he saw them.

Mrs. Singh was faster. She shot twice, and the man fell.

There were other bodies on the first floor, all Orchestra agents and security personnel. Faces that Kitty recognized. People she knew, more or less. They were dead now because of Smythe.

Tears stung Kitty's eyes and an overwhelming pressure began to form inside her skull. This was too much to think about. Too much to look at.

So she didn't look. She just kept going, following Mrs. Singh and Verity down the stairs into the basement. The guard on duty by the door was dead too. He had a shotgun across his knees, and he had fired it. Another one of Smythe's men was lying at the foot of the stairs. Kitty stepped over him and forced herself to keep breathing.

There was some mercy in it being so early in the day. Not many people had been in the building yet, which was good because Smythe's men had gone through quickly and violently. Kitty didn't look at the bodies. They became blank places in her field of vision. She saw everything else but them. She couldn't look at them, so they weren't there.

Except that they were there.

A few more of Smythe's men appeared from the radio room. Mrs. Singh shot them without a moment's hesitation. They passed an office where another man was busy planting documents in the desk. Mrs. Singh shot him too, as he reached for his gun.

It was terrifying how easily Mrs. Singh could do that, but it did grant Kitty some measure of comfort. These men were horrible and wanted to murder them, and to blame them for all sorts of terrible things. At least Mrs. Singh was a shield against their plans.

As they neared the armory, Kitty heard more gunfire. She peeked around the corner and saw the man called MacIntyre and two of his soldiers lurking on either side of the armory door, firing half-blindly into the room.

"You can't keep this up forever!" MacIntyre shouted. "Drop your guns and we won't kill you."

Kitty heard Saul shout back, "I have a better idea! You drop *your* guns and I won't kill *you*! You bleeding bastard!"

Saul's voice sounded ragged with pain, but it still thundered just as Kitty remembered it. MacIntyre scowled and looked at one of his men.

"Give me a grenade," he ordered. "Think they can barricade themselves in there? I'll get them out."

The other man removed a hand grenade from inside his coat pocket, but then he hesitated and looked down at it. "Sir, there's kids in there," he said.

Kitty gasped and then bit her lip to silence herself. Kids. That meant at least some of the Young Bloods were with Saul. He must have brought them to the armory to protect them, only now they were all going to die anyway.

"So?" MacIntyre demanded.

"I didn't sign up to kill no kids, sir."

"You signed up to follow orders!" MacIntyre shouted. "Now give me the damn grenade!"

Mrs. Singh looked at Verity and held up her hand. Verity nodded, and Mrs. Singh slowly counted down on her fingers. Five. Four. Three. Two.

"Shite, who're you?" exclaimed someone in the hallway behind them.

Kitty looked and saw another one of MacIntyre's soldiers approaching from the direction of Mr. Pryce's office. He had an empty valise in his hand. More documents being planted.

Kitty started to panic. What was she to do? She couldn't bring herself to shoot someone again, not so soon. The thought was unbearable. But here was a man who wanted them all dead, and he wouldn't hesitate to shoot.

He wouldn't hesitate to shoot once he had drawn his gun. It was still holstered, since his hands were full with the valise.

"On your knees!" Kitty shouted at him. She braced her pistol and made sure that she had good form, to make it clear she knew what she was doing. It didn't convince her, but hopefully it would convince him. "'Ands back of your 'ead! Get on your knees!"

"Ah, shite," the man cursed, but he did as he was told, dropping the valise and slowly kneeling on the ground.

"'Ands on your 'ead!" Kitty repeated.

The man laced his fingers together and put them behind his head, still swearing under his breath.

From the direction of the armory, Kitty heard MacIntyre's voice: "Bollocks, what's that?"

Mrs. Singh and Verity dashed into the hallway in front of the armory and Kitty lost sight of them. There was another burst of gunfire, and then silence.

"Mrs. Singh?" Kitty called fearfully. Who had shot, and who had been shot?

Mrs. Singh poked her head around the corner. "We're fine, Kitty. Bring our new friend along, will you?"

Kitty nodded. She turned back to her prisoner. "On your feet," she snarled.

The soldier got up slowly, still keeping his hands on his head. Kitty nodded toward the armory, and the man went. As he passed her, Kitty was certain he meant to jump her, but he looked at her gun again and went peacefully.

In the next hallway, Kitty saw MacIntyre on the ground, bleeding from gunshots in his leg and his arm. Another man had fallen, and the third had surrendered. Verity took charge of the prisoners, shouting commands at them.

"Hands up, against the wall! You've just shot a bunch of my friends, so don't get any clever ideas!"

Kitty rushed past and went into the armory. A metal table had been upended and set facing the door, offering some measure of cover against MacIntyre's bullets. Crouched on the other side of it was Saul, holding a revolver. Boxes of ammunition were scattered on the ground around him. Debby was huddled next to her uncle, with two more revolvers in her lap. She was in the midst of reloading one of them, and she relaxed at the sight of Kitty.

"Kitty! Oh, I thought we were done for!" she exclaimed.

Saul chuckled. He was bleeding from the side, but he flashed a smile at Kitty. "Miss Granger, very nice to see you. How are you this morning?"

"Now is not a time for jokes, sir!" Kitty exclaimed.

Saul grunted. "Nonsense. Always a good time for jokes." He glanced at the pistol in her hand. Kitty still held it at the ready, with the barrel pointed down since she wasn't planning on shooting. "Good to see you remember your discipline under pressure."

There was another upended table farther back, and as the room grew quiet, Kitty saw Faith, Tommy, and Liam get up from their hiding place. They all looked shocked by their ordeal, and equally relieved that it was over.

"Kitty? Is that you?" Faith cried, rushing to join her. "And Mrs. Singh? Oh, thank God!"

"I'm here as well!" Verity shouted from the hallway.

"You a'right?" Kitty asked Faith. She looked at Tommy and Liam as they joined her too. There were a few scrapes and bruises, but they all looked unhurt.

"Yeah, thanks to Saul and Debby," Liam said.

"I tell ya, Kitty, that man's a bloody tiger or somethin'!" Tommy said.

Saul grimaced as he tried, unsuccessfully, to get up. "This? This is nothing. Let me tell you about Arnhem . . ."

Debby sighed with exasperation. "Oh, shut up, Uncle Saul! You're bleeding!"

"Here, let me help," Liam said. He grabbed a first-aid box from a shelf and knelt by Saul.

Mrs. Singh crouched next to Saul and rested an arm on the table. "How are you doing?"

"Better than the chap who gave me this, that's for sure," Saul answered.

"What happened?" Mrs. Singh asked.

"Bunch of bastards got in upstairs, then forced their way down here. I got the kids to the armory and covered their retreat, and, well . . ." Saul looked down at his wound. "You've seen what happened. What is going on?"

The others gathered around, eager for an explanation.

"It's Sir Richard Smythe," Mrs. Singh explained. "Our suspicions were correct. He and Lord Lowell are plotting to attack the government today."

"How?" Debby asked. "What, like this? Like what they did here?"

"They're gonna use bombs," Kitty said. "If their MPs are the only ones still alive, they'll control the government."

"Yes, but . . ." Liam looked flabbergasted. "No one will stand for it."

Mrs. Singh shook her head. "We've seen the plans. They'll blame us for the attack—declare a state of emergency, martial law—and then bang goes British democracy."

Debby looked confused. "Blame *us*?"

"That's what this attack were about," Kitty explained. "Plantin' evidence that we was the ones behind the attack. Or will be the ones, I guess. Claim it's a Communist uprisin'."

Mrs. Singh stood up again and began rummaging through the supply of ammunition. "So," she said, "we're off to Westminster to stop them. I had hoped we could get some backup here, but you all have your hands full."

"I could come with if you really want," Saul offered. Even

Kitty knew it was a joke. Saul gestured at his side wound. "Just the thing to walk off this damn gunshot."

Mrs. Singh gave him a stern look. "That's enough, Saul. Debby, call in reinforcements. Let's get this place locked down. And I want the prisoners interrogated. I want to know how deep this conspiracy goes."

"Or how high," Faith added. "How did they know to come here?"

"The Old Man's in on it," Kitty said.

"Bloody 'ell," Tommy murmured. While the others gaped in disbelief, he set his face into a determined expression. "Look, you can't do this alone, Mrs. Singh. I'm comin' with ya."

"Me too," Faith interjected. "I may not be a fighter, but I've got my basic training, and a handbag full of gadgets, so that must count for something."

Kitty grinned at her, feigning a jaunty attitude that she didn't actually feel. "That's a lot better 'n me. I don't even 'ave the 'andbag."

CHAPTER 26

Given the state of things, they had to wait until reinforcements arrived at the Orchestra before moving against Smythe. It just wasn't safe leaving a handful of injured people to secure the entire facility. Every minute that passed was agony to Kitty.

She sat against the wall in the armory, pretending the be studying the map of Parliament, while most of the time she just let her mind turn in circles to work out the tightly coiled mass of stress and fear. Memories of the bodies kept resurfacing no matter how hard she tried to keep them at bay, and all of them had the face of the man she had killed. There was just no escaping it.

Three agents arrived within an hour of the call. George Harman was one of them. The crusty old security guard turned ashen-faced at the sight of the bodies, and Kitty heard him confide to Mrs. Singh that he wished he had been there. Better he had been the one shot than the young fellow who'd been on duty at the time. Harman's guilt was palpable, and shared by the other survivors. Kitty practically tasted it.

By midmorning, headquarters was sufficiently secure enough for Mrs. Singh to leave. Parliament would be sitting soon, so there was no question that the bombs would be in place by now. Smythe would surely be in the area, ready to oversee detonation himself.

Mrs. Singh was at first resistant to letting the Young Bloods accompany her, but finally she had to accept that with the prisoners to worry about and the danger of another attack on the orchestra, Harman and his men had to remain at headquarters. Debby and Liam stayed too: Debby to call up their contacts in the security services and alert them to the threat, and Liam to tend the wounded—including Saul, who was still grumbling about being left behind. Mrs. Singh's backup could only come from Kitty, Verity, Faith, and Tommy.

They took an unmarked van to the Palace of Westminster. Kitty sat between Faith and Verity, with her hands tucked between her knees so that no one could see her fingers tapping against each other. Not that anyone was paying attention to her. Faith was busy organizing her "handbag of gadgets"— really, a large satchel filled with whatever equipment she'd been able to grab before they left—while Mrs. Singh, Tommy, and Verity were discussing what was to be done when they arrived.

"We can't very well storm in with guns blazin', can we, Mrs. Singh?" Tommy asked.

Mrs. Singh frowned. "No, Tommy, we certainly cannot."

"Take the pistols and hope for the best?" Verity offered.

"If we get caught, we'll be detained," Mrs. Singh said matter-of-factly. "And if the worst happens, that will be confirmation of Smythe's lies. We need to be inconspicuous."

After a long time of silence, Kitty found her voice. "Smythe's gonna have soldiers with 'im. We can't be empty 'anded. Is there any quiet way of doin' it?"

Faith's eyes turned wide and she rummaged through her satchel. In the process, she pulled out several unmarked bottles and handed them to Kitty. Kitty just took them without protest. She often did important, frantic things without explanation. Why should she complain if someone else did too?

"Well, I've got chloroform," Faith said, holding up yet another bottle for Mrs. Singh to see. "Will that help?"

"That's perfect, Faith." Mrs. Singh made a face, both gratified and exasperated at the same time. "To think that I'm reduced to fighting fascists with chloroform . . ."

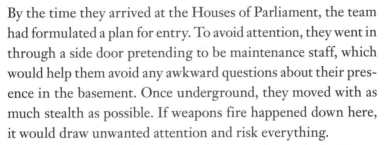

By the time they arrived at the Houses of Parliament, the team had formulated a plan for entry. To avoid attention, they went in through a side door pretending to be maintenance staff, which would help them avoid any awkward questions about their presence in the basement. Once underground, they moved with as much stealth as possible. If weapons fire happened down here, it would draw unwanted attention and risk everything.

As they neared the maintenance room beneath the House of Commons, Kitty spotted a pair of armed men standing guard near a crossroads in the passageways.

She made a hissing noise to get everyone's attention, and pointed. Nobody seemed to find the hiss odd, probably assuming it was to preserve secrecy, but really she was having a little trouble forming words at the moment. They kept getting lost in the maelstrom inside her head, and it was better not to say anything than to say the wrong thing.

"Chloroform," Mrs. Singh muttered. She held out her hand to Faith, who handed her the bottle. Mrs. Singh pulled a handkerchief out of her pocket and wet it with the chemical. Then she slowly advanced on the men.

Kitty wasn't sure how Mrs. Singh was going to handle two men at once, since she only had the one cloth, and anyway, chloroform didn't go into effect instantaneously, whatever the films pretended.

As Mrs. Singh neared the men, she pulled a stone out of her pocket and tossed it underhand past the men. It skipped along the floor, pinging loudly against the stonework. Both men glanced in its direction.

"Whassat?" one of the men said.

"You heard something too?"

"Yeah."

"I'll check it out."

One of the men drew his gun and slowly moved along the corridor toward the noise. The other man looked after him, reaching for his own weapon. Mrs. Singh advanced on him with rapid, quiet steps. As the first fellow moved out of range, Mrs. Singh grabbed her target from behind and shoved the chloroformed cloth over his face. There was a struggle, of course, but Mrs. Singh kept a firm grip until the man slumped in her arms and she lowered him onto the ground. She then advanced again, and did the same thing to his companion.

"That worked better than I expected," Mrs. Singh admitted, as the rest of them joined her.

Faith gave Mrs. Singh the bottle of chloroform to re-supply the cloth. "You doubted me, Mrs. Singh?" she asked.

"As the Russians say, Faith, *trust but verify*," Mrs. Singh replied.

Kitty moved past the others and led the way toward the main room under the Commons. She remembered the shape of the floorplan almost exactly. Sometimes it was fuzzy as she tried to conjure up the specific twists and turns of the passages, but she flicked her fingertips together and exhaled in short, sharp bursts, and the image came back to her.

They encountered and subdued another pair of guards before they finally reached the room they were looking for. It was dingy and dim, with a low ceiling like the rest of the basement. Inside were several men with submachine guns. They clearly meant business and were prepared for a hard fight to carry out their objective. That made sense. Smythe had probably trusted this mission to only the most devoted of his followers. Most people would balk at destroying a building full of civilians, so these men obviously had no qualms about anything at all.

Kitty pressed herself against the wall and peered into the room. She saw the guards, and she saw Smythe standing in the middle of the room, holding a revolver in his hand. There were large boxes all around the room, covered in wires and dials.

Bombs. Those were the bombs.

In the very center of the room was a man tied to a chair. He wore a rumpled suit, and he looked very annoyed at his predicament.

It was Mr. Pryce.

"Look here, Smythe," he grumbled, "if you're quite finished slapping me about, why don't we talk about this like gentlemen?"

Smythe gave Mr. Pryce a disdainful glare. "Shut up."

"What do you think you're going to accomplish here? Blow up Parliament and declare victory? This isn't Germany. You can't burn down the Reichstag and assume control of the government. We are still a democracy. The people won't stand for it."

"We're going to wake up the British people, Pryce," Smythe snarled. "They must take a stand against the *hordes* invading our country! If the Englishman doesn't act against the tide of Africans and Indians and Communists ravaging our shores, we will be drowned in rivers of blood! But when we destroy the men holding open the floodgates, then true Englishmen will stand up and join our ranks! You'll see." Smythe paused, and a cruel smile crossed his face. "Well, actually, you won't see, because you'll be dead."

"Going to blow me up with Parliament?" Mr. Pryce asked, his tone snide and taunting. "I suppose you'd better get a move on, Sir Richard. Don't want the bombs going off while we're still having this nice chat."

"Thoughtful of you, Pryce, but there's no need to worry," Smythe replied coolly. "I'm not about to give you the chance to wriggle free and disarm anything. The bombs are on a twenty-minute timer. Once all the MPs are in their seats, I will set it, and leave you and them to your collective fate. And you, Pryce, can die with the knowledge that all of this will all be laid upon your doorstep."

Mr. Pryce's jovial façade fell away. "What do you mean?"

"My men have already destroyed your little 'orchestra.' When the police arrive to examine the scene, they will find a mountain of evidence that John Pryce and his agents are secretly Russian spies. Your death will open the door for our new government."

"No one will believe that, Smythe!" Mr. Pryce retorted. "They will see you for what you are: a pathetic husk of a man playing at being a dictator. This mad venture will end in failure."

"We'll see," Smythe said. "Oh. Wait. *I'll* see. You will not."

Kitty glanced at the others as they joined her.

"Is that Pryce?" Mrs. Singh gasped. "Well, that explains where he's been."

"There's five of them," Verity said. "What are we going to do?"

"Need to split 'em up," Kitty whispered. "Then jump 'em. Can we cause a distraction?"

Faith fumbled with her satchel. "Wait, I've got just the thing." She produced two small metal balls. Each one was divided down the middle into separate hemispheres. "These are automatic chimes. Twist 'em and they'll ring."

"Right, that'll do it," Kitty said. She took one of the chimes and twisted it until it stopped. "Like that, yeah?"

Faith nodded. "Roll it where you want it to go. Give it a few seconds and it'll make a racket."

Kitty crouched and threw the chime across the room. It made a little noise when it bounced on the ground, and one of Smythe's men perked up. "Anyone hear that?"

Kitty took a second chime from Faith, wound it, and tossed it into the opposite corner. Then she waited. After a few seconds, she heard a loud, ringing noise, not exactly a wind chime, or a bell, or a rattle, but sort of all three at once. Smythe and his men turned in its direction.

"Someone see what that is!" Smythe shouted.

Two of the men broke off to investigate. As they went, the second chime began to ring, and everyone turned toward it. Now the men were scattered, spread across the room, looking in different directions. Mrs. Singh grabbed whatever cloth was ready to hand—kerchiefs, scarves, even scraps—and doused them in chloroform.

"Right," she whispered. "Tommy, with me. We're going to the right. Verity, take Kitty and Faith and deal with those two on the left."

Kitty followed Verity along the dimly lit wall toward the

nearest two men. Mrs. Singh and Tommy went in the opposite direction.

"Bring your man down and don't let him aim his gun," Verity said quietly. "I'll help you as soon as I can."

She leaped on one of the soldiers and grabbed him from behind. Her chloroform-soaked cloth covered his mouth and she held on tight as he struggled against her. Kitty and Faith rushed the other man. While Faith pinned his arms, Kitty grabbed onto his coat and shoved her cloth against his face. The man tipped over onto the ground, and they held him there, smothering him until he slipped into unconsciousness. Kitty found herself acting almost automatically, too overwhelmed by the noise and stress to think beyond the task in front of her. Chloroform, cloth, face. It was a simple sequence of actions.

Simple was good. Simple was easy. Simple would get the job done.

In the middle of the room, Smythe looked around, startled by the noise. They were hidden from his view, but he knew something had gone wrong.

"Sam?" he called. "Martin? Lads, someone say something!"

Mr. Pryce chuckled. "I think you're in for a spot of bother, Sir Richard."

Smythe growled in anger and shoved his gun against Mr. Pryce's head.

"One more word, Pryce," he snarled, "and I'll put a bullet through your brain!"

"If the only way you can win an argument is through threats of violence, you are in for a poor career in politics," Mr. Pryce said sagely.

Kitty saw Mrs. Singh sneaking up behind Smythe, but she

couldn't grab him as long as the gun was pointed at Mr. Pryce. At that range, even the slightest disturbance could be fatal. She could see in Mrs. Singh's face that the agent was unsure how to subdue Smythe and rescue her friend without the one act making the other impossible. Kitty inhaled and exhaled three times. She knew what had to be done.

"'Ello, Sir Richard," Kitty said, leaving the shadows and approaching him. She walked with a jaunty step, to keep his attention on her.

Smythe pointed his gun at her. "Who are you? Keep back!"

That surprised Kitty. She had expected Smythe to recognize her. Maybe her disguise during the Lowell trip had been more transforming than she realized. That made some sense: she was disheveled and bruised, a far cry from the refined houseguest. And she definitely didn't sound Canadian right now.

"What have you done to my men?" Smythe demanded.

"They're just enjoyin' a little nap, sir," Kitty said. "Thought the rest might do 'em good."

Smythe narrowed his eyes. "You're not alone. Who's there with you?"

Mrs. Singh crept up behind Smythe and fell upon him in a flash. She circled his throat with her arm, and with her other hand she grabbed his wrist and shoved the gun toward the ceiling, before he could pull the trigger on Kitty.

"Just another one of Pryce's socialists, Sir Richard," Mrs. Singh said. "Easy, easy," she continued, as Smythe struggled against her. "Drop the gun and give in. It will be much less painful for you."

As Mrs. Singh subdued Smythe, Kitty rushed to Mr. Pryce and untied him.

Mr. Pryce stared at her and blinked a few times. "My goodness—Miss Granger? What are you doing here?" he asked.

"I thought that were obvious, sir," Kitty replied. "We're 'ere to rescue you."

Mr. Pryce chuckled as he got up. His movements were very stiff, and he rubbed his wrists, which were raw from the rope. "Much obliged, Miss Granger."

Mr. Pryce stepped aside as Mrs. Singh disarmed Smythe and shoved him into the chair. Smythe started to get up again, spitting fire and vengeance, but he stopped when Mrs. Singh pointed his own gun at him.

"How the tables have turned, old boy," Mr. Pryce said cheerfully. "Verity, if you'd be so good as to tie up Smythe's accomplices . . ."

"On it, Mr. Pryce," Verity replied.

Mr. Pryce crouched in front of Smythe and looked him in the eye. "I'm not a resentful man, Sir Richard, but after the past twelve hours, I look forward to hand-delivering you to the authorities."

"Ah, shut up, you bloody ponce!" Smythe shouted. "It's degenerates like you who are destroying this country!"

Mrs. Singh grabbed Smythe by the collar and snarled, "Unless you'd care to start confessing, Sir Richard, I suggest you hold your tongue."

Smythe snarled at her. "You don't frighten me, you Punjabi dilettante. Playing at a man's game, are you? Got tired of parading around with your fancy dresses and parties, eh?"

"Rant and rave all you want, Smythe," Mrs. Singh replied. "Some of us work for a living, unlike you."

"You have lost, Sir Richard," Mr. Pryce said. "Be a good sport. Blowing up Parliament didn't work for Guy Fawkes.

Did you really believe the second time was the charm?"

"Parliament or no Parliament, it doesn't matter!" Smythe shouted. "You think you've won, but you haven't! There are more of us than you can imagine, just waiting for a signal to rise! The trueborn Englishman cannot be stopped by the likes of you! The purification of Britain will come to pass! If not now, then soon! If not by my hand, then by one who has yet to arrive! You've only delayed the inevitable."

The sounds of boots in the corridor interrupted him. Kitty turned and saw a dozen men in British Army battledress rush into the chamber, carrying automatic rifles. They circled the team and held them at gunpoint. Kitty felt herself starting to panic. She hadn't expected this, and going from a hard-won victory to capture by armed men was frightening. The world started getting hazy again.

Head together, Kitty. Head together.

Kitty couldn't risk flicking her fingers in case the soldiers got the wrong idea, so she clenched her jaw and pressed one foot against the ground. It wasn't perfect, but the pressure helped draw her back from the cloud of stress.

The two soldiers in the middle parted, making room for Gascoigne to come forward. He was stern-faced, but he looked slightly triumphant.

"What have we here?" he asked.

Mr. Pryce approached his fellow agent and held out a hand. "Easy, Gascoigne," he said. "We're on the same side."

A couple of the soldiers shifted their aim to Mr. Pryce, but Gascoigne waved them off.

"Don't even try explaining this away, Pryce," he said sternly. "I find you here, surrounded by explosives, preparing to blow up the House of Commons as soon as it's in session . . ." He looked at Smythe. "My God, man! Is that Sir Richard Smythe?"

"It is," Mr. Pryce answered, "and if you would only listen—"

Gascoigne grabbed Mr. Pryce by the lapels of his jacket and yanked him forward. "You really have lost your mind, haven't you? The Old Man said you were obsessed with Smythe, but I never imagined you'd *kidnap* him to make sure that he dies too!"

Smythe seized on Gascoigne's words immediately. "Officer! Please, you must help me!" he cried. "These people are insane! They kidnapped me from my house last night! They're going to murder me!"

This blatant lie was really too much. Kitty looked at Smythe long enough to give him a furious glare.

"You bloody lyin' bastard!" she shouted. "You was the one what planned to blow up Parliament!" She turned to Gascoigne and pointed a finger at Smythe. "It were 'im, sir. We only just rescued Mr. Pryce."

The combination of speaking and making eye contact under this much stress was rather difficult, but Kitty knew that it was important to make as strong an impression as possible. She fixed her eyes on Gascoigne's collar, which was near enough that the man would hopefully think she was looking at his face.

"Look, there is no point in telling stories, girl," Gascoigne scolded her. He turned back to Mr. Pryce. "The Old Man already warned me that you might be up to something. Said he was sending a team to investigate your headquarters to be safe, and he put me on standby here in Westminster. And it's a damn good thing he did. One of my men saw your people sneaking in. We assumed you were going to assassinate someone, but this? Blowing up Parliament, Pryce? You Welshmen really are full of surprises."

"I am telling you, Gascoigne—" Mr. Pryce insisted.

"He's lying!" Smythe interrupted.

Faith pushed her way forward, holding up a mechanical pen for Gascoigne's inspection. "Sir, if you'll just—"

The soldiers immediately aimed at her, and Faith backed away in fright.

"Drop the weapon!" one of them shouted.

Without thinking, Kitty planted herself between Faith and the soldiers, shielding her friend. "It's not a weapon, it's a bleedin' pen!" she snapped. "An' we're on your side, might I add!"

Gascoigne motioned for his men to lower their weapons. "Easy lads, I'll handle this." He beckoned Faith forward. "What do you want, girl?"

Faith approached Gascoigne cautiously and showed him the pen. Kitty gasped as she recognized it as a recording device. Faith must have brought one in her handbag of gadgets. Well, of course she had. Faith probably kept one on hand at all times, like any sensible person would do. It was still a pen, after all. One could never have too many of those.

"I think you might like to have a listen to this, sir," Faith said. She twisted the top of the pen to rewind the tape, and fiddled with it to make it play.

"You have lost, Sir Richard." That was Mr. Pryce's voice, crackling a little from the recording, but easy to hear. "Be a good sport. Blowing up Parliament didn't work for Guy Fawkes. Did you really believe the second time was the charm?"

Smythe's voice answered, "Parliament or no Parliament, it doesn't matter! You think you've won, but you haven't! There

245

are more of us than you can imagine, just waiting for a signal to rise!"

The color drained from Smythe's face as his full rant played back. He began talking over the recording, stammering excuses, but no one listened to him. Gascoigne's expression fell as he realized how badly he had been duped.

"Smythe was the one behind the plot?" he asked in disbelief.

Mr. Pryce smirked in triumph. "It may shock you to learn this, Gascoigne, but my lot of foreigners and socialists have successfully saved Britain from a coup. So perhaps you would like to have your men put their guns down."

Gascoigne held out a hand and slowly lowered it. His soldiers pointed their weapons at the floor, all of them looking confused and apprehensive.

"I'm sorry, Pryce," Gascoigne stammered. "I . . . I assumed . . ."

"I know, Gascoigne. Maybe next time you'll see fit to trust me and my agents."

Gascoigne still looked unsettled. "But—the Old Man. How could he not know?"

"The Old Man were in on it!" Kitty exclaimed, forgetting to keep out of the conversation. "We got photos of 'em an' everythin'!"

"Is this true, Pryce?" Gascoigne asked.

Mr. Pryce looked at Mrs. Singh for confirmation.

"It is," Mrs. Singh said to Gascoigne.

Gascoigne hesitated for a few seconds, considering something. Then he motioned to his men. "Take Sir Richard into custody."

"This is outrageous!" Smythe shouted, as a couple of the soldiers hauled him out of the chair. "This is not the end of this, Pryce!"

"Oh, shut up, you whiny fascist," Mrs. Singh said to him. "Gascoigne, there are some more of Smythe's men there, and there . . ." She pointed to the corners of the room. "And a couple more in that corridor over there."

Gascoigne nodded, and motioned to his men to handle it.

"And those are explosives," Mrs. Singh added, pointing to the boxes. "The timer on them hasn't started, but I'd get the bomb squad down here as soon as possible."

"I second that notion," Mr. Pryce agreed. "I've just narrowly avoided death by explosion. I'd prefer not to risk it a second time."

Gascoigne slowly nodded. His expression made it clear that he didn't enjoy being wrong, but he understood the situation and accepted it.

"I'll have my men lock down the scene and deal with Smythe and his men," he said. "You ought to get back to your headquarters and put your evidence together. I fear this is going to be a rather complicated affair to untangle, especially if one of the traitors answers to the Minister."

"We also need to work out where the Old Man and Lowell are," Mrs. Singh added.

"Lowell?" Gascoigne asked. "You don't mean Lord Lowell, do you?"

"He's one of them," Mrs. Singh said.

Gascoigne wrinkled his nose. "Conspiracy between an MP, a lord, and a senior intelligence officer. This is turning into a bloody scandal!"

"Not if we can catch them all in time," Mr. Pryce said. "I'd like to avoid a public panic, and I'm sure the government will agree. If we can capture Lowell and the Old Man before they do any more damage, no one need ever know."

"Fine." Gascoigne still looked worried, but he gave Mr. Pryce a nod. "Take your people and see if you can locate Lowell and the Old Man. I'm going to deal with this mess, and inform the Minister." He grabbed Smythe by the scruff of the neck and leaned in close to him. "As for you, Sir Richard . . . . I don't like being made a fool of. You're in for a miserable time if I have anything to say about it."

CHAPTER 27

Kitty followed Mr. Pryce, Mrs. Singh, and the rest of the team upstairs and out into the street.

"So the question is, where do we find Lowell and the Old Man?" Mr. Pryce asked.

"They could be anywhere," Mrs. Singh said.

No one had a good answer, and they walked to the van in silence, broken only by a few half-hearted suggestions that ultimately went nowhere.

"Bloody—" Mr. Pryce grumbled, before he remembered himself and held his tongue. Kitty knew he wasn't a man given to swearing, except under the most trying of circumstances. "There must be a way to narrow down the possibilities. They have to be someplace with communications equipment, to stay in contact with Smythe and their allies. It would be near London . . ."

"But not *in* London," Mrs. Singh said, "in case something goes wrong. Lowell is a coward, and the Old Man is too smart to let himself be trapped in a box. He would leave open a path for escape, just to be safe."

Verity gasped. "Wait! Lord Lowell has a private plane. It's at an airfield a few miles outside of London. But I don't know if he would be there."

"Well, if 'e decides to run, it'll be where 'e goes, won't it?" Kitty offered. "Aeroplane's the best way outta the country if it all goes wrong, innit?"

"She's right about that," Mrs. Singh told Mr. Pryce. She checked her watch and glanced back at Westminster. "And you know, Parliament is due to be sitting right around now. By the end of the hour, the Old Man is going to start wondering why there's been no explosion."

"Aye," Tommy chimed in, "an' that's assumin' 'e don't know about Gascoigne moving on the basement early. I'll bet he tipped 'em off thinkin' Gascoigne would get there after the explosion. Gascoigne goes in early, the Old Man knows about it, an' 'e'll assume the plan's gone wrong."

"If it were me, I'd run for the airfield straightaway," Kitty agreed. "Smythe checks in an' gives the all clear, they can always go back. But if not . . ."

"They can fly away and escape," Verity finished.

Mr. Pryce nodded. "I daresay that's about right. Return in triumph, or slink off under the cover of the chaos. At this rate, they might already be gone!"

"No time to waste then," Mrs. Singh said. "Pryce, are you sure you're up to this? After the night you've had, you deserve a little rest."

"And miss out on all the fun?" Mr. Pryce exclaimed. "Perish the thought!"

It took about forty minutes to reach the airfield, following Verity's directions. As they drove up, Kitty immediately spotted the small silver plane on the tarmac, and the workmen who were loading it with crates and luggage cases. The airfield was surrounded by a chain-link fence, and men with guns stood at the only gate. Something told Kitty that the Old Man had taken over the place with his own guards.

The team assembled behind some shrubs a little ways away from the fence. Mr. Pryce looked troubled by the situation.

"A bit of a higher-security setup than I expected," he admitted.

Mrs. Singh frowned. "We need to lure the guards away from the gate. There's no doubt this is the Old Man's work. If he and Lowell aren't on that plane already, they'll be boarding soon. We have one chance to grab them. After that, they're in the air and gone."

"Can't we get someone to shoot them down?" Verity asked.

Mrs. Singh raised an eyebrow at her. "You mean ask the Royal Air Force to open fire on a civilian plane belonging to a British lord?"

"Ah, yeah," Verity said. "I suppose the Minister wouldn't sign off on that."

"If we don't take Lowell and the Old Man alive, I don't know what the Minister will think about all of this," Mr. Pryce said. "We are making outrageous accusations against some very powerful people. The more evidence we can get, the better for all of us."

"We need a distraction, then," Tommy interjected. "Right? Like an explosion somewhere else. Somethin' to make 'em leave their post to investigate."

"But what?" Verity asked. "Set the van on fire, maybe?"

Tommy looked shocked and then furious. "You are *not* settin' fire to one of me vehicles, Verity. I've spent hours fine-tunin' that bloody thing!"

Kitty blinked a few times as ideas turned around in her head. She ran through all of the possible—and impossible—options. Driving by with the van would attract attention, but on its own it wouldn't lure anyone away from the gate. Driving into the gate would only get them shot. They needed something to spark a panic. Faith's noisemakers weren't loud enough to work in an open space like this. They needed something like an explosion.

Explosion.

"Cigarette lighter!" Kitty exclaimed.

"What?" Mrs. Singh asked.

Faith looked at Kitty. Her eyes widened. She understood. "Cigarette lighter!" she echoed.

"Is this code or somethin'?" Tommy asked.

Faith rummaged in her bag until she found her lighter and held it up for everyone to see. "My pocket flamethrower."

"I thought it didn't work," Verity said.

"It doesn't work because it *explodes!*" Faith answered.

Mrs. Singh looked at Mr. Pryce, and Mr. Pryce looked at Mrs. Singh.

Finally Mr. Pryce asked, "Can your lighter explode on demand?"

"I turn it on, it starts burning, and it blows up within a couple of minutes," Faith replied. "It doesn't have a timer or anything."

"Well, we don't have a better plan, do we?" Mrs. Singh said to Mr. Pryce.

Mr. Pryce sighed. "We do not." He turned to Faith as Mrs. Singh dashed back to the van. "Faith, set the lighter to go off a few meters down that way." He pointed along the fence. "Then get back here as quick as you can. I'm afraid I have to conscript you and Kitty into our little army."

Mrs. Singh returned from the van with the spare guns. The very thought of more violence made Kitty feel sick. Still, she wasn't going to back down now, not when the others needed her.

"What about us, sir?" Tommy asked.

"You're our best driver," Mr. Pryce replied, "so I need you to get the van away from here. Once the bomb goes off, drive past the gate on your way out. Make a show of it and try to lure out the guards. Verity, go with Tommy in case they give chase. I don't want the two of you getting into a firefight, but if it happens, protect each other."

Verity and Tommy both nodded. "Yessir."

"And after that?" Verity asked.

"Get back to headquarters and wait for us."

"What are you going to do?" Verity asked.

Mr. Pryce gestured to Mrs. Singh, who handed the extra pistols to Kitty and Faith. "Capture the plane and fly it out with our prisoners onboard. I hope."

<hr />

Kitty clutched her pistol nervously as she crouched behind Mr. Pryce and Mrs. Singh. She watched Faith plant the bomb and hurry back to them, hidden from view by a dip in the ground. When Faith got there, Kitty handed her the second pistol. From Faith's grimace, she knew that they shared a similar discomfort with holding the weapons. But they had the training to use them, and under the circumstances, there wasn't much choice.

Thirty seconds passed, and a small fire appeared on the ground near the fence. The ground was mostly dirt so there wasn't much risk of a conflagration, but a few scattered bits of grass and shrubbery began to burn. The guards near the gate looked in that direction and started shouting.

Thirty more seconds passed, and suddenly the lighter exploded with a bang and a shower of fire and heated metal.

The shouting from the guards got louder. The men at the gate abandoned their posts, and they ran to see what was going on. More men came from the airfield buildings, carrying fire extinguishers instead of their guns.

Mr. Pryce raised a hand as he watched the guards. As the men crowded around the fire, he motioned to Verity and Tommy, who waited in the van. At Mr. Pryce's signal, Tommy hit the accelerator and the van roared past the guards. It banked sharply at the edge of the fire, and raced toward the highway.

The guards were clearly starting to panic. Some of them ran to a truck parked inside the fence and gave chase along the road. The others continued to fight the spreading fire. The gate was unguarded, and everyone was too busy to pay attention to it.

Kitty followed Mr. Pryce onto the tarmac and across the landing strip to the plane. Faith was close behind her, clutching her bag of gadgets, while Mrs. Singh brought up the rear, protecting the two girls.

As they approached, the plane's engines fired up. A couple of attendants, looking confused and frightened, grabbed the rolling stairway next to the plane and started to push it away.

Kitty pointed her gun at them and shouted, "'Ere! 'Ands off it! Get outta 'ere!"

These men weren't soldiers, and they didn't argue. As the attendants ran for cover, Mr. Pryce led the way up the stairs, taking them two at a time. Kitty dashed after him as quickly as she could. As they reached the top, a man appeared in the plane's doorway, reaching for the hatch to close it. Mr. Pryce leveled his weapon at the man's forehead and motioned him back inside.

The interior of the plane was cramped but very expensive. There were a few seats upholstered in plush velvet, and a table in the back. Kitty had never been inside of an aeroplane before, but she hadn't expected this. It was part private office and part gentleman's club as far as she could tell, and also it could fly. Kitty couldn't even imagine affording something like this, and the fact that it belonged to a man like Lowell was doubly galling.

Lowell and the Old Man were already buckled into their seats. They were looking over some papers, and at first they didn't seem to notice the team entering their cabin.

"The first thing we want to do is liquidate the Swiss bonds," the Old Man said to Lowell, sounding very cool and collected. "We also must divest the network, in case James or Richard decide to talk."

"They wouldn't do that, would they?" Lowell asked. He was ashen-faced and sweaty. "Sell us out?"

Mr. Pryce cleared his throat to interrupt them. Lowell looked up, did a double-take, and then tried to jump out of his seat, only the seatbelt held him fast. The Old Man looked up more calmly, his expression resigned but not panicked.

"Ah. Pryce," the Old Man said. "I suppose it was gambling too much on good fortune to assume we would get away."

"You are quite right about that, sir," Mr. Pryce replied. Even facing down an enemy, he was polite to a fault.

In the back of the plane, a couple more of Lowell's men got up from their seats, grabbing for their guns. Mr. Pryce and Mrs. Singh turned their weapons on the men to stop them before they could draw. Kitty and Faith exchanged a look and quickly covered Lowell and the Old Man.

Mr. Pryce closed the aeroplane door and gave everyone a pleasant smile. "That's right, no sudden movements," he said. "I would prefer not to shoot anyone today, if that's all right with the rest of you."

Lowell's men awkwardly nodded their assent.

"Guns on the ground, if you please," Mr. Pryce continued. "And take off your belts. It seems I forgot to bring my handcuffs."

As Kitty and Faith covered the men, Mr. Pryce and Mrs. Singh tied the men's belts around their wrists to secure them, and locked the guards into some of the unused seats.

"Mrs. Singh, if you would be so good as to relieve the pilot, I think we should be going," Mr. Pryce said.

Mrs. Singh answered with a crisp salute. "Aye, aye, Captain."

"Now look here . . . Pryce, is it?" Lowell said. "Let's be reasonable about this. I have money. A lot of money. I can make you a very attractive offer if you let us go."

Mr. Pryce raised his eyebrows. "Bribery?"

Lowell laughed nervously. "Let's call it an understanding between new friends. I have a quarter of a million pounds' worth of bonds here on the plane, and almost a million more in a Swiss bank account. If you let us go, I'll pay you whatever you want!"

The Old Man gave Lowell a disapproving look. "Henry, stop it. You're embarrassing yourself."

"You could retire to the Caribbean on that!" Lowell sputtered. "Just let us fly away and tell your superiors you arrived too late!" As Pryce remained unmoved, Lowell looked at Kitty and Faith. "You two! Pryce doesn't care about you. He's using you! How much is he paying you? I can top it! I'll—I'll give you a hundred thousand pounds each if you turn your guns on Pryce! That's probably more money than you've ever dreamed of before!"

"Now you're embarrassing *me*," the Old Man said.

Kitty made a face at Lowell, furious and insulted. "I thought you said the offer were a quarter million."

"Or do we get paid less for treason because we're girls?" Faith asked.

"Well, I . . ." Lowell stammered.

Mr. Pryce snorted with laughter, then tried to compose himself. "Lord Lowell, please stop trying to bribe my agents," he said. "You already have enough crimes to answer for."

Lowell continued to shout and sputter, mixing offers of money with threats of violence. "You will regret this, I swear!" he shouted. "Release me now, or your families will suffer!"

The Old Man looked at Lowell and said, "Shut up." He turned to Mr. Pryce and smiled. He seemed amused at his situation. It wasn't the reaction Kitty had expected, but perhaps it was his only way of coping with the failure of the plot. "Well done, Pryce. A game jolly well played."

Kitty stared at him. He thought of this as a *game*?

"You shouldn't congratulate me, sir. I was unconscious most of the time." Mr. Pryce nodded at Kitty and Faith. "My agents did all of the real work. If you want to heap praise on the people who foiled you, give it to them."

From the cockpit, Kitty heard Mrs. Singh call, "I helped too, you know!"

"I said 'my agents', didn't I?" Mr. Pryce called back.

"So I'm just an agent now?" Mrs. Singh asked.

"Well, when I say agent, I mean someone who works for me," Mr. Pryce replied.

"*For* you?"

"Alongside me," Mr. Pryce corrected. "In a junior capacity."

Mrs. Singh laughed. "Keep digging that hole, Pryce. There had better be a bottle of champagne at the bottom of it."

Mr. Pryce grinned. "Your wish is my command, Mrs. Singh. And it's the least we deserve after saving Britain."

CHAPTER 28

The day dragged on for what felt like forever, even after Lowell and the Old Man were taken into custody. There were interviews and reports with Mr. Pryce, Mrs. Singh, Gascoigne, and some people from the Ministry. Kitty did her best to stay focused and relay everything that had happened precisely and clearly, which was extremely hard. Her brain clicked on endlessly, and it was all she could do to avoid drifting off into peculiar tangents instead of answering the official questions.

By the time it was all done, Kitty was too tired to go home. The Orchestra had a small barracks for the agents to use, and she just wandered in and collapsed onto one of the beds. The room had no windows and Kitty had no idea how long she slept, but eventually she woke up and saw Verity reclining on the next bed along, apparently having drifted off in the middle of reading some reports.

Kitty smiled. Verity looked very peaceful, and peaceful things were a welcome change from the mission. She slowly got up, and the bedsprings creaked. Verity snorted softly and opened her eyes.

"Oh, I, um . . ." Verity said, disoriented. She looked at Kitty and smiled. "Oh, you're awake. I was just, um, waiting for you."

"'Course," Kitty replied. She stretched and gave a tremendous yawn. "What time is it?"

Verity checked her watch. "It's tomorrow morning."

"Oh Lord!" Kitty cried. "'Ow long 'ave I been asleep?"

"I'm guessing twelve hours," Verity replied. "Don't worry, you needed the rest."

"But there's things to do! I'm not in trouble, am I?"

Verity shook her head, looking almost as if she might laugh. "You just saved Britain from a fascist coup, Kitty. Why would you be in trouble?"

Kitty frowned and looked down at her hands. Feeling like she was in trouble for something was familiar. It was easier to assume that than to hope for the best and be disappointed. "I dunno," she said quietly.

Verity put an arm around her. "You're a bloody hero, Kitty Granger, and don't you forget it."

"Thanks," Kitty mumbled, uncomfortable at being complimented. "I s'pose I'd better go 'ome. I mean, Da don't expect me back for a few days, but the sooner the better."

"That is probably best," Verity agreed. "Here, let me have a look at you first."

She examined Kitty's face and hands gently, but with intense scrutiny. It didn't exactly make Kitty feel uncomfortable, since Verity felt less intrusive than most people, but all the same, Kitty shifted her feet nervously.

"No bruises or marks on your face," Verity said. "That's good. Hands are a little scraped, but I don't think your father will notice that."

"I doubt it," Kitty agreed. "'E don't notice much about me, 'cept when I'm bein' trouble. I'll just be on me best behavior for a few weeks, an' 'e won't think twice about it."

Verity nodded. "Yes, we can't have your family being tipped off that you're a dangerous spy getting into scrapes all the time. Then they'll start to ask questions."

Kitty laughed at the joke. Laughing was nice. It helped relieve some of the tension.

"You know, I was wondering, Kitty," Verity said. She hesitated, like she wasn't sure how to broach the subject. "Have you ever thought about moving out?"

"What, leavin' me da, you mean?"

To be honest, Kitty had never considered it a possibility. She had always assumed she would have to live at home until her father died, and after that . . . she had no idea.

"You don't have to decide now," Verity told her, "but I have a flat in downtown London. There's plenty of room for two, and it's much more convenient for both the magazine and the Orchestra. Plus, it means you wouldn't have to worry about your father asking why you keep odd hours. This won't be the only mission that takes you out of town for a while."

Kitty stared off in silence, pondering the offer. It represented an independence she had never really thought possible for herself. And maybe she wasn't quite ready to take that plunge just yet. Leaving home was a huge step. But thanks to the new hires, her father didn't need her to help in the shop anymore, and it might be nice not having to worry about him being overbearing at the worst possible moments.

"I'll think about it," she said. "Is that a'right?"

"Whenever you decide, just let me know," Verity said, smiling. "Now then, let's get you back home. You deserve a rest."

Kitty followed Verity into the hallway, where she saw Mr. Pryce, Mrs. Singh, and Gascoigne standing outside of Mr. Pryce's office. It looked like they had just finished a meeting and Gascoigne was getting ready to leave. Verity put out a hand to stop Kitty, and the two of them hung back to avoid interrupting the conversation.

"I don't believe the Prime Minister is going to make an impassioned speech about one of the lords plotting to blow up Parliament, if that's what you mean," Gascoigne said to Mr. Pryce, as he put on his hat. "But there is ample evidence of conspiracy and treason, so the courts will deal with them accordingly. We'll simply keep the full extent of what almost happened out of the public eye."

"Sensible," Mr. Pryce said.

"Don't want to spark a general panic," Mrs. Singh agreed.

Gascoigne nodded. "Or undermine confidence in the Conservatives. We cannot allow this to hurt the party in the next election, Pryce."

Mr. Pryce frowned. Kitty guessed he was offended at the notion of concealing information from the public for political reasons. Mrs. Singh's reaction was far more dramatic.

"Bloody hell, Gascoigne," she exclaimed. "Is that all you can think about?"

Gascoigne didn't answer her. "In the meantime, Pryce, I've spoken to the Minister about your new assignments. As we discussed, you will be taking orders from me now. You will find that I run a tighter ship than the Old Man did."

Mrs. Singh looked angry at this news, but Mr. Pryce gave Gascoigne a cheery smile. "Need I remind you about our agreement? You give the Orchestra full autonomy, and I'll back you up when people start asking questions about why you were so eager to follow the Old Man's orders on the day of the attack. A mutually beneficial arrangement, I'm certain you will agree."

Gascoigne coughed uncomfortably. "Yes, well . . ." he stammered. "You and I will discuss this later. Good day."

Once Gascoigne had left, Mrs. Singh folded her arms and said, "That man is going to be trouble. You know that."

"I predict we have a year or so before Gascoigne becomes too much of a problem," Mr. Pryce replied. "I'll work on the Minister to get us made a separate agency now that the Old Man is behind bars."

"Honestly, Pryce, you're always so bloody cheerful," Mrs. Singh said. "Doesn't it bother you that *we* saved the country, but Gascoigne gets the promotion?"

For a moment, Mr. Pryce's countenance fell. "It does bother me, my dear, but that's inter-service politics for you. If I'm going to do my job, I have to put up with this sort of nonsense some of the time. Well, most of the time."

"Ever think about taking me up on my offer?" Mrs. Singh asked.

Mr. Pryce laughed. "You mean going into private enterprise? Spying on the rich and powerful, and blackmailing them into doing some good in the world?"

"That's the one. Could be rather fun if you ask me."

"Not my style," Mr. Pryce said. "I believe Britain can be a force for good, and far more effectively than some blackmailed millionaire. I just need to protect the country from men like Smythe, who would rather use our resources to hurt people than to help them."

"I respect that," Mrs. Singh told him, "but you don't set policy. What happens if a government's elected that wants what Smythe wanted? A new British Empire. England for the English. Will you just stand at your post and hope for the best?"

Mr. Pryce looked troubled by the question. "God willing,

we will never come to that bridge, but if we do, we'll cross it then."

Mr. Pryce went into his office and closed the door. Verity nodded to Kitty, and they turned the corner into the hallway like they had only just arrived.

Mrs. Singh smiled at them as they approached. "Back on your feet, I see," she said to Kitty.

"Yes, missis. Sorry, I didn't mean to sleep so long."

"You had a very long day yesterday. It's understandable. Come on, I'll drive you home. No reason for you to take the bus after what you've been through."

"Thank you, missis," Kitty said. Truly, she hadn't been looking forward to taking public transportation all the way to the East End.

"Be seeing you," Verity told her with a parting wave.

Kitty smiled. "An' you."

She followed Mrs. Singh out to the parking lot and into one of the cars. They drove for the first few minutes in silence, but after a bit, Mrs. Singh spoke.

"I'm very proud of you, Kitty," she said. "I hope you know that. Pryce is too. We all are."

As always, Kitty felt embarrassed at being complimented. "Oh, I dunno 'bout that," she mumbled. "Just doin' me job."

"You were given a first assignment that was supposed to be safe and easy," Mrs. Singh replied. "It turned out to be dangerous and difficult, and despite that you pulled it off and saved hundreds of lives. You should be proud too."

Kitty bobbed her head but didn't say anything.

Mrs. Singh continued, "I spoke to Pryce, and he's going to give you a few days off to recuperate. But I thought perhaps you might like to come to the magazine tomorrow anyway."

"I'd like that, missis," Kitty said. "I like to work." Perhaps she'd have some time to stop by the garage and see if Tommy needed any help with car repairs. That would be calming.

"You and I can sit down and discuss what you've been through," Mrs. Singh added.

"No need, missis," Kitty insisted. "I'm fine, honest."

Mrs. Singh gave her a long look. "Kitty, you shot a man and you were nearly killed. Now that's not unusual in this line of work, but it's a lot for a young person like you to process. I know from experience. We are spies, not machines. We think and we feel, and we are affected by things. You can't simply shrug off what happened to you. You need to talk about it and work through it. If you'll let me, I'd like to help you with that."

Kitty nodded slowly. She understood. The idea of confronting what had happened made her hands twitch, but she couldn't just leave it unaddressed, festering in the back of her head as she tried not to think about it.

"I think I'd like that, actually," she admitted.

Mrs. Singh smiled. "Good. We can't have our most promising new recruit succumbing to fatigue, can we?"

"No, missis," Kitty agreed.

The drive was nice and quiet, and Kitty was already feeling a little better by the time they reached home. Mrs. Singh accompanied her into the shop, and Kitty saw her father behind the counter, talking to one of his new employees. Another local lad was sweeping the floor across the room. Everything looked better than Kitty remembered. The money coming in had paid for new stock, fresh paint, and a host of other little improvements. She had no idea whether sales were any better than before, but the place certainly *looked* more successful. And her father seemed happier than Kitty had seen him in a long time.

"'Ello, Da!" she called from the doorway.

Her father looked up from his newspaper and smiled at her. "Kitty! Back a'ready? Oh, an' 'ello, Mrs. Singh. Good to see ya 'gain."

Mrs. Singh gave him one of her most charming smiles and offered him her hand. "Hello, Mr. Granger. A pleasure as always. My goodness, but doesn't the shop just look wonderful!"

"I 'ope Kitty weren't no trouble on your business trip," her father said, even as he hugged Kitty. The irony of the juxtaposition was lost on him. Kitty sighed in resignation. How quickly he jumped from being happy to see her to reminding people that she was a burden.

Mrs. Singh laughed. "Nonsense, Mr. Granger. Kitty is the best secretary I've employed in years. I have no idea how she keeps track of everything so well, but thanks to her the trip was a complete success. You should be very proud."

"Oh, I am, I am," he insisted.

"In fact," Mrs. Singh continued, "it was such a success, I intend to celebrate with some friends of mine. I don't suppose I could trouble you for some groceries while I'm here? You have such a good selection."

"Certainly, missis," Kitty's father said. He snapped his fingers at one of the new clerks. As the young man took Mrs. Singh's grocery list, Mr. Granger leaned over the counter and said to Mrs. Singh, "You read the paper this morning, missis?"

"I have not, in fact," Mrs. Singh replied. "Anything of note?"

"Well, says 'ere they've arrested a Member of Parliament."

"My word!" Mrs. Singh gasped. "Mr. Granger, whatever for?"

He gave Mrs. Singh a sage look, preparing to educate her. "Well, missis, seems there were a plot to assassinate the Prime Minister."

Mrs. Singh put a hand to her heart and looked like she might faint from the shock. "No!"

"'Tis true. An' there's trouble brewin' in Northern Ireland. I tell ya, Mrs. Singh, I dunno what's become of this country these days, I really don't."

While the two of them kept chatting, Kitty slipped away from the conversation and went upstairs to her room.

She dropped her suitcase by the bed and hung up her coat. She rummaged through her desk drawer for a pencil and an old crossword she had left unfinished ages ago. Sitting on her bed, Kitty settled back against her pillow and took a few deep breaths to steady her nerves. Her eyes focused on the puzzle in front of her, and gradually the rest of the world started to slip away. The tension in her head eased, and Kitty was finally at peace again.

Author's Note

A note about our hero:

Kitty Granger is autistic. It is a fundamental part of who she is, inseparable from her as a person. Nevertheless, the word "autism" never appears in the text of this story, because autism was not well understood in the 1960s. The criteria for diagnosis was extremely narrow and focused on children with severe developmental delays, which meant that the majority of autistic people went undiagnosed at the time.

In addition, diagnosis was heavily skewed toward recognizing signs of autism in boys rather than girls, a problem that persists today. It is extremely unlikely that Kitty and her family would even have heard of autism, and virtually inconceivable that her autism would have been recognized as such during her childhood.

The ways that Kitty's autism manifests and affects her experiences have been based on modern information and perspectives, in an effort to make her portrayal as realistic and as respectful as possible.

A note about the villains:

Smythe and Lowell are old-school British fascists from the 1930s, who successfully distanced themselves from mainline fascism during World War II and cloaked their political leanings behind the cover of conventional right-wing politics. They are completely fictional, but their ideology is based on real examples from British history.

Their associate Oswald Mosley was real, and his British Union of Fascists existed from 1932 to 1940, when it was banned during World War II. After the war, Mosley attempted to reenter politics with a new party, the Union Movement. In 1959 he ran for Parliament on an anti-immigration platform, calling for the deportation of Caribbean immigrants. He lost with less than ten percent of the vote, lost again in 1966, and finally retired.

In addition to Mosley, there were many other fascists or fascist sympathizers in Britain before, during, and even after the war. They included the likes of Archibald Henry Maule Ramsay, a virulently anti-Semitic Member of Parliament who organized a group called the Right Club aimed at unifying Britain's far-right; Hugh Grosvenor, 2nd Duke of Westminster, who was reportedly obsessed with anti-Semitic conspiracy theories; Admiral Sir Barry Domvile, who was invited to attend the Nazi Party's Nuremberg Rally in Germany in 1936; and Ronald Nall-Cain, 2nd Baron Brocket, a Nazi sympathizer who attended Adolf Hitler's 50th birthday celebrations in 1939. Evidence suggests that none other than Edward VIII, who reigned as king for most of 1936, was a fascist sympathizer.

Britain's fascists came from all walks of life, from the working class all the way up to the nobility. Many were imprisoned as a security risk during World War II, but some were not. Smythe and Lowell are, clearly, among the latter group, whose beliefs persisted well beyond the end of the war.

Topics for Discussion

1. Kitty is autistic. Her brain works in a particular way, which she knows that some people consider "peculiar." What are some ways that she uses this to her advantage?

2. What coping mechanisms does Kitty use when she experiences sensory overload or feels otherwise overwhelmed? How do these coping strategies help her manage difficult situations?

3. Why does Kitty want to work for Mr. Pryce and Mrs. Singh instead of continuing to work in her father's shop?

4. What is Kitty's relationship like with her father? How do her colleagues at the Orchestra treat her differently than her father does?

5. Why do the Young Bloods at the Orchestra stick together, according to Verity? What do they accomplish that the more senior agents don't?

6. How does Saul advise Kitty to deal with bullies? How could his advice apply to day-to-day situations at school or in your neighborhood? How do you think it could apply to a political situation?

7. Tommy assumes that most girls aren't interested in cars. Kitty tells him, "Girls can be interested in all sorts of things, only we don't talk about 'em 'cause people keep tellin' us we're not s'posed to like 'em." Think of an instance in your life when someone (perhaps you) made an assumption similar to Tommy's. What do you think Kitty would have said about this?

8. Mr. Pryce believes that the secret fascists within Britain's Conservative Party could never take over the government by nonviolent means. Do you agree with his assessment? Why or why not?

9. Kitty speaks in an East End accent, but she switches to a posh Canadian accent for her cover. Why do you think she prefers her natural way of speaking, even though she knows how to speak in other ways?

10. What does Kitty come to understand about Diana and the way she treats people? How is Diana's behavior connected to her father's social position and worldview?

11. How does killing a man—and seeing several others killed—affect Kitty? What does Verity tell her about this? What is Mrs. Singh's perspective?

12. How do the Old Man and his fascist accomplices try to undermine the Orchestra? How might a group like theirs do something similar in the present day?

13. What role do racism and xenophobia play in Sir Richard Smythe's plans for "the purification of Britain"? How do the members of the Orchestra refute his ideas of what "true Englishmen" are?

14. Mrs. Singh asks Mr. Pryce, "What happens if a government's elected that wants what Smythe wanted?. . . . Will you just stand at your post and hope for the best?" Mr. Pryce dodges the question. What do you think his answer should have been?

15. How does the possibility of moving out of her father's home and becoming Verity's roommate change Kitty's ideas about what her future might hold? What do you think the next few years of her life will be like?

Acknowledgments

First and foremost, I am extremely grateful to those members of the autistic community who have written or spoken publicly about their experiences with autism. Thanks to their efforts, there is a wealth of firsthand information about life on the autism spectrum readily available, if one simply takes the time to look. Many such resources have proven invaluable to the writing of this book, both in informing Kitty's portrayal and in giving much-needed context to the rest of my research.

I would like to thank my marvelous editor, Amy Fitzgerald, whose edits have been consistently keen and insightful, and helped make *Kitty Granger* the book it is today.

I also want to thank my agent, Jennifer Unter, for her tireless dedication and excellent representation. Thank you for finding the perfect home for Kitty.

Finally, my thanks to all of my readers, both new and old. Words cannot express my gratitude for your support, encouragement, and enthusiasm. I hope that you enjoy the worlds that I create and the tales that I tell.

About the Author

G. D. Falksen is the author of *The Secret Life of Kitty Granger*, *Maiden of War*, *Doctor Cthulittle*, *The Transatlantic Conspiracy*, and The Ouroboros Cycle series, and has been a contributor to the award-winning anthologies *Mine!* and *Cthulhu Fhtagn!*. He is also Chairman of the Advisory Board of Writers and Artists Across the Country, a nonprofit organization dedicated to facilitating author visits to underserved schools. Falksen's Ouroboros Cycle series is currently being developed for television. Read more at www.gdfalksen.com.